Gold in the Mud

About *Gold in the Mud* (*Sárarany*, 1910)

Torn between the torpid bliss of his home life and a seething quest for prosperity, Dani Turi, the peasant Don Juan and leader of Kiskara village, follows his urge to break the bonds of his low social status, only to find his path barred by the aristocratic landowners bent on maintaining their centuries-long hold on the reins of power. Zsigmond Móricz (1879-1942), one of Hungary's greatest novelists and the first to portray the peasant classes with full regard for their human aspirations, reveals in this riveting narrative his mastery in drawing complex characters and evoking the unique atmosphere of rural Hungary.

Gold in the Mud

A Hungarian Peasant Novel

Written as *Sárarany* in 1910 by

Zsigmond Móricz

Translated from the Hungarian by

Virginia L. Lewis

Most fog kapni az ember valamit,

Csodásat, szépet és nagyot

Vagy semmit.

- Endre Ady

Contents

ZSIGMOND MÓRICZ

Translator's Introduction

Published as *Sárarany* in 1910, *Gold in the Mud* was written by Zsigmond Móricz (1879-1942), one of Hungary's foremost novelists, whose literary career extended from the turn of the twentieth century to the Second World War. Móricz was the first Hungarian author of note to have been born and raised among the peasantry. His father, Bálint Móricz, was descended from impoverished peasants and farmed a small parcel of land in eastern Hungary, in the village of Tiszacsécse, then numbering all of 300 souls. One can still visit the house he built for his family there when Zsigmond was a youth, the "Móricz Zsigmond Emlékház."

Zsigmond was the first of nine children, eight boys and one girl, two of whom died in infancy. His family was well acquainted with the poverty he often depicted in his narratives. But this did not prevent his parents from nurturing cultural ambitions in young Zsigmond, whose mother, Erzsébet Pallagi, was a Reformed pastor's daughter and presumably descended from ancient Hungarian nobility, a claim that son Miklós Móricz, also a writer, later proved false. The author's father went to great lengths to secure an education for his first-born son, and Zsigmond began his studies at the Debreceni Református Kollégium in 1890. After trying a variety of career directions including law and theology, Móricz eventually took up journalism, moving to Budapest in 1900. He devoted energy to the study of Hungarian folk culture, which he prized, while at the same time entering the urbane cultural world of Hungary's capital and acquainting himself with important authors of the time, including several who have gone down in the annals of Hungarian literary history: Dezső Kosztolányi, Mihály Babits, Kálmán Mikszáth, and the revolutionary poet Endre Ady, with whom Móricz forged an influential friendship in 1909.

Naturalism and Realism, literary trends that were already fading in western Europe, gained in importance in countries such as Hungary, Romania, and Poland during the era dominated by the experience of the First World War and the halting rise of capitalism in these traditionally agrarian societies. Móricz's experiences as a reporter at the front during the Great War, and as a witness to the sometimes promising, but more often disappointing political upheavals that took place in the wake of the conflict, strengthened his commitment to recording the plight of his nation's poorest classes in his writings. His early fame was founded on the novella "Seven Pennies" ("Hét krajcár") published in 1908 in *Nyugat* ("West"), a journal of such significance for Hungarian literature that an entire era is named for it, extending from 1908 when the first issues appeared, and lasting until the time of Móricz's death in 1942. The poignant portrayal of the value a mere seven pennies can have for an impoverished family sealed Móricz's reputation as an author with an unprecedented ability to lay bare the suffering of society's most neglected members.

Móricz's career as an author, grounded in ten years' work as a journalist, had begun. Tragically, only a fraction of his novels have been translated into English: *The Torch* (*A fáklya*, 1917), *Be Faithful unto Death* (*Légy jó mindhalálig*, 1920), *Very Merry* (*Úri muri*, 1928), and *Relations* (*Rokonok*, 1932), along with the story collection *Seven Pennies* (*Hét krajcár*, 1909). His works have fared better in other languages, especially French and German, but nonetheless the lack of availability of his novels in English translation has caused prominent historians of Hungary to lament the loss to English-speaking readers. In his article "How Modern Was Zsigmond Móricz," Péter Nagy points out the following: "In [Móricz's] own life-time, two modern spokesmen of the peasant world, Władysław Reymont and Frans Sillanpää, were awarded the Nobel Prize. His life-work is of no lesser importance than theirs, he is their equal in the beauty he created."[1] Of all the novels Móricz wrote that have yet to be translated into English, his first: *Sárarany*, or "Gold in the Mud," is perhaps most deserving of the international readership it has lacked until now.

---

[1] Péter Nagy, "How Modern Was Zsigmond Móricz," *The New Hungarian Quarterly*, vol. 77 (1980), p. 42.

Sárarany first appeared in 1910 as a serial novel in the influential *Nyugat* magazine, to be published in book form a year later. It was the first Hungarian novel to portray the peasant, here embodied by protagonist Dani Turi, as an ambitious individual who bows to no man, thus ushering in a new era of Hungarian literature. The novel's central theme is the deplorable waste of human potential resulting from the repression of the peasantry in what was still a largely feudal society, even in 1910. Móricz relies on the techniques of Naturalism to get his message across, creating memorable scenes that will appeal to modern readers in their vivid imagery and brutal directness. His descriptive powers are at their height in such scenes as the nighttime flight of Dani's wife Erzsi to her uncaring parents after he's beaten her, Dani's passionless tumble in the hay with a peasant girl during the wheat harvest, his claustrophobic encounter with his aging, hopelessly apathetic parents in their decaying cottage, and the gambling scene at the home of the alcoholic schoolmaster with his large, impoverished family, among many others.

But Móricz's skill goes far beyond such revealing vignettes of village apathy and disillusionment. The author's reputation rests also on his unflinching account of how Hungary's long-standing social and economic injustices stripped its peasantry of access to agency, happiness, and success. Dani Turi is a progressive farmer whose skill at making the land profitable through the application of modern agricultural techniques sets him apart not only from his downtrodden peasant peers, but also from the backward-looking landowners who see land merely as a means to maintain their powerful social status, rather than as a resource for the benefit of society as a whole. In order to realize his vision for a successful agricultural enterprise, Turi must secure the approval of Countess Helene, member of the comital Karay family to whom the estate surrounding Kiskara village belongs. The confrontation between Turi and the Countess towards the novel's end is one of its most memorable moments. But the traces left on the reader by the murder scene involving Helene's paramour, Count László, are if anything more indelible, as Móricz exposes how the weight of Hungarian history turns Dani Turi's enormous positive energy into a brutish force of pointless destruction.

Gold in the Mud is arguably the most powerful novel Zsigmond Móricz penned. In rendering this text into English, the translator has worked to remain as true as possible to the original Hungarian prose. Translation inevitably involves compromise, and in the case of *Sárarany*, a peculiar challenge is posed by the novel's unique publication history. More recent editions omit scenes and passages from the first version published in the pages of *Nyugat*. Some of these omissions strengthened the novel, by tightening the prose and improving its coherence and flow. Others resulted in a loss of detail, background, or clarity in terms of a seamless unfolding of the plot. The present translation is based on two versions of *Sárarany*, the second Hungarian edition from 1939, published by Athenaeum a few short years before Móricz's death, and the German translation by Armin Schwartz put out by Ernst Rowohlt Verlag in 1921, which is largely faithful to the first edition of *Sárarany*, though it contains several glaring translation errors, errors that have been corrected in this English version.[2] The resulting text has been edited for its faithfulness to Móricz's wording and punctuation, as well as for consistency in details of plot and character development, with the goal of allowing the reader to experience the original novel as authentically as a polished English version will allow.

Although this translation of *Sárarany* is a century overdue, it is nonetheless a timely work. Hungary's history is unique, yet also representative of the experience of those European nations that struggled with often tragic failure to keep up with the revolutions brought about by capitalism and industrialization, to say nothing of democratization and embourgeoisement. Hungary is still struggling to realize its full potential as a free, democratic country, a struggle informed by precisely those historic social and economic problems diagnosed so vividly by Zsigmond Móricz in his

---

[2] Zsigmond Móricz, *Sárarany*, 2nd ed. (Budapest: Athenaeum, 1939); Zsigmond Móricz, *Gold im Kote: ein ungarischer Bauernroman*, trans. by Armin Schwartz, 2nd. ed. (Berlin: Ernst Rowohlt Verlag, 1921).

early prose works. But *Gold in the Mud* is also a worthy literary experience in its own right, apart from its value as a historical document. Móricz's depictions of eastern Hungary's landscapes and the impoverished circumstances of many of its inhabitants at the turn of the twentieth century are unparalleled. And the often chilling confrontations he narrates between husbands and wives, parents and their children, peasants and nobles, the rich and the poor, will keep readers on the edge of their seats for generations to come.

First Part

I.

Burning hot summer. After the many downpours that had prevented the wheat from ripening, the sudden arrival of scorching heat has left the grains to wither. The rugged, thoughtful peasants only shake their heads quietly and conclude: "Even God himself has forgotten his handwork." But they don't grumble, they don't lose their nerve, and they don't cry. About the weather? Some things you just have to take as they come.

Dani Turi strode along the village street toward his home. Pretty young peasant girls followed him with their eyes, but he paid them no mind. His head was full of worries; from time to time he tilted it as though to pause over a particular thought. He brooded over great plans. In the manner of the man who seeks to get rich quickly, he embarked on ever bolder enterprises.

As he walked through the door into the carefully cleaned yard, he lifted from the ground a withered cornstalk, broke it into pieces, then tossed them among the shavings and twigs by the iron stove as he entered the kitchen.

His wife was working busily near the kitchen door. Her face was reddened, her bodice left her narrow, snow-white shoulders and neck free, and the skirt of blue-dotted chintz didn't quite cover her feet in their worn black slippers.

When she saw her husband enter the yard, she turned her face halfway toward him, her features tainted by envy and rage. Neither their five years of marriage nor the two children born to them had compromised him in any way. Everything turned to good for him. The tanned man with his red cheeks was more handsome today than he'd been before their marriage, given the good care she's taken of him, practically fattening him up. She, on the other hand, is not what she once was; the brats have sucked the flesh from her limbs, while all the work and trouble have taken care of the rest.

Dani had left the house before dawn – soon it would be midday; he thought he should greet his wife or at least speak a friendly word to her. But greeting her would be beneath his dignity – the wife was to greet the husband, who then responded with a sober nod of the head. His wife Erzsi had missed the proper moment, and as Dani looked into her astonished, large black eyes, it struck him that he must owe her something. He looked out past the kitchen door at the sky, turned his gaze partway toward the woman and said:

"If it's going to rain, it should rain!"

He stroked his moustache, from which he'd gotten the nickname "Turi with the good-looking muzzle." His wife winked grudgingly back, and with that the matter was over.

Dani turned his steps toward the front room. Again he felt the urge to say something, as though not everything were as it should be between him and his wife.

4

"Where's my red notebook?" he asked.

"Where else? In your coat. In the wardrobe."

Dani went into the room. He, too, knew he'd find his notebook there.

The air in the room blew coolly on him. It was filled with the odor of the yellow clay coating the floor, alongside that of the rather musty bed linens and the food they kept in the carefully cleaned room, the rancid butter and souring milk. The wardrobe was a fine piece of furniture, nice enough for a nobleman. Dani opened the door and retrieved his red-bound notebook from his coat pocket. He sat down at the table and began to calculate in the dim room with its shuttered windows. From time to time he guided his pencil to his mouth, and tossed words and ciphers in large schoolchild writing onto a clean page.

"I'll kick the soul from your body, you dog!" he suddenly heard his wife yell. "May God punish you, you brat – you've knocked over the milk jug!"

Slap! Slap! was heard from outside, as the mother struck the child's scrawny behind with her flat hand. The boy didn't start crying until several moments had passed, then it was as though a piglet were being slaughtered.

Dani listened for a time to the din, then continued with his work. The children belonged to their mother, they were none of his affair; if the woman weren't at least in charge of the two children, she'd leave home.

Soon after that the door opened and the woman stormed in in a rage to inspect the milk jugs arranged along the wall.

"What in God's name should I do now!" she grumbled fretfully. Not because she sought anyone's advice, but because she couldn't suppress her anger. "There was still a pint left in the jug, it would've been just enough. Now I have to start in on a full jug, and that means worrying with skimming the cream off the top."

"The butter won't harm the cake," Dani threw in. He sat with a worried look, all but ignoring his wife's anger.

Erzsi gritted her teeth and reached for one of the large milk jugs, one that had cracked long ago. She was still waiting for the tinker, but as he refused to come, she'd taken to handling the container with care, since she had so few milk jugs left that suited her. But now in her agitation she forgot that the jug was cracked, grabbed it forcefully, and just as she turned with it toward the front room, it flew to the floor and broke into a thousand pieces.

"Broken to bits," Dani said, not letting himself get upset. "Never mind – if it breaks, it breaks, there's nothing to be done about it. Just let it go – it's hardly a disaster ..."

Erzsi turned angrily toward her husband and raised her arm with the apparent intent to hurl the handle left in her hand at his head. Had a better impulse not held her back in the last moment, things could have ended badly. But the wife isn't there to lash out in anger; she takes things out on herself rather than venting her ire on others.

She turned and left, tossed the broken handle into the trash, fetched the broom, the dustpan, and a rag, then returned to clean the floor.

Hot, burning tears flowed from her eyes, and a volcano of anger threatened to erupt inside her.

Dani regarded all this in good humor. He told himself it probably would not be advisable to start a quarrel with his wife, but it so happened he was in the mood to tease her. He turned the pencil back and forth between his thick fingers distractedly and smiled quietly at her. He thoroughly enjoyed watching her clean the soiled floor with a nimble skill that defied her anger.

"You see," he remarked softly, "now it'll look really nice. You should always scrub the floor with milk. But you're so stingy with it ... "

The unexpected insult numbed the woman; she struggled to find words of response.

At that moment they heard loud hissing and crackling from the kitchen stove.

"Oh no, now that milk has leaked out too!" the woman yelled and ran out.

Dani laughed out loud. Through the open door he could indeed smell the stench of burning milk.

Now from the other room one could hear a child's piercing cry. The baby had awoken and loudly announced his presence.

"Drop dead!" the mother yelled into the room. "You'd be better off dead than growing up to be a dog like your father!"

Dani just laughed quietly to himself.

But the woman continued her rant: "Where in the heck is the little wretch? You!" she cried out into the yard where the older boy still sat sobbing on a crossbeam below the porch roof. "Get in here! I don't want to hear a sound, otherwise I'll kick you in the head. Go into the room and rock your brat of a brother ... But take care that you don't fling him out of the cradle!"

Dani laughed again. She's full of concern for her children. She tells the bigger one not to fling the little one out of the cradle! Typical woman!

In the meantime, Erzsi had set everything to rights on the stove and now returned to the front room to sweep up the shards of broken jug.

"I could be torn to shreds ... ripped to pieces ... " she grumbled.

"The jumping about doesn't hurt you a bit – just freshens you up!" Dani retorted.

"Shut up!" she yelled at him, her face burning with anger. "Or else I'll drop dead here in the middle of the floor! Or murder the lot of them." She was foaming with rage.

"The tramps!" she yelled. "They should be poisoned! That would be the best. They do nothing but drain me of life. And if there were a hundred of them, they'd all be albatrosses around my neck. I'm nothing but their servant."

"What are you here for, then?" Dani responded with disdain. "How many maids should I get to help you out?"

"That's the last thing I need!" Erzsi retorted with disgust. "Your maids – let the hangman take them ... They're only good for you. None of your girls shall set foot in my kitchen. Not a woman in this village may touch my white dishes."

Dani laughed out loud; it was a healthy, hearty, happy laugh. "Well, well," he cried. "Is there any in the village that you wouldn't have pilloried with me?"

"Yes. My grandmother, who's been rotting in the ground for the past twenty years. There's none besides her."

Dani laughed again, flashing his handsome, healthy white teeth. He tossed back his powerful bull's neck, and his ruddy face with its daring gaze shone with manly good looks. He stroked the brown hair lying atop his white, sweat-covered forehead, so that it fell in broad waves off to the side. His eyes sparkled in intimate, carefree satisfaction.

The woman stared with hate-filled eyes at the man for whom she'd jumped into a well years ago. The first-born daughter of a well-to-do peasant, her father had bristled at giving her away to a cottager's son. And nothing had come of the wedding until the strapping fellow, whom all the girls chased after in any case, had had his way not just with Erzsi, but with her mother as well. Erzsi discovered this too late, after she could no longer change it and every other woman in the village could boast of having enjoyed her husband's love; the mother-in-law lost her mind over it – it was she who'd informed her daughter. Erzsi was filled with disgust, and from that point on could no longer look her mother in the eye. Had her husband made do with just one lover, it would have been a tolerable marital relationship. But sharing him with ten or twenty girls and ladies, including, as she knew, her mother, was unbearable. The young wife felt more disgust at the sight of a woman she suspected of having been with her husband than in the face of a corpse. Yet as she had nowhere else to go, she chose to stay with the man without whom, as she so keenly sensed, she could not live.

The man merely gazed at the woman with her fiery black eyes, her features distorted by anger. A peculiar, ambiguous emotion came over him as he considered the hell of those dark eyes, flashing from beneath her black, daringly arched eyebrows, her well-formed, snow-white forehead, from the framework of her starkly prominent cheekbones, sharply profiled, narrow nose and embittered mouth, those eyes that were nonetheless powerless to affect him ... He understood why he had lately grown cool toward this woman, and yet it astonished him how quickly his blood began to boil these days. How beastly this woman was, simply beastly, made for kneeling, praying, and hating, but not for loving. A Catholic! Hardy and passionate, incomprehensible to him. With his own nature of a stout Calvinist, as easy to appease as he was to inflame, angry in moderation, often cursing, yet tending toward mellowness, toward constant cheerfulness ... And still this woman excited him, captivated him far more than all the other women of the world. He wouldn't trade her for anyone else on the globe. He was filled with her, delighted in her great cleanliness, the immaculateness of her physical and spiritual life. He was proud of her, as of someone who was without equal, and when he roamed about the flower garden of fleeting joys, he always thought with happiness of the woman at home who saved her pure calyx for him, and prayed on her knees to her strict gods, who were foreign to him.

The eyes of the strong, healthy man with his ruddy cheeks flashed; with his left hand he grasped his wife's tensed forearm and hastily drew her toward him. In her other hand she held the dustpan – with a jerk the shards it held flew clinking across the room. Dani again laughed heartily, as though relieved. He embraced her, holding her arms fast; and the strong, sturdy peasant woman felt her power dwindling beside that of her husband – in his hands she was as helpless as her children were in hers. He could do with her as he pleased. He forced her onto his lap, bent her over his shoulder and stroked her arms.

"You nasty bug!" he said. Then he held her with outstretched arms so he could look into her face.

The woman let the dustpan fall from her hand; it hit the shards with a clank. She yielded submissively – she was completely at her husband's mercy.

"You China rose, you! What's troubling you?" Dani asked and regarded his wife with a victor's satisfaction. "What's the matter? How could I possibly harm you? You can barely stand to have me kiss you! It honestly makes you ill, you hothouse flower. I'm just too much for you, you little dew blossom! You'd wither in my arms if I kissed you till *I've* had enough!"

He stretched his wife across his arms like a gangly child. Erzsi thought she was floating on air. The secure feeling of firm ground disappeared beneath her feet and from her soul, she grew dizzy and faint; then she felt how she lay in the arms of her husband, and it seemed as safe a place as the hands of God. The thought flashed in her narrow mind that there existed no man as strong as hers on the entire earth; only half conscious, she let him do what he wanted with her. She forgot her kitchen, her milk; her roast could burn and turn to coal – what did she care.

Dani laid her warm, supple torso against his chest and shoulder and hugged her tenderly. Her steamy body, barely clothed, felt ever cooler to the touch in the shaded room, yet radiated such heat as though it were molten bronze.

"You see, you see?" the peasant said softly. "You're like soft mud. What'll I do with you? When I touch you with just one finger, you're done for. Dammit, a hundred women wouldn't be enough for me ..."

He embraced the woman, hot with passion, and held her tightly against him; then he furrowed his brow and fell silent. He thought about his business deal, which quickly took him over completely, and as he sat there, his wife in his arms, he surveyed his previously interrupted planning attempt clearly and calmly, as though he once again held a pencil between his fingers, and not a woman pining away with love, his betrothed partner in marriage.

The woman's body snuggled ever closer to him. Her naked arms embraced the man's neck and shoulders; her restless, able, caressing fingers tingled as she felt through the man's soft, supple shirt to his glass-smooth, elastic skin. They began to play and soon gripped feverishly, tautly into his flesh, pressing, kneading, torturing it, mashing the yielding cushions of muscle beneath his shoulder as they filled her hand. The woman's mind became the passive helpmate of her passionate desire's sudden storm, and as her strong, tan arms slung themselves round her husband's head, her lips pressed burning hot on the nape of his neck, where it shone white from beneath his shirt, and she forgot all worries, all bitterness, all heartbreak. She wanted only her husband, desired him, yielded to him.

The man roused himself with a smile from his ruminations. He felt as though something had happened in his wife. He patted her soft, swelling limbs and said calmly, guided by his thoughts: "If this business takes off, then we'll be free of all our worries and troubles."

The woman flinched and pressed the man desperately against her, as though wanting to smother every alien thought within him, as though expecting from his body some help against the alienation of her soul.

The man wanted to push her away, but couldn't; she embraced him doggedly and voluptuously. He smiled at her, all but forgetting how she'd ended up in his arms.

"If I can make this lease turn out the way I want, I wouldn't trade places with the Deputy County Chief himself."

The woman's arms fell limply, much as the four o'clock does when singed by the sun's rays. Dani was quickly done with her; he held her away from him with outstretched arms, as was his wont, and looked in her face.

"You'll become a real lady yet," he said with radiant joy.

But Erzsi's expression was so sad, so deeply depressed and frightened; her eyes begged and quivered, tears sparkling in their corners, and her features grew slack and tired. Her thin face was lustful, her lips throbbed with heat, her nostrils widened and her eyelids drooped across her pupils.

Yet in his excitement, the man noticed none of that, he was consumed by his plans. It seemed he'd resolved everything that had occupied his mind up to that point. "There's not as much silk in all the shops of Szatmár as you'll be able to get for your dresses!"

The woman shut her eyes and lowered her head.

"I'll lease you the whole of Nagyszeg, do you hear? ... I've already spoken with the steward about it. The landlord is upset with the Jewish leaseholder, and besides, the whole thing depends on the lady of the manor anyhow. I want to go up there myself, it's not like she'll eat me alive. I'm not afraid of a lady, I've seen others before. Even if she's Her Excellency herself, beneath it all she's still just a woman!"

Erzsi jumped up as though a snake had bitten her. Every ligament in her body tensed. She only now understood what her husband had said.

"Wwwhat?" she yelled, her voice faltering. "What did you say? Her Excellency? The Countess? ... You want to go to her? But ..."

"Hold on, hold on, I tell you, she won't eat me alive! What have you got to be afraid of?"

"Now her, too!" the wife screamed hoarsely and sprang from her husband's lap. She clapped her hands together, raised them over her head, then let her arms fall back down. She started racing back and forth across the room as though she feared the unavoidable death of one of her dear children. "Now her too, her too!" she repeated.

The husband spent several moments watching her uncomprehendingly. "What is it that's got your goat?"

"My God! My God! My savior stretched out on the cross! When will my suffering ever end? Oh blessed Mother of God! ..."

"Don't bellow so!" the man yelled. "That's just what I need, just that! You bird brain." He hurled the pencil angrily onto the table. "Instead of being happy and dancing, the fool goes on like an idiot. It's true, a woman is worse than an animal ... Don't you get it? If this thing works out – because nothing is certain yet – I'll close a deal with the landlord that'll finish him. I want to lease the entire property of Nagyszeg, the entire Puszta itself; in the Tisza bend there are cabbage fields I could easily sublease for eighty, maybe a hundred forints rent a quarter acre."

"A thousand."

The man grew silent. That was at least an intelligent word, one that related to the business at hand. The wife is always thinking in terms of worst-case scenarios, not like him, who sees his plans with rose-colored glasses, his imagination chasing around so swiftly it can't be brought to a standstill. Often enough it was the wife who proved right, so rather than interrupt her talk, he pondered and considered the matter anew.

He started from the beginning and told her everything, with all the details, as he was accustomed to doing. Erzsi stood in the middle of the room, gazing distractedly with lowered eyes, and listened. After a bit, she went out to the kitchen, tidied things up on the stove, chased the dog out, closed the door behind it and returned to the front room. Her husband looked up from his notebook and continued his speech:

"If you were to have sixteen little chickadees, you'd be able to leave all of them a proper fortune. So enough with the sour faces, I can't see the point."

"I don't need the fat from your women."

"There she goes again ..." Dani muttered angrily.

"I'd sooner take your brats on my arm and go begging with them. I don't need that kind of dirty money."

"What dirty money?"

"Egh! Money for which I have to fight over you with others."

Dani grimaced indignantly.

"Sure, sure," the wife continued, "now he runs after the high-born ladies; the ones he had before weren't enough for him! Just go, go, till the ladies are tired of you and throw you in with the hogs. May God grant that you get what you deserve at last! You've gotten far too shameless! ..."

Dani stared at her wide-eyed; he now understood her suspicion, it was like getting a nail to the head. Maybe she's not so wrong. A lady is just a woman, after all! ...

He furrowed his brow and turned toward the window.

Erzsi trampled a shard with her foot. She leaned down and collected the splinters. Then she burst out: "I tell you, enough of these vile deeds! The day that my anger reaches the boiling point, may God in heaven have mercy on us all."

Dani rose. He looked at his wife, his eyes aflame. "And I tell you," he commanded sternly, "that you should look after your own affairs, and nothing else. You've got your kitchen, your yard, your children. You have nothing to do with my business ... If you can't stand by me, then don't get in my way ... You're not lacking for a thing. You know I love you. I live for you, for you and the children. I want to gather up the entire world and lay it at your feet. To this day I haven't given a single other woman the tiniest of gifts. So what are you feeling sorry about? Have my kissing skills gone sour? God knows! What does it matter to you how I go about my business, as long as I succeed!"

The woman swallowed her tears; she sensed the fight could yet end harmlessly, but could just as well take a turn for the worse. Her husband's stern tone silenced her like a scolded child.

He, too, grew quiet. He sat back down in his chair and, with a serious expression, tried to collect his thoughts.

"You know, Dani, I need very little," she said sadly and softly. "I would be happy if we lived as poor cottagers in your mother's hut. But if we already own so much, what do we need with more? Why so many kids, all the money and worry? Why shouldn't we live like my father and mother? Quietly, decently. We shouldn't lust after the entire world, shouldn't disregard what we have. Why trouble yourself like this if you don't need to? You'll see ... things will end up badly one day!"

"Be quiet, for God's sake!" her husband interrupted her irritatedly. "Listen when I tell you to listen ... Don't compare me with your father, I'm not an old *Scarecrow* like him!"

The young wife blushed at the sound of this spiteful nickname for her father, whom she loved and honored with all the warmth of her heart. She flashed a look of hatred at her husband. "Leave my father in peace! Just watch out: one day you, too, will have your nickname – and no amount of water will wash it away!"

Dani hesitated. He looked searchingly at his wife, wondering if she already knew something. For some time he'd noticed how people on the street laughed when he passed, whispering some word or other. He still hadn't learned exactly what sort of word it was. Nor did he dare ask, for fear someone might reveal it to him.

"May God spare anyone who tries to stick me with some nasty nickname," he grumbled, forcefully suppressing his anger.

Their argument finally stagnated. Half an hour ago it had begun as an impending tempest, only to peter out like an autumn fog, leaving a depressive atmosphere and dull apathy behind, the results of a tension neither the man nor the woman could ignore.

When Erzsi saw that her husband had nothing more to say, she went out into the kitchen. Dani leaned his arm on the table and lost himself again in his plans.

II.

Kiskara is a pretty little village on the Hungarian plain, numbering barely a hundred houses. The lots are long and regularly shaped, the gardens planted with fruit trees, and in the village center the wooden clock tower stretches its spire into the air like a spear rising up from a green grove. On the tip sits a cock with ruffled feathers, announcing abroad that here resides a pure Hungarian people of Calvinist faith.

The village is the hereditary seat of the comital Karay family, who also gave it their name.

At the time of the Reformation, the Karays took up the new faith, and the Hungarian population of their far-flung estates followed them into this faith of the Transylvanian princes, not from spiritual necessity, nor even for political reasons, but simply to annoy the Viennese court. When Catholicism regained its popularity during the time of the Prince Primate Pázmány, the Karays returned to the Catholic religion, but this attempt to curry favor with the Emperor was in vain; the people refused to follow their example. The Hungarians had quickly accustomed themselves to the free, independent religious life the new confession afforded them. And when the persecutions came, the people's soul steeled itself and found heroic satisfaction in its attachment to the faith.

The hostile relationship between the village and its landlord originated in this period. The village boundaries mark no less than eight thousand acres; of these some six hundred belong to smallholders, the rest to the Count.

This land was for ages the ancestral inheritance of the Karay family. But the peasants' right of possession was just as old. Since time immemorial, one and the same people had resided here. It was an especially favorable turn of fate that neither the Tatar vandals nor the Turkish plague destroyed this people; they lived here courageously from one century to the next as serfs of the Karay counts. The village population provided the servants needed by the landlords, and the excess love of the gentlemen and their ladies poured itself out here in the old days when fussiness was not in wide circulation. There existed a certain feeling of racial communion between the lords and the peasants, but after the great treason, the peasants in Old-Kara despised Count Pál Karay with a hatred that only comes about between blood relations. It's the most savage hatred, absolutely irreconcilable.

Count Pál Karay endeavored futilely to come up with a simple, concrete legal formula to justify his treason – every peasant saw through him. And what good did it do him that, according to the great peace treaty that was reached, it seemed a natural and wise thing to put down the insurgents, causing everyone throughout the country, from the last prince who'd been sent into exile all the way down to the lowest servant in Kara, to look on him with hatred and rage? And what use was it that he acquired the properties of those adherents of the Prince who'd emigrated not by accepting them as gifts, but by purchasing them? Everyone knew he'd bought 130,000 acres of land for 100,000 ducats, and that 50,000 ducats had been paid not by him but from imperial coffers, the rest eventually being waived by the most gracious Queen. Everyone also knew that the poor Hungarian soldiers did not put down their arms on that famous plain, the Alföld, until the treaty lay signed and sealed in the general's pocket ...

When Count Karay, with his hard Kuruc skull, got himself involved in this business, he counted from the start on the advent of national hatred, and shook off the contempt like a komondor shakes off water. He was, after all, already an old man – by the time his grandchildren were grown, all of this would be forgotten.

But as he withdrew to his ancestral estate and the ancient castle of his forebears, every peasant looked at him with fire in his eyes.

The old Count snorted and angrily clenched his teeth, in an attempt to break the peasants of their hatred. It didn't work. The Hungarian peasant was in those days on a par with the petty nobility; he may not have obtained his political rights, but he certainly bore all the political burdens.

The landlord could boil in his own anger, for all the peasants cared. The "Count" was no longer the landlord in their eyes. Their stubborn, hardened Calvinist necks resisted His Excellency's dignity. And their compulsory labor contributions had brought them precious little thanks; from this point on, they harnessed their strong, unwavering stubbornness and practiced sabotage wherever they could.

"Just you wait!" Count Pál Karay growled in his rage, and he hurried to Vienna to lodge a formal complaint with the Queen.

After a few months, he'd chased the entire native Hungarian population off of his far-flung estates, away from this blessedly fertile, rich land, and settled "in the place of the cringing Calvinist dogs pious Swabians who profess our holy Catholic religion." He insisted on people who, rather than sitting before their houses moping and sobbing forth sad, plaintive songs, sent pious psalms to heaven, eyes lifted upward; people who, rather than spit when they heard the name Karay and call after him: "our traitor," crossed themselves and praised him as the "patron of the Swabians!"

For a long time one heard not a single Hungarian word in this ancient Hungarian territory. The old Count's business officials had depopulated sixteen villages and three market towns. The people had emigrated to other, more distant counties; only here and there was a village –

including Kara – indemnified with a small, strictly measured urbarial possession. The Count had designated the "Hangman's Heath" for the residents of Kara: "That's where they belong from the first to the last!" And one dismal autumn the people left their dear homeland for oblivion, there to found a new village, which they named "Kiskara" or Little Kara ...

Throughout an entire winter the houses of the abandoned villages stood empty. Snow lay on the roofs, rain ran unhindered through the farmyards, frost wreaked its havoc. Wolves took up residence in the village churches, and when lightning struck one of the towers, an entire village went up in flames. Here and there, those who'd been chased from their homeland set the abandoned houses ablaze, so that the familiar nests so dear to them would not become a breeding ground for ravens.

When, in the springtime, the Swabian usurpers arrived, the air was filled with their foreign jabbering; the immigrants complained that what they found here was far from the paradise promised them. The famished Swabians, who'd fallen prey to plague in their homeland, weren't satisfied with what they received: the fertile, blessed earth, the cows and horses, the wagons, the five-year exemption from taxes and labor duties, even the housecat his lordship the Count had provided for them ...

It happened that old, blind Karay, who didn't understand a word of the language spoken by his new people, could not decipher a German-written letter they'd intercepted, not even with the help of the 25,000 men in his camp. Once again his anger flared. He would have preferred to send the new arrivals to the devil, but that wasn't possible. The Swabians who'd settled in the Tisza River valley enjoyed the special protection of the Viennese court. This settlement initiative enabled the Queen once again to extend her favor to the old Kuruc leader, whose appearance and demeanor were such that, whenever he appeared in the Vienna castle, the ladies-in-waiting whispered among themselves what a dangerous game the Queen played by allowing this hungry bear free reign.

Old Karay returned from Vienna, as angry as the peasant who thrashes his vine stock after hail has destroyed it: "Let's just see, Lord God, who can do it better!"

As if there weren't already enough unpleasant newcomers on his estates, now he would bring an even lowlier, fouler tribe! Needed was an even more servile sort, a hungrier, filthier people. Bring on the Wallachians!

Who had even noticed their presence on earth before now? But they're here, after all. They wander down unnoticed from the oak- and beech-covered hills, where no wheat grows, but only acorns and juniper – this is where the penniless Wallachian pastures his few goats, the poor, tired, tattered Wallachian with his long, curly hair, his short-trimmed moustache and hungry, always hungry stomach, blowing his endless sad songs on his shawm. Until now, he's been seen here as the bear in the forest: in the vast, measureless forests where the Wallachian hasn't an inch of earth to call his own, just like the bear. He so resembles the little cub – are the two not alike when they come into town to attend the market and dance to the monotonous beat of the leather drum? With what a sympathetic look – at once astonished and shy – do the Hungarians, sustained by their hearty wheat bread, enjoy observing the Wallachian.

So the Count settled this half wild people in the very villages the Swabians had rejected. In this way, some twenty Wallachian communities sprang up on his estates.

Thus it came that, in the soul of the Kiskara peasants, hatred toward their rulers existed side by side with the fear of God. This helpless anger, stored up over centuries, has now grown entirely unconscious. Who could explain to the children today what sin the Count had committed against them! Yet everyone knew to spit when the Count's name was mentioned, and if the occasion arose, the peasants were easily enraged and prepared to beat down the hereditary Count.

III.

The Hungarian folk had been living their monotonous, quiet existence in Kiskara for two centuries. Each fall and spring they plowed and sowed, in days past with a wooden plowshare, in more recent times with an iron one. One would never have thought that this good, black earth could produce anything besides wheat, wheat, and more wheat. People grow no more corn than needed to fatten the pigs. What potatoes are grown certainly suffice. What else should the God-given earth bring forth? A bit of broomcorn for making brooms, a few rows of sunflowers to press some oil from, turnips for the cows, squashes for the children, a little hemp for the spinning gatherings. The rest then brings forth wheat, wheat, wheat.

This life is so simple, so familiar, without change or variation. The moon waxes and wanes, as if to tell everyone what they should do when. In summer there's the hard, tiring work in the field, which seems less the working of the soil than the struggle waged by a small group of bitter, orphaned people for their daily bread on the back of the great, apathetic, merciless earth. And their struggle is a hard one; the strenuous work wears the people of Kiskara down before they attain a respectable age.

But the struggle is dictated to them by centuries-old custom – the individual need think very little. What is there to think about? Agriculture? ...

There in the soul, in the conscience of these peasants lives, as an unconscious faith, the worldview of the ancient pagans, a strangely ardent nature worship passed down to them as a fundamental inheritance the scholars know nothing about. Over a thousand years, little has changed here, this ancient worldview merely wears a new dress: the dress of Christendom, adorned with crosses. But these people's hearts remain pagan. And in their theological conscience, so often labeled as superstitious, they regard the house of their Christian God solely as a place to honor their own unnamed, eternal lord and God. Old storytellers among them, who likewise manifest the hardened type of Kirghiz heathen, possess detailed knowledge of the stories concerning the twelve daughters of the king, the significance of the phases of the sacred moon, and when they scoop water from the sweep well, they know to pour a bit back from the bucket they've just filled. Who could say why? Perhaps to honor the eternal God enthroned in the middle of the earth.

Everything spoken and done here tells of the ancestors left behind in the high, icy North; the race of people who migrated westward preserves here the soul of the East. On this earth, where millennia ago only the sea whirled and thundered, they still know the great whale at whose back the world stands ... For how many thousands of years those who sowed their seeds here preserved the fantastic notions of the seafisher, perhaps only their Finno-Ugric ancestors could say.

And regardless of which men stand at the head of the government, whether in times of absolutist rule or constitutional protection, all of that is registered here only in muffled tones, like a roar from the endless distance. Who even cares about it? When spring comes with its sunny days, the plowshare must sink into the earth. And as the little bee flies toward the blossoms in spring, so does the farmer return to the soil. Though war and revolution may come, the peasant sows the seed of bread, so that he may think of life in times of death.

Into this calcified world, where the minds of some have grown hard while others have moldered, there suddenly entered a strange new era of upheaval.

A man had been born, grown up, served three years with the military, then married. Just like the others. Many had attended his baptismal feast, many his wedding. But who would have imagined what would become of him?

It so happened that, during the first year of having his own farm on a plot along the Tisza River his wife had received as dowry, he grew not wheat, but rapeseed.

When the man brought the seed back from the city, the people shook their heads. Who'd ever heard of such a thing?

Coming here with a new crop! One shouldn't toy with the earth!

"This Turi is insane!" said the one ... "No, not a fool, a squanderer," said another. "He's wasting the earth! ... He came into money and wealth overnight, and now he's lost his head, he doesn't know what he's doing."

They scorned him, told him their feelings to his face. He just laughed. And when the oil-rich, fleshy plant had grown to the height of a full-grown man and the entire plot of rape lay resplendent with fresh, bright-yellow blossoms, and finally when the harvest arrived and the richly blessed earth yielded Dani Turi eight hundred forints per acre of rapefield, boundless incredulity took hold of the people.

For as long as anyone could remember, no event had ever unleashed such excitement among the people of Kiskara. Throughout the winter they spoke only of Dani's rapeseed. The next year his rape crop was again successful. The following year, the entire bank of the Tisza was yellow with rapefields as far as the eye could see.

The skeptical peasants shook their heads and, from time to time, suspiciously crushed a clod of earth on the edge of the rapefield; it would never have entered their minds that this soil could produce anything other than what it was accustomed to producing. They would gladly have vented their anger on this earth, which up to now had failed to return all the nice money they'd invested ...

In the following year, Dani Turi's fields produced an even larger, more startling harvest boon. Dani Turi, this cheerful young peasant with his handsome moustache and numerous love affairs, who lived life with such ease and joy that the peasants, so used to regarding the plowman as a grumpy, suntanned, wrinkled, apathetic, somber fellow, had nothing to say about him but: "The devil take that Dani, he succeeds at everything!"

This year Dani planted cabbage along the Tisza, on the very fields where, in the first year, the rapeseed had done so well. He had to win over the women to this project – it was the only way to succeed where no one else would in cultivating these far-flung fields successfully. When it came to winning women over to harvest cabbage, Dani didn't even refrain from giving hugs to the Gypsy women dwelling near the village.

An earthquake could not have aroused the astonishment Dani Turi did when he earned the sum of three thousand forints from a plot planted with cabbage which previously, when planted with wheat, had brought in barely two hundred. It was a splendid cabbage crop, free of stalks, dense and smooth. People fought over this Kiskara cabbage at the markets.

And then, the following winter, all the women of the village offered themselves to him just so he would grant them a single cabbage plot along the Tisza. Not knowing any better, the people laughed when the old Scarecrow, Dani's father-in-law, out of pure stinginess, turned over to him as a nuptial gift the low-lying field that had until then lain useless and fallow, rather than his superbly worked wheatfields.

Dani Turi divided the entire stretch along the bank of the Tisza into narrow strips and now rented these out at high prices: without lifting a finger, he got more from the land than he would have if he'd worked himself to death.

New plans unfolded in his head: the revitalizing of the old, used-up earth; fertilizer one could buy at the store and scatter from sacks; deep plowing of the soil, viticulture ... He didn't succeed in everything, but nor did any of this cost him extra money. All the women of the village were his vassals, his work slaves.

He'd been married for barely four years when the boundaries of Kiskara grew too narrow for him. These boundaries were limited by the monstrous estates of the Count. Why should one not be able to get a few fields from there?

When, during the winter, he first came up with this idea, the peasants responded with the same curt hand gesture of rejection that meant: forget about it. That all belongs to the Count. The Jew is master there. The entire property has been let out.

Dani didn't rest. He was often seen on the Count's estates – he had an inexhaustible supply of excuses. He'd already made the acquaintance of the entire staff, and his fabled good luck with women soon made him right at home on the Count's fields. Before the year was over, he knew these fields better than the Count's own steward, and every detail of the lease agreement was more familiar to him than to the Count's attorney. There were two smaller sections of the domains that were independent from the main complex under lease. The first was the Nagyszeg, which at the time of the leasing had been under water; this section lay in a mighty enclave of the Tisza. The other was the Pallag, a nice piece of pasture extending for two hundred acres. Dani also learned that the Count did not want to lease these two sections, but to sell them. Yet the current landlord, "Count Miska," would have nothing to do with peasants; he was put off by the aura of drudgery surrounding them and did not believe he could get any money out of them. Word was that the leaseholder, Lichtstein, had already all but finalized his purchase of the Pallag, at a bargain price. Dani couldn't imagine entering into competition with the young Jew, whom the peasants dubbed "Liscsán."

But in recent days something odd had happened. The Karay counts had a pretty little forest castle near Kiskara where no one from the Count's family had shown his face in fifty years. Count Miska's wife had inexplicably come up with the strange idea of taking up residence here. No one could say whether it would be for a longer period of time or just one day. Master workers had come from Pest to get the castle into shape, and one day Dani Turi learned that Her Excellency the Countess was in fact there.

"I'll speak with her!" he told himself, and right away he pictured his plow working the Nagyszeg parcel. Three hundred acres! Nearly as much as half of Kiskara. And in a single section, twice as much land as he and his father-in-law possessed together.

IV.

He didn't have a moment's rest. His body shook with fever, he felt a tingling near his heart and spasms in all his limbs that sapped his strength and held his thoughts hostage. For some time now this struggle had raged within him. Ever since the days when he'd learned how to forge great plans and then realized there was no human possibility of realizing them. Today he was angry with himself and his heart for this senseless struggle; he kept telling himself amidst curses he had nothing to fear, so why should he tremble so?

But now suddenly such incredibly far-flung plans stormed down on him that he nearly lost his head in his greed-induced excitement. And constituted as he was, he could not possibly overlook the fact that, when it came to realizing these plans, he was a small man, terribly small, even smaller than he had been back in the day when, as the son of the poor cottager Mihály Turi, he'd cast a glance at the peasant Takács's daughter.

Yet one thing bolstered his confidence, and that was the fact that he'd succeeded in everything he'd tried thus far!

As he sat stiff with thinking at the table in the dimly lit room, he resembled an Indian idol; he could have sat like that for ten thousand years.

His gaze fell on his fist, which was so brown it looked almost black as it rested on the table in the dim light.

It was the first time in his life that he'd noticed his hands.

How could he dare embrace a noble lady with such hands?

His thick, coarse fingers lay there spread out, studded with jagged nails, and were so strong and so accustomed to hard gripping that they were incapable of holding anything gently. Held by such fingers, a tender white woman's body must melt like a sculpture made of butter ...

Such asinine words. It was out of the question that a well-born, aristocratic woman could take a liking to him.

Then, with a firm movement, he stretched out his arm and struck the table powerfully with his iron fist; he held his arm out like this for a moment, rigid as steel, and as he looked boldly with his handsome, sparkling eyes into the great whirlwind of his life, he said to himself: "That's what will be! No matter what. Regardless of what happens, it will be! If it's worked out so far, it'll work out now too!"

And he was no longer the man from before, but another, nimble, energetic man, not wasting his time in thought, but chasing his dreams with gusto.

Just then the door opened and his little boy entered the room. "Father," said the child timidly, "come to dinner."

"I'm coming, son!"

The father rose, approached his son, bent down and lifted the child up high in his iron fists. "Hey there, my little brat! You'll become a count one day! ..."

As this thought flashed up within him, a sudden ray of light struck him like lightning shooting through an oak tree.

But the lightning didn't destroy him, it only made him harder. Far from turning into a self-consuming flame, he was ablaze with energy.

V.

The family ate in silence. Father and child sat across from each other along the two long sides of the white kitchen table. The narrow end had been set for the woman, but rather than sit at the table, she served the others, then took her earthenware plate and ate standing by the oven, quickly tossing the few bites inside her. Afterwards she squatted down on a little chair, took her one-year-old boy onto her lap and gave him pre-chewed bits of the food she ate, mumbling softly as she did.

Dani looked thoughtfully at his son sitting across from him – in his handsome little face all the pleasant features were united that he could possibly have inherited from his father and mother. The large, dark eyes he had from his mother, the fine, high, intelligent forehead and white skin from his father.

"Don't slurp so!" Dani admonished the boy, who was sucking his soup distractedly from the spoon.

The child looked up at his father and noticed that his voice was calm, which strengthened his courage.

Dani paid no more attention to the child; he was occupied by other thoughts.

"You're slurping too, father," little Béla said in a serious tone.

Dani looked sternly at the boy. "I'm allowed," he said with importance. "I'm just a peasant! ..."

And he observed the fine, narrow, white hands of his son.

After a moment, he added: "Why didn't you wash your hands before eating? A little student must always have clean hands."

The child failed to understand the hint and didn't move.

His father pressed him: "Well? ... Go and wash your hands, this minute."

The child got down from the tall chair and, somewhat mystified, went to the water jug, took some water into his mouth, then washed his hands and his face a bit too, as he generally did in the morning. Admittedly it had never happened before that he washed himself twice in one day, but if his father demanded it! The hand towel of coarse linen hung on the door hinge; he dried his hands and face, then sat again at the table with reddened cheeks, shiny nose, and dripping hair.

His father laughed quietly. No gentleman's child could be more handsome.

Erzsi watched all these goings-on and turned up her mouth. She surmised where her husband's thoughts were headed. But this time she didn't grumble at him.

She took the little one on her arm and went up to the older boy, stroking his damp short curls away from his forehead – a man doesn't notice such details. She grabbed the comb and combed him, parting his hair to one side in the manner of a little gentleman.

VI.

Once they'd finished their meal, Dani rose from the table, wiped his mouth and went to work.

Until suppertime he occupied himself with laying in the hay; then he returned to the house, shaved and put on his Sunday best.

Erzsi watched him quietly, neither saying a word to the other. Their son Béla played on the floor with baby brother Sanyi, which did not prevent him from following his father's actions with interest.

When Dani was finished dressing, he reached for a walking stick and turned to leave. In the middle of the hall he stopped and searched for words of farewell. "Well ... if ..." he began, thinking after each word, "... if Pesta comes in, tell him that tomorrow all six of them must be here. We want to start gathering up the hay. It's still lying out in rows, prey to the rain."

Then he nodded and left.

In the yard he stopped again, shaking his head. *How obstinate she is!* he told himself. *She doesn't ask me where I'm going. God knows, what a struggle it is when one's wife is not truly her husband's helpmeet! ... I have to do everything against my wife's will. It's not enough that she doesn't support me, she has no faith in my undertakings and works against them ...*

He went out to the street in a bad mood. No new thought entered his mind and he felt oppressed.

The street was empty – only here and there a child could be seen. Everyone who had sound limbs was to be found in the fields.

Out in the middle of the village street, a rather pretty girl dressed in a red floral skirt came running toward him – it was the Jewish leaseholder's servant girl. In that moment Dani transformed himself into the man who loves to flirt with women, and when the sun-tanned girl tried to hurry past him laughing, he poked her with his thumb in the middle of her apron.

The girl stopped short and drew back a step. "Ooh!" she cried.

Dani stood in front of her: "Where to, huh?"

The girl was in a hurry and sought left and right for a way past the man, but Dani had spread out his arms to block her, so she stood still. "Don't hold me up, since I'm in such a hurry ..."

"Then just stop, if you're so rushed."

"Let me be!"

"Where are you off to? What's the matter?"

"Something awful has happened."

"And?"

"I was told not to tell anyone."

"Not to tell *anyone*, but they didn't say you couldn't tell *someone*!"

The girl snickered. "The young gentleman has passed."

"What? ... Liscsán?"

"He was riding home from the fields on Csillag; the horse shied when he reached the gate and threw the young gentleman off, and right away he broke his neck."

A sudden spasm, as terrible as a lightning bolt in the winter sky, crossed Dani's face. "Is he dead?" he asked frantically.

"Yes," the girl answered, terrified, and gaped at the man.

"Swear to God?"

"Yes, of course! I'm telling you, he's dead." The girl swore it to him anxiously.

"All right then, go back to your work."

And he sent her off without bothering to look any further after her than after the block that held the neighbor's gate ajar.

For a moment he stood as though nailed to the street, then he lifted his head, looked around him and headed straight for the large house on the left, where his cousin-in-law Gyuri Takács was watering four horses at the trough.

"Gyuri, loan me your Ráró. My horses are all out to pasture today."

"Where are you headed?"

"You'll find out tomorrow."

"Will you ride the horse hard?"

"Don't worry about it, even if Ráró bites the dust, it'll be worth it."

"Then ... take Kesely instead."

"I said Ráró!" Dani insisted.

Gyuri studied his cousin-in-law, but didn't answer. He knew the man and his obstinacy.

"Hey," he called to the stable boy, "bring out the horse blanket ... Or a saddle?"

"Ah, the blanket'll do."

They laid it across the horse's back. Dani set his left foot on the horse trough and swung up on top of the horse, grasped the halter and nodded goodbye.

He rode off calmly, at an even, steady gait.

After a few minutes the village was behind him and he rode along at a quiet trot, deep in thought, leaving a light cloud of dust in his wake.

VII.

As darkness fell, Gyuri Takács shook the dust and hay remnants from him and went over to see his cousin, Erzsi.

Dani Turi's house stood at the end of the village, facing the street. A large, new, wooden fence surrounded it; it was an impressive building when compared with the rather small village houses beside it. Dani had bought it when he'd brought his bride home, and with his accustomed good fortune he'd acquired it cheaply. Since then, the house had increased at least four or five times in value.

"Good evening!" Gyuri greeted her.

The young woman was in the process of chopping up dried stalks and readying a fire to cook the evening meal. "Good evening, Gyuri!" she replied cordially.

The man stood in the door, darkening the room inside. Erzsi looked at him cheerfully.

"Where did your husband go off to?" Gyuri asked.

The woman studied him. "He's gone?"

"He asked for my Ráró," Gyuri answered, then he edged his way inside and leaned with his shoulder against the door post. "He rode off with him. He said, 'it'll be worth it even if the horse bites the dust.' So where did he go?"

Erzsi shook her head hesitantly. "I don't know. I didn't ask him."

They stood silently for a time.

"So are you always just cooking and baking?" Gyuri asked then.

Erzsi tossed the dried stalks aside. "You know, my husband's so finicky ... He wants to have his hot meal at night, just like the Reverend."

"He was terribly spoiled at home!" Gyuri remarked with his peasant's scorn.

Erzsi felt shame for her husband. It bothered her that Gyuri expressed such disdain for the day laborer's son when he was together with her. She countered sharply: "At least his mother didn't nurse him through his fortieth year!"

Gyuri's face darkened. He grew silent. The village residents joked that he didn't marry because his mother still nursed him.

The man's thick moustache quivered. He wanted to say something, but he swallowed the insult and merely looked at his cousin, who pouted and turned her eyes from him in a sulk. No one could insult her husband to her face!

"If I get used to a woman," he said then, "I'll stay with her until my death ... I'd know how to be faithful to someone. Albeit not just anyone. I wouldn't bring just any woman home to mother."

Erzsi's face turned flaming red.

Six years ago, Gyuri had courted her; but she'd merely laughed in his face. How could she love her own cousin? And shortly after that she'd jumped in a well for Dani.

Since then, Gyuri hadn't once mentioned the matter; he thought he himself had forgotten it. As though one could forget such a thing.

They both fell silent for a while. Erzsi put the cleaned dishes back onto the plate rack. Gyuri followed the woman's movements with his small brown eyes just as quietly as the housedog lying on the floor was accustomed to doing.

"Certainly, you were a good-looking girl, Erzsus ..."

A shiver ran through the woman's body when this nickname from her childhood met her ears.

Her children had been taken to their grandparents, so Erzsi was alone with Gyuri. There was no work left to do in the clean kitchen, nonetheless she cast about for something to occupy her so as not to have to stand there idly. Gyuri was well aware of this.

"If only we could go back there once more!" the man said.

Erzsi was silent.

"So? Erzsi?"

"Leave me alone! ... One shouldn't tempt God."

"God has other things to do besides bothering with us ... At the most, if he's angry with us, then ..."

Erzsi grew depressed. "You're just as much of a heathen as the others."

"I'm no angel ... Otherwise, you'd love me."

"Don't I love you? ..."

49

Faint twitches furrowed the man's sturdy, fleshy face. His eyes began to burn. He could have sighed, but suppressed the urge, preferring to control his nerves.

Finally he spoke: "You know, it's very hard to weld together what's once been broken apart."

"Especially when it was never actually together," the woman added.

"True, true!" the man admitted.

His voice shook with such sorrow that the woman looked over at him, and what she saw there helped her truly to understand the sad, empty hopelessness of his life.

"Other folks have their burdens, too, Gyuri ... Gyurika ..." she said softly, tenderly, sadly.

The man suddenly lifted his head, causing it to strike the edge of the door post. "None of them like I do."

The woman took her time answering, her voice choked with tears: "You kind soul! ... What problem do you have, then? And what do you know about others?"

"A lot!" cried the man suddenly and unexpectedly, then he moved forward a step. "Everything! Do you hear? I'm descended from the Takács line! ... I see your life! You unhappy woman! I sigh with you over every pain that afflicts you! ... If only it weren't for that!" He choked forth the words. "If it weren't for that! Then I'd have no problem!"

Erzsi stood there as though turned to stone. It both pained and heartened her to know that there was still one soul walking the earth who shared her horrible inner torment.

"You can't stand him, right?" the man asked her point-blank.

The woman stared at him, her face as expressionless as a wall.

"You hate him! You feel no love for him! Thank God! Don't be afraid, I'll settle the score with him! For your sake!"

"What do you want?" Erzsi asked, terrified.

"To spill his blood," the man gasped with bulging eyes.

"Get out!" the woman screamed. "Get out of my sight! Holy Mother of God! Have you lost your mind?"

"I want his blood!" the man cried bitterly.

"As God is my witness, I'll be after yours if you so much as harm a hair on my husband's head! To think you want to harm *my husband*! ..."

Gyuri suppressed his rage, but didn't abandon it.

Slowly he turned to leave. He stopped on the threshold. "Erzsi," he said hoarsely, "on the day when you tell me you no longer love him, Dani Turi will end up – just like this spider." And violently he smashed a spider on the door, crushing it, so that nothing remained but a small, moist blotch.

The woman shot back with contemptuous pride, almost gleefully: "My husband will be there!" And with an air of confidence, she followed the grave man with her eyes as he left, without saying a word of goodbye, and disappeared into the dark of evening.

And as she watched her cousin walk heavily along, his head bent, a sense of foreboding descended on her soul, like fog.

"A Takács knows how to suffer, but not murder," she told herself. "He knows how to work, how to save, to suffer and die ... Certainly if he were strong enough to act, then I would now be Mrs. Gyuri Takács! ..."

VIII.

Dusk turned into black night as Dani reached the city. The air was sultry and so thick with dust one could almost bite into it. He wiped the sweat from his forehead and grumbled scornfully: "The devil take this stinking Swabian dust!"

Like every peasant, he felt strange in the city, although he came here often enough. Only in his little village was he a whole man. Those who didn't live here, but came for gain or loss, were alien villagers; for this reason, when they arrived in the atmosphere of the city, they furrowed their brow and found themselves having to fight off the strange feelings that assailed them here. The houses on either side of the street concealed themselves in dense shadow behind wooden fences, as though lying in wait. And the Swabians who lived inside them were well-known to him; he had to bargain with them in an entirely different manner from his peers. Whoever wants to sell something to a Swabian has to muster his wits; when his own eyes tell him he's struck a good deal, he can be fairly certain that the Swabian is somehow gaining while he himself is losing.

He'd gotten used to these neighbors a long time ago. He'd been born into this state of affairs and held no grudge against the Swabians; it seemed to him the natural, inevitable, and ultimately only conceivable order of things that matters were as they were. But he didn't feel comfortable in their midst. He was perfectly willing to engage in conversation with them, but his innermost gut feeling did not draw him to these people, instead pushing him away and dividing him from them.

The street he now rode along retained a completely village appearance. It was as though he were at home – it was even called Karai Street. From this he turned off into another street where the houses didn't stand behind fences, but faced the street with their fronts. They were adorned with red-tiled terraces framed by columns. Above the windows, triangles had been built into the wall whose purpose could not be discerned by a Hungarian brain. But the provincial master-builder claimed: "It's aristocratic this way!" When Dani reached Market Street, he turned toward the marketplace. There the giant tower rose against the blank sky, standing like a great warning sign, absent of its church, bearing witness to the heathen spirituality of the ancestors from beyond its ruins. The faint-hearted citizens of the town were unable to restore the monumental creation of the fathers. In the end the government stepped in, and now there rises between the trees the properly restored tower, its new tin roof bordering the gable in a pleasing manner.

"Damned tower!" Dani said to himself. "How many loads of stone were invested in that! Enough for half the County, for an entire winter ... And all that belonged to *us*! ..."

He scowled and rode on, toward the market square. Along the way he glanced off to the right at the monastery, to the left at the three-towered parish church, where to this very day the sermon is given in German on every second Sunday. Dani furrowed his brow even more and made a fist. His aged uncle on his grandfather's side was still alive and had many a story to tell about the olden days, about this very city and how it had been *back in those days*, when the "Great Tower" still belonged to the "Hungarians." But they'd taken the tower away from them, even though "God didn't want it that way." When they'd placed the cross on the tower, lightning had struck it the following day, burning both tower and church to the ground. The church walls caved in and it was never rebuilt. The Calvinists asked for the stones in order to build a new church of their own where space had been allotted to them, on the other side of the bridge, beyond the main city, in the hospital district. But they didn't get them; later the stones were used to build a cowshed at the parish house.

Whoever tells these tales today and whoever hears them merely shrugs his shoulders. "It was such a long time ago that it might not even be true ... It's pointless to keep harping on the same string ... What good does it do if we were once lords, when we're now beggars."

But Dani heard these stories with different feelings. Even though his father was a poor man, he was descended from the old Karaite families who'd inherited their place on this land from the servants of the Count's court. Dani often remembered a quote of his grandfather's: "There flows just as much Karaite blood in your veins as in those of many a count ..." But the old man never explained what he meant by that. Dani knew that the Turis had once been well-to-do. They'd only grown poor later on. But the haughtiness and overambition they'd received by way of inheritance remained forever. And along with that, seething anger over their oppressive poverty.

It occurred to him now that this feeling also lay at the bottom of the plan he'd devised along the road. He pressed his teeth together and gazed resolutely ahead. He felt as though he were facing a fierce battle with an entire army at his back. He wanted to gain land, to conquer it; not just for himself, but for his entire land-hungry village.

And suddenly his many-buttoned vest grew so taut across his swelling chest that the seams all but burst.

"Wait, you dogs!" he said to himself, and he thought not of the Swabian and Wallachian peasants who worked themselves to the bone on narrowly measured strips of land, thus sharing the misery of their Hungarian brothers, but of the great lords who lived out their luxurious lives, without worries and without work, and most especially of the Count, whose high-towered castle lay spread out there on the other side of the market, with its grand park, its ornamental trees, and its wrought-iron enclosure, made of heavy chains and orbs. "Wait, you dogs! We'll suck out your blood, just as you have sucked out ours."

IX.

He stopped in front of a large private gate and jumped down from his horse.

In order to overcome his nervous excitement, he stretched his limbs and yawned out loud. Then he smiled faintly, shaking his head. "We'll see how many sackfuls it takes. For the time being, it's the only game around."

He led his horse through the small gate and entered the beautiful courtyard with its beds full of flowers, where glass balls shimmered in the fast descending darkness, and tied the horse to the fence. Then he climbed the few steps to the vestibule, which was enclosed by glass and draped with flowers and wild grapevines.

It was dark there – he dared not take another step. He was familiar with this home and knew that small, priceless furnishings were to be found everywhere. He didn't want to knock anything over.

"Good evening," he called out loudly, doffing his hat in greeting.

A moment later a lamp in the room inside shed its light into the vestibule. And Dani saw that he stood directly in front of a rocking chair, its seat cushioned with a rug. How glad he was to have stopped where he did, otherwise he would certainly have knocked over the rocker and the little table beside it ...

A servant girl brought the lamp to where he stood, followed by the beautiful young mistress of the house.

Dani quickly straightened himself and forgot all the thoughts that had been occupying him. He gazed blissfully at the beautiful Jewess.

"Good evening!" he said once again in a calm, cheerful tone. "Is His Excellency at home?"

"He's in the casino," the lady responded, regarding the handsome peasant with marked curiosity. "Why do you seek him?"

"There's a business matter I'd like to discuss with him," Dani answered with a smile, cocking his head to one side.

"Aren't you from Kiskara?" the woman asked.

"Yes, I am."

"You're Dani Turi, aren't you?"

"I don't deny it."

"Well then, good evening! Have a seat. My husband will be here momentarily ... I just put my little girl to bed."

They took a seat on the veranda, the lady in her rocking chair, Dani across from her in a straight-backed chair beside the large dining table.

In the harsh, yellow light of the lamp, the young lady's complexion had a favorable appearance. Dani observed her with surprise. This was the first time he'd actually seen a true genteel lady up close. Until now this opportunity had been so far removed from him that all curiosity had seemed pointless. But now, under the influence of the strong perfume, the unfamiliar aroma of heliotrope, he was seized by an unaccustomed physical excitement. The Countess must surely also be a lady such as this, but doubtless a thousand times more beautiful! ...

The beautiful lawyer's wife noticed the peasant's arousal and did not fault him for it.

"What's new with you, Master Dániel?" she asked; she was somewhat at a loss, because she didn't know what to talk about with this man. She was acquainted with Dani and knew that he was wealthier and smarter than the other peasants, nonetheless she searched long and fruitlessly for a topic to converse with him about.

Dani was in no hurry to answer her question; he just shrugged his shoulders slightly, raised his eyebrows and smiled again. His smile only enhanced his sharply profiled, manly countenance. His expressive blue eyes with their intimate gaze reveled in the beautiful lady and seemed intent on penetrating the elegant housecoat with its fine lace trim. His fascinated stare began to embarrass her. Her large dark eyes, in which the childish spontaneity of youth was paired with the clarity of rare intelligence, looked up toward the ceiling, and in this position she fully exposed to the visitor her beautiful, silky-soft face with its youthful, plump, kissable lips. Dani at first observed the lady with a certain awkwardness – something displeased him about her, this refinement struck him as unnatural; yet the lawyer's wife with her white skin and black hair was so pure, so lacking in affectation, that his eye, so experienced when it came to the fairer sex, soon discerned how one ought to regard this exotic gem, this noble lady.

His blood, quick as it was to boil, soon was seething like a cataract. There at arm's length before him was the very woman he'd thought of today, yet she was so distant from him that he couldn't possibly conquer her. He foresaw the revulsion that must take hold of this woman if he dared touch her with his hand ...

He had to turn his eyes away; he looked around the room, surveying the splendid furnishings whose purpose was not entirely clear to him.

The lovely Jewess had, in the meantime, found a topic of conversation. "Listen," she said, "I'm actually upset with you."

"With me?" Dani asked with a smile.

"Yes, with you. I've heard nice things about you."

"About me?" Dani asked again.

"I was just saying, let this man come see us once, and I'll give him a proper dressing-down."

"Well, here I am!" Dani said and waited cheerfully. The lady spoke with a tone of superiority, in gracious condescension, as one would when lecturing an inquisitive child, or a peasant.

Dani was no longer excited. His struggle with the woman began. And it gave him pleasure, like when the dog toys with the cat.

"Very well! So you hate the Jews?" the lady spoke.

"Me?" Dani responded in shock, for it had never occurred to him to nurture such ideas. But then he remembered that the lady must be confusing him with Dani Farkas. He didn't defend himself against the accusation, that wouldn't have befitted a man. He embraced the little battle.

"I've been assured that you hold a grudge against the Jews," the lady continued.

"That's not true," Dani replied smiling, and with that air of superiority that a sensible man derives from his masculinity when confronted with a woman.

"So you don't, then? You don't resent the Jews?"

Dani gave a sly wink of his eyes and replied: "Not all of them ... only every other one."

"I see," the lady said cleverly. "You don't resent them all, is that it? Not the good ones, only the swindlers?"

Dani shook his head with amusement. "That's not how I differentiate them."

"How, then?"

"Well ..." and Dani stroked his handsome, well-groomed, chestnut-brown moustache. "I don't resent the ones that wear pants trimmed with lace."

At first the lady didn't understand. She would never have imagined his dishonorable intent. "Trimmed with lace? ... How trimmed with lace?" she asked.

Dani flashed a devilish smile. "The ones one can't get at, the pretty ones, with crocheted or tatted trim."

The young woman's face grew flaming red.

She understood the brazen joke and sat for a moment in amazement before the peasant. But in the next moment she burst into uncontrollable laughter. She spread her arms so that her lace sleeves exposed their delightful roundness, reared back and roared out loud. Dani watched the splendid play of her charmingly beautiful forms with the desire of a hungry wolf.

The beautiful little Jewess renewed her laughter two, three more times. Her pretty white teeth sparkled, her blue-black hair came loose, falling over her white forehead, and a few tears fluttered on her large eyelashes when at last she looked eye-to-eye at the man. "So then, Master Dani, you love Jewish women?"

"The pretty ones."

"Me as well?"

"You? ... For you, gracious lady, I could hang an entire week at the end of a noose."

Once again the lawyer's wife burst into resounding laughter. "But you wouldn't like to become a Jew for my sake?"

"I'd like to become Christ himself!"

"What? Would that be such a great sacrifice for you?"

"Since it was the Jews who crucified Christ and not He the Jews."

A new fit of laughter rocked the young lady. "Oh, Master Dani, Master Dani," she said then, "how do you come up with such things ... See here, you know how to court a woman better than the gentlemen do."

In this moment, her husband appeared in the vestibule. "What's this, what's this?" he cried. "Who's here?"

"There's no one here but our incomparable friend Dani," the young woman returned and jumped up to meet her husband.

"Ah, Master Turi? ... A splendid man!"

Dani rose and pushed his chair away in peasant fashion. Then he regarded the lady and the gentleman as they hugged each other with gentle ease. The lady's white arm rested with such delicacy on her husband's shoulder, as though a rose had fallen there. And the man, with his plump face and red moustache, breathed such a soft kiss onto her hand, as though he hadn't touched it. And when they'd kissed each other in this same gentle manner, like the touching of butterflies' wings, Dani saw clearly that unattainable something that was missing from his women, his love affairs: this elastic tenderness, this subtle touching. The fanning of the flames, the non-corporeal quality of the body.

He perceived nothing of their conversation.

X.

"**S**o what can I do for you, Master Turi?" the lawyer asked as he led the peasant into his study. It bothered him to see these overly sociable people bring the gentlefolk down to their level. He didn't like the peasants at all, he had nothing but trouble with them, due to their ignorance, their pettiness, their cunning. But he had to deal with them, that's what made him his livelihood.

He proffered his cigar case to Turi. "Have a smoke."

Dani took a cigar, inspected it, and put it in his pocket. "I'll smoke it at home. Right now I want to talk."

"Be my guest."

"The young Master Lichtstein is dead."

"What do you say?" the lawyer asked abruptly.

"This afternoon, when he was returning home from the fields, his horse got spooked and threw him. He fell with his head against the gate post and died instantly."

The lawyer was shocked. He began to pace the floor with large steps. He didn't even look up. Sadness filled his face as he paced back and forth, taking no notice of Dani for minutes on end.

The peasant kept his cool. He waited patiently.

Then he just thought quietly to himself. He reached across the table for the cigar case and took another cigar. He squeezed it, bit off the tip, spit it out, and took it between his teeth. He retrieved his lighter and lit the cigar attentively. He sent a few smoke rings into the air and thought now only of his cigar. When everything was as he liked, he placed the cigar between his teeth and sat back down on his chair. He realized he didn't cut an especially good figure with the unaccustomed tobacco roll in his hand, but he gained an advantage of sorts in any case. It gave him a certain gentlemanly confidence and pride as he watched the lawyer pace nervously back and forth.

"So, what do you want, Master Turi?" the lawyer asked at last, having calmed down somewhat and surveyed the situation objectively.

"Me?" Dani asked, then waited.

"Well, out with it then."

"Why ... that's all I wanted to tell you! ..." And he put the cigar back between his teeth.

The lawyer turned away glumly and resumed his agitated stroll. This is what irritated him most about the peasants – this vulpine cunning. This dirty skullduggery. He could easily just say what's on his mind, but now, when he's being asked, he shuts up. The lawyer struggled to suppress the expletive on the tip of his tongue. He couldn't afford to say it out loud, because he knew that Dani was a wealthy, resourceful, lucky man, the bellwether of his village. In a word, this was a man he could accomplish something with. Perhaps even a great deal!

"Well, sir," Dani began at last, taking the cigar between his fingers.

"Go on," the lawyer spoke with the air of a professional at his client's service.

"How do ... things stand?"

"What things?"

"This" – Dani searched carefully for the best word – "contract."

"What contract?"

"The one concerning the Pallag meadow."

A light shone in the lawyer's eyes. Now he understood what the peasant was after. The pasture regarding which the purchase agreement was to be signed in the coming days.

"Everything is in order," he responded.

"That's good ... What I want isn't much. It's just that, as long as the young gentleman is dead – I'd like to take his place ..." Dani lifted his head and looked the lawyer in the eye, as though he'd said something significant.

"If the Count accepts you ..." the lawyer replied thoughtfully.

"At the very least!" Dani said. "Tomorrow I'll go to the Countess, she lives by us now. I'll tell her."

The lawyer looked rigidly at the peasant.

Then he resumed his pacing.

After a time, he came to a stop in front of Dani, who'd quietly returned to smoking his cigar. "Look here, Master Turi. I'd like to suggest something to you ..."

Dani listened without so much as removing the cigar from his mouth. From behind it, as though from behind a weapon, he eyed the lawyer guardedly.

"See here, why don't you take over the entire lease ..."

Dani didn't bat an eyelash as he heard this monumental proposal. He acted as though it were a mere trifle.

"You see, my friend," the lawyer pressed on, "never before has there been such a promising opportunity. How fortunate for you that you came to me at this precise moment ... You know, this parceling out is an old idea of mine. You can take over the lease with your village, and then we'll get the matter taken care of. What do you say to that?"

Dani stood silent for a time, then finally answered: "These cigars you've got are quite bad ... A person has to spit and spit when he smokes them."

The lawyer shook his head. Once a peasant, always a peasant.

"I've got better cigars as well." He opened the glass door to his bookcase and took out a case of fat cigars, which he held out in front of Dani.

The peasant studied them with a smile, alongside the lawyer's soft, effeminate, snow-white hands, and as he reached clumsily inside the case with his awkward, iron hands, he thought to himself: *If only I could have such hands as yours for just one hour!*

XI.

Erzsi did not comprehend what her cousin Gyuri had said to her until he'd disappeared beyond the gate and along the street. At first she'd only understood that he'd threatened her husband; and almost mechanically, like some animal instinct, the bond that connected her to her mate, the feeling of belonging to each other that awakens in every couple the illusion of being one and the same body and soul, burst forth in her. But then Gyuri's thinking became more and more clear to her, and once again she felt shame for her husband in front of this man, whose great perseverance was a trait that linked his soul with hers. She didn't believe the time had come for Gyuri to avenge her, the time when all other options had been exhausted, but nonetheless it was good to know she could count on his support should that time arrive.

If she were ever to admit that she abhorred her husband! ...

My God, how much more must happen so long as she was incapable of uttering this fateful word? She'd already traveled the entire length of Calvary. What station could possibly remain on her personal Via Dolorosa? Or was the worst yet to come?

She shuddered as the thought of the Countess seized her mind. What if he went as far as attempting to gain access to her! What was this man to her, then? What of his belonged to her? The moment he set foot outside his house, he belonged to another, to every woman that met his eyes. And when he was at home, it was impossible to speak a word to him, his head was filled to the brim with worries.

She broke out into bitter tears.

Then she lit the lamp.

At that moment her children arrived home. It was Mrs. Kovács who brought them, an old cottager woman who'd worked faithfully for her parents for as long as she could remember. Erzsi was as attached to her as though the woman were her own mother. In her father's home, everything was so constant, their life, the daily routine, the people, even the perpetual nagging between her father and mother. Erzsi couldn't get used to this new life, where with each passing day her wealth increased and yet every minute brought her new losses to lament. It had been her intention to make everything perfect in her own home that had been flawed in her parents' home. She'd inherited her father's blood and was glad for the chance to become a homemaker herself and achieve the very orderliness and cleanliness that had eluded her mother. But now things were only worse in her own home. At her husband's side, she could realize what she yearned for on only the tiniest of scales; the big things rushed past her like a storm. In her parents' home at least the basic things of life were as they should be! ...

Heaving many a sigh, old Mrs. Kovács lifted the baby, who was already asleep, from her lap and laid him in his cradle. The older child soon noticed that his mother was upset, and his cheerful face grew sad. He opened wide his large dark eyes and sat silently on his little chair by the wall. He bobbed his head back and forth like an old man, as his grandfather was accustomed to doing: yes, yes.

Erzsi staggered about like a sleepwalker – she barely knew what was happening.

"Goodness, how tired I am all of a sudden!" the old woman sighed.

"What were you working on, Aunt Mari?"

"Nothing, really, but the hardest work is the fact that, in order to move forward, you have to put one foot in front of the other. That's what tires me out the most ..."

Erzsi looked at her sleepily; she barely understood the joke. "So what's new at home?"

"Oh, dear, little that's good. But then, where can you find anything good in this world? Good things have gone out of fashion like laughing. It's been at least a year since I opened my mouth in order to laugh."

Most of the time, these exclamations on the part of Aunt Mari induced at least a chuckle, even though the seriousness behind them was sincere. But Erzsi didn't chuckle. With effort she struggled to get the words to leave her throat, so taut with the weight of her sadness: "What happened, then?"

"They went at it with each other again."

"Who?" Erzsi asked with dismay, thinking her parents had had a fight.

"Old Turi passed by."

Erzsi thought she would choke. Much as a haystack set ablaze, the anger heaped up inside her toward her husband's family began to flare and burn. "What did he say?"

"He said the lousy Scarecrow should be grateful his daughter's been made into a noble lady by his son Dani."

Erzsi grew dizzy, she felt a rage-induced stroke coming on. She could find no words, her mouth merely opened and shut.

For a time a painful quiet filled the air as the old woman regretted what she'd done. To be sure, she couldn't have kept the matter to herself and was relieved once it had slipped out of her. But now she felt sorry and ashamed. "It was like this," she began, trying to explain and appease her, "as old Turi was walking by, he passed in front of our gate, and your mother called him and told him to stop a moment. It all had to do with this godforsaken roof that your father-in-law, the old bungler, had done such an abominable job of repairing for you. Old Turi stopped. Your mother said to him: 'Listen here, godfather, the roof is leaking again!' The old man answered rudely: 'How can it leak when it hasn't even rained? Let it rain in buckets! The corn needs it!' To which your mother responded: 'Which is why this is just the right time to get the roof fixed once and for all, since it's not raining. 'Cause what'll we do once the water starts running into the room?' 'Put a tub beneath it, and a washing trough. If you haven't enough, you can borrow more from your daughter. She's a wealthy lady ...' At this point, your father came out. He was very angry, as it certainly is scandalous that that old dog Turi, who makes himself out to be a master strawbinder, messed up the roof so badly – may his hand wither away! Your father said then: 'Listen, godfather! Either you know how to do something, or you don't. Either you're going to fix the roof, or I'm going to sue you for damages.' That's when all hell broke loose. Such a foul-mouthed old man! Goodness me! You never heard such words come out of a man's mouth like the ones he slung about. Good Lord in heaven, just listening to such cursing would doom a person to hell. My oh my, I was only sorry it rained hellfire and brimstone just the one time. It should have happened again, even at the risk of me being damned in the process! The old loser said then: 'A lousy Scarecrow should be grateful that my son's made a noble lady out of his daughter!'"

Erzsi listened to this story and burned with rage.

"So what do you say to this, Erzsus? What do you say about a man like that, a day laborer who lives off the work of his two hands, who hasn't inherited an inch of earth from his father, and dares open his mouth up like that in front of a wealthy peasant? ... What do you say?"

The young woman shuddered as a chill took hold of her. With a shrug of her shoulders she said: "And you would do better to forget how to speak, rather than bring such gossip from one house to another."

The old woman was taken aback. She pulled her scarf around her face, veiling her traits in shadow.

For a while they sat there silently; the child on his chair against the wall just bobbed his handsome, neat, round head back and forth, like a little old man.

Then the old woman rose. "Well I never, it's time to go home ... All of a sudden it's black as night out. The sun is tired, it's retreated into its hole. How can an old, useless woman keep from growing tired herself? ... Good night, Erzsus."

"Take care."

And the old woman stepped out from the bright light into the darkness, disappearing into the night like an old witch.

XII.

"Do you want to eat something?"

"No."

"Then go to sleep."

The child quickly got up from the table and began to undress. He took off his little black jacket and pulled his shirt out from the waistband of his underpants. Then he went to the back room and waited until his mother had cleared off the large bed. He slept in the same bed as her, at her feet.

Once in bed he sat up, folded his little hands and repeated the evening prayer after his mother. Then he slid quickly under the covers; he wasn't cold, he just wanted to bury himself there. He curled himself up and soon slept with regular breaths.

His mother watched him for a time; then she looked after the other child and settled him into his cradle.

She wiped a tear from her eye and sat down at the table where a long-stemmed oil lamp burned with a small flame.

She stared sadly before her for a time, then thought of something to do, rose, went to the dresser and retrieved some white linens from the bottom drawer that needed mending.

Occupied with her sewing, she waited and listened to the ticking of the wall clock, whose face was painted with a beautiful wreath of red roses.

It was nearly midnight when she heard the clip-clop of a horse's hooves. Her husband had returned home.

While Dani tied the horse up in its stall, she warmed his dinner amidst heavy sighs, fueling the fire with dried corn cobs.

"Good evening!" Dani greeted her cheerfully.

Erzsi aimed her large, serious eyes at him, then turned away. It hurt her to see his beaming face when her own soul was filled with lethal sadness.

Dani felt like his hot body had been dipped into ice water.

So that's still the way it is, he thought to himself, and his good mood vanished. Heavy apprehension weighed down his chest, and as he seated himself at the white table, he sensed the unbearableness of this situation. While away, he'd long since forgotten what things were like at home. His coming and going, his contact with other people, the constantly changing impressions, his plans, the work and ideas that had occupied his mind had all drawn his attention away from the one thing which, in the whole circular movement of his active and colorful life, was to him merely one of many dimensions; to his wife at home, however, it was the only dimension, because it constituted her entire life.

Dani remembered the circumstances in which he'd left the house today and once again had that feeling of wordless tension that had accompanied their parting. And now he found himself caught up in this tension yet again.

Bitter anger took hold of him toward his wife over her awful tenacity. Was there no end to their marital bickering, then? She was never willing to forgive, to look the other way. Quick to flare up in anger, yet equally quick to forget, the husband shot furious looks at his frosty, implacable wife. He felt the urge to give in to his rage, to hurl something to the floor, to grab the woman and shake her violently. He wanted to do something terrible. If only that would help! But an inner voice told him to control himself and try to appease his wife with gentleness. But for this he also lacked the strength, so that his impotent anger turned to agonizing sadness.

With blinking eyes he stared into the lamp's small flame, and when the woman placed his meal before him, he set to eating in silence, choking chunks of meat down unchewed.

Neither of them spoke.

They went across to the bedroom. The woman blew out the lamp and, in the darkness, took off her clothes and lay down.

Dani stood in the middle of the room and was overtaken by such exhaustion that he could barely move a muscle.

Every part of his body was drained of energy, his limbs drooped with fatigue.

At last he moved. He sat down on the edge of his bed and removed his boots. He undressed from head to toe.

Then he went over to his wife. He often lay beside her a bit before going to sleep, just for a chance to cuddle up to her, kiss her, feel her warmth. For he loved this woman, he couldn't live without her. He couldn't even imagine life in her absence. She was the healthy, strong emotional ground that he trusted, upon which he stood, and from which he daily derived renewed strength.

The woman shuddered as he neared her, as though a snake had touched her. "Go, go!" she gasped hatefully. "Go to your own bed."

The man was stunned. Was it then impossible to overcome her obstinacy? The blood rose to his head; he balled his fists and held out his arms. "Watch yourself, Erzsi!" he said, his voice rasping. "Watch yourself. This could end badly."

The woman sat rigid with anger.

The man lay down forcefully beside her and stretched himself out on the bed, all but shoving her off.

The woman shuddered with hatred and rage.

Dani laid his arm around his wife, who struggled in vain to loosen herself from his embrace. "Bastard!" she said.

Dani swallowed the expletive on his tongue.

"Like his whole tribe!" the wife gasped again.

The man quaked.

"His miserable father, the scandalmonger!"

Dani's fingers balled themselves into a fist and he lay there, rigid with outrage. His wife had struck a painful blow to his heart.

"He dares to call someone 'lousy'? ... That pig. That lowlife. That bastard. How dare he use that word against my father!"

Dani realized his father had once again said something in his exasperation that would stick in *those people's* craw for an entire year.

The woman was delighted to see that she was ripping her husband's heart to pieces, and went on, gasping with hatred: "So he can't fix a roof, the bungler, but he knows how to swear?"

"Leave me in peace, Erzsi. All this over the roof, again?"

"The wretch! ... My father, lousy?"

"Enough!" Dani burst out, and in the darkness his eyes shone like flames.

The woman grew silent.

Dani got up from the bed. He stood there before her barefoot on the cool, stamped-earth floor.

His head burned with fever and threatened to explode.

"What a miserable life, a miserable life!" the woman blurted out. She pressed her hands to her face and began to cry bitterly and loudly. "Wretched scum! ... Oh, good God, oh, blessed Virgin! What's become of me, what's become of me! I'm abandoned in this world. And it didn't have to be this way! It's my doing that I'm cursed like this, since I chose him for myself. I could have become the companion of someone who's strong before man and God. With him I would have been happy, I would have been the only one. My life would have been heaven on earth, absolute paradise. And now look what has become of me, my God, my God, my God, what's become of me. The worn-out shoe of a fool, the laughing stock of a dirty pack of scoundrels!"

Dani's fingers tingled with the urge to choke this woman.

"I'm lost, doomed. A helpless lamb trapped among wolves. Every moment they're holding the knife, ready to plunge it into my heart ..."

Dani let his arm fall again.

"You!" the woman said now in a more normal, natural tone. "Tell your father to hold his tongue, otherwise he may regret it."

"Erzsi!"

"The loathsome old buzzard."

"Why doesn't he just crawl beneath the earth!" the man grunted, cursing his father to the woman's face.

Erzsi grew silent and turned away.

They remained this way for minutes on end, in funereal silence. The man stood rigidly in the black darkness. The woman was totally spent, now that she'd vented her anger.

After a good quarter hour, Erzsi collapsed in a cold fever and drew the covers around her, covering her bare arms with her blanket.

"I'll kick the life out of him myself!" the man yelled out suddenly, his anger now coming into its own. "And out of my mother, too, the old witch! Why did she even give birth to me? Why did she raise me up for this damnable life? ... What sort of life is this? Nauseating hell. Is this a life? Even the wolf in the meadow is happy to return home to his wife and den. For me it's slow, torturous death. In my house I have to endure all the torments of hell."

The woman's heart grew hard again. She clenched her teeth, wrinkled her stiff eyebrows, and listened stonily to her husband's curses.

"Oh, I'm damned!" the man screeched with such force that his throat all but burst open. "I'm doomed! But I've only myself to blame! I'm not a man, I'm not even a person. If I were, I wouldn't have to put up with a woman's jabbering, everyone would respect me without talking back to me. Most of all my wife. But I'm nothing but a rag, I'm mud." And he struck his head violently with both fists.

With furious, club-like strokes, he beat his own head.

"You fool! You idiot!" his wife screamed at him, and she jumped up and tried to hold his arms still.

The man staggered as his wife restrained him, and stared with bulging eyes into the darkness.

The woman shuddered over her entire body. Then she broke into loud sobs. "My God, My God! What a life! What a horrible life! But I'm getting what I deserve, living with such a man."

She put her hands to her face and slid from her husband's shoulder onto the edge of the bed, then cried herself out with bitter tears.

The man stood there in a daze, barely conscious, and waited.

Finally he too sank down, kneeling by his wife, and laid his head on her lap; soon his sobbing echoed hers.

"How come a man can't kill himself just by saying the word ... How I'd love to turn this ragged corpse over to the worms."

The woman let her tears fall thick onto her husband's head, and answered Dani's anguished cries with renewed sobs.

At last she softened and took pity on her husband as he struggled with his grief. She laid her hands on his head and stroked it at length, pausing only to stroke him again.

"What a life! What a life!" she whispered.

"That's because we love each other, Erzsi," the man said, lifting his head. "We're practically dying of love for each other. Why would I care about your suffering if I didn't love you? ... Why would you care about me if you didn't love me? ..."

The woman started crying all over again.

The man suddenly embraced her and pressed her so passionately to him that he nearly crushed her. But the woman didn't resist, she yielded, all but losing consciousness.

And as they held themselves in each other's arms, the child at their feet suddenly broke into bitter cries, frightening them with his painful, halting sobs.

The parents listened to him with dawning horror. Their conscience afflicted them as they realized what all the child had had to hear; they were deeply ashamed.

Beyond that, they saw clearly that the enormous conflict between them remained unresolved, in contrast to previous disputes after such heated arguments as this. A deep, festering wound, bleeding out so much pain, eating away at them, incurable. They felt only a vague weariness, but each of their saddened hearts shuddered as it sensed the other's torment.

XIII.

When the child repeated his sobbing, his mother abruptly sat up in bed. She pulled him from the foot of the bed and laid him between her and her husband.

"My little son, my sweet little boy, dear child of my heart! My poor soul, my pearl, my little flower. You have a bad father and a bad mother who hurt you!" she spoke to the boy, soothing him like an infant. "They hurt you, dear soul, my poor little lamb ..."

She pressed his sad head to her breast and the child buried his face in his mother's bosom, as though his nursling feelings had been reawakened. His sobbing gradually subsided and he listened, comforted by his mother's tender words. Soon warm, fragrant sleep descended on him, numbing his poor little head, and he fell asleep.

His mother continued murmuring comforting words to him, words that were meant, however, for another, for her husband, who stretched out wearily on the boy's other side.

"Oh my poor son, what a father you have! ... You have no father, my orphaned son ... When has he ever spoken to you? When has he taken you on his knee? Has he ever played with you? ... My poor child, you're an orphan like your mother, your poor, orphaned mother."

The bed went round and round with Dani as his insides were seized with dizziness – he felt like he was hurtling down into an abyss. His wife's every word struck him in his heart. From behind the bulwark of their child, she set him in her sights and he was defenseless against her arrows.

"Life is so very bitter," the woman went on, "so wretched and miserable, forcing me to watch as the entire world robs me of my husband. Dear God, everyone else has a bigger piece of him than I do. I'm just there to fatten him up for others ... Such a rewarding life, so very rewarding ... Nothing good can ever come of it, never. Such a life isn't fit for a human being. No angel could bear it. Oh God, oh God ..."

The man lay silently, waiting for the next blows.

The woman grew quiet. This wasn't the way to air the bitterness in her heart – she needed contradiction, argument, in order to fully open the valve that would release the flood of her torment and allow it to run freely.

"Your father is sleeping, my little son!" she began again, pressing the slumbering child to her breast. "He's sleeping, with a clear conscience he's dozing away."

The man quaked over his entire body, but otherwise lay still.

After a time, the woman asked him: "Are you asleep?"

Dani shifted impatiently and heaved a deep sigh.

Erzsi again fell silent, but only for a time.

"No matter whether he's sleeping or not, he refuses to speak. He says nothing. Not a word. He has no words to comfort me with. He's nothing but a dog – no use complaining: that's how it is."

Dani sighed again.

"He comes home as though he were arriving in hell. Everywhere else he's happy and jolly, he looks at everyone he meets like a shining sun; but once he passes through this gate, it's all over. When he steps across the threshold to my home, it's with the face of a mourner. That's how much he cares for me."

"Oh, good God!" the man said with suppressed anger, "how am I supposed to be happy and jolly, with you always looking at me as though I'd murdered your father and mother!"

"Well, isn't that how you are? Can I look on you with friendly feelings? Can you stand my father, my blood relations? Wouldn't you rather drown my entire family in a spoonful of water?"

May God let them drown, Dani thought to himself. But he didn't say it, he bit his lip.

"Do you ever do anything for me? Do you? Can you think of just one nice thing I've gotten from you? And yet you have nothing to reproach me for, that's certain, Dani. Don't I provide you with everything imaginable? Are you lacking for anything? Well, tell me – are you?"

When the man only gestured in annoyance, she continued: "Or do you think it doesn't hurt me that we don't get along with your parents? Is it my fault? Aren't they the ones who've estranged me from themselves? In the first year, they treated me like one of their own, didn't they? But how many times since have they insulted me? I'd need a mountain of paper to write it all down on. Have I done anything wrong, Dani? ... Have I? ... Tell me!"

"No!" the man sighed.

"All right, then," Erzsi said, clinging to the word, "that's the most important thing. In the five years of our marriage, have I as much as looked at anyone else? What would you do with me if I kept a lover?"

Strangle you! the man thought to himself in his rage; but he said nothing, only clenching his fists.

The woman sighed. "But you! What do you do to me? Why are you never with me? You can't stand us? And yet you're with all the women of the entire village? Shouldn't I cry over that from morning to night?"

The woman's voice rippled along so calmly, softly and painfully as never before. Until now these laments had always released a storm of passion in them, but now she enumerated all her complaints with such directness, clarity, and profound suffering that the man's heart shrank within his body; he fully understood the woman's dismal, hopeless life.

"What do you want, Erzsi? What should I do?" he asked.

"What, Dani? What? Nothing. What I'm asking is so little! ... Be mine, Dani."

Her voice was tainted by tears, tears that released a holy oath in the man's heart.

"What could I ask of you, Dani? Nothing – only as much as I offer you ... Look, the way I live is that, in everything I do, I think of you: what would you say if you saw that? Would you find it good? Would it make you happy? Would you be content with me? ... That's how you should treat me too, Dani."

Profound stillness descended on them after these words.

And in the man's soul a feeling of worship grew, as though he were in a church. He breathed in the great spirituality of this woman, this pious woman, and said in the end: "I'll try, Erzsi!"

Now she wanted to hug him, but the child was in their way. Seeing this, Dani stood, gently took the sleeping child in his arms and carried him over to his bed.

Then he snuggled up to his wife once again, embracing her so gently, so intimately, so heart-wrenchingly that her blood flooded her brain.

XIV.

They'd slept for a mere hour or two when someone knocked on the window.

"Peasant, we've come."

Dani's eyelids blinked open. He awoke in a sullen daze, his head buzzing.

He got up sluggishly and pulled on his boots.

"Just sleep," he told his wife, who stretched drowsily in their bed. Then he went out.

He'd learned from his father that three hours sleep should be enough for a man, but he felt now like an entire week's sleep would not rid him of his lethargy.

The air outside was fresh; in the east, daylight was breaking.

Four men stood waiting in the yard, bearing pitchforks and rakes over their shoulders, or holding them at their sides.

"Is it you, Pesta?"

"It's us, peasant. Let's go ..."

"Wait, have a shot of brandy, then you can go."

"Aren't you coming?"

"Me? ... I have other things to do."

The men drank their brandy.

An old man among them, wrinkled and bent, who could barely drag a pitchfork anymore, turned to the peasant: "Dani, are you ill?"

"Me, ill?" Dani responded scornfully – like all hale and hearty people he had no regard for the sick. "Illness is ill, but not me!"

"Hm, hm," the old man grunted, shaking his head.

Dani turned and walked away. He knew that the old man saw through him. He could read even in the dark that he was unhappy with his wife.

With a sigh he turned his steps toward the stall. There he awoke the stable boy, who lay in a deep sleep, then jumped to his feet like a soldier at Dani's call. Dani gave him a few orders, after which he patted Ráró down, then ordered the stable boy to lead the horse back home. This done, he went back out to the yard.

He felt strange, like never before. He had no desire to work.

On this beautiful morning, filled with the songs of birds, he felt like a tired old man in the evening of life. His head spun, his heart was oppressed. He recalled the feverish stress induced by his ambitious plans, then waved it all off in his mind: *What good is it all if the wife wants no part of it? Why should I bother working if she doesn't want to hear of my work? What's the point of living if she doesn't want me as a living man, only rotting flesh? I'd be a good enough man for her if I lay around at home, always hanging on her. All women deserve to be kicked and then left in the lurch ... But where would that get me? My life is in her hands! ...*

Slowly, almost without realizing it, he walked back into the house, stopping in the middle of the room. The morning peered through the window and he saw his wife lying in bed.

Erzsi smiled at him sleepily and gladly shifted toward the wall to make room for him.

Dani sat down on the edge of the bed, bent over her and kissed her quietly. Erzsi reciprocated with eagerness.

Then he kicked his boots off and lay down.

His wife nestled up to him passionately.

V.

It was broad daylight when he awoke. Noon was fast approaching.

His first thought was to jump out of bed and get to work, but instead he just lay listlessly under the covers.

He listened to what was going on in the world beyond. The window was open and the sunlight fell between the leaves of the hollyhocks to the middle of the room. Outside, Dani heard his son's voice. The boy was playing in front of the house with his baby brother and spoke with the little devil as though he were as smart as himself.

"Will it turn out well, Sanyika? Will it be good? Have I done a good job braiding it? Will it be a nice whip? Will it?"

"Ooo, ooo!" said the little one.

"Good, good, good? Mama! Sanyika said 'good'! Good, Sanyika? Good? I've made you a really good whip, haven't I – just listen to how it cracks!" And he cracked the whip loudly.

The baby gurgled again: "Ooo, ooo, ooo!"

Dani closed his eyes and listened. He smiled in his thoughts, but his face remained unmoved.

Suddenly a song could be heard through the window, soft and dreamlike:

> I'm drawn to Kara village,
> Where the roses bloom in droves ...

Dani's heart quaked. That had been his favorite song when he was courting Erzsi. For years his wife hadn't sung. Her small, bright voice crept into his heart, and Dani felt a tightening in his throat as the second, even livelier verse sounded:

> The cherry leaves are rustling,
> A girl is growing up for me.
> Her mother would suit me as an in-law,
> The blue-eyed maid shall be my wife.

The woman's voice faltered; the last line no longer flowed out so freely, as in her heart the bitterness returned, aroused by the word *in-law*. In order to banish the painful feeling, she began singing a jollier song:

> I've wrinkled boots with yellow spurs,
> And I've chosen an orphan girl for me.
> The sweet little orphan will love me so true,
> If mother and father leave us in peace.

This had also been a favorite song of his. And even the sigh he heard following the song belonged to him. It was true, if they were both orphans, much suffering would be spared them!

Now a new, joyful song sounded. It was as though the happy days of his bachelorhood had returned:

> My house stands in the little alley,
> My beloved lives in the broad avenue;
> That doesn't worry us a bit,
> We meet both morning and night.

This verse was meant for him, but the second she sang for herself:

> Because I jumped into the well,
> Dear rose, you didn't take me.
> Because I didn't call out to you,
> I remain as I always was.

> There's a little sage bush in my garden,
> It grows with the rose's gratitude.
> From eve to dawn he fails to come,
> Nor does he fill me with love.

Dani released a heavy, heavy sigh. All of these songs were being sung for him. His wife was singing to him, from one heart to the other. And to top it all off was this other song she intoned now:

> My rose, who now is leaving!
> Give me your hand in farewell!
> I want to kiss you on the lips,
> So that you never forget this hour.

Oh don't leave, don't leave,
My heart can't bear it,
My heart can't bear it,
Sleep with me this evening! ...

"Erzsi!" Dani called.

The woman fell silent there outside, even the noisy clanking caused by her work ceased as she suddenly bolted up, flung open the door and rushed into the room. Her face was red as fire.

Dani looked at her, his eyes beaming; she fell onto the chest of this man she so loved, and her young woman's beauty flooded her face as she looked into her husband's eyes.

They kissed and held each other at length, as though they were still a young couple. The woman was so fresh, so happy, like Dani had known her only during their first year of marriage. He kept looking at her as though he were dreaming, as though he wanted to see through her skin, into her body, deeply, to the wellspring of her thoughts. Because behind every kiss, behind every smile, every sweet word he suspected some attempt at bargaining.

That's how you want to repay me for my work, my life! he thought to himself.

But he took care not to ruin his wife's mood. Nor his own, for he had the feeling he'd become a different man. No, he no longer desired his work, his great plans had lost their appeal – he only remembered them as some vague dream. And as he moved among his little family there through the morning, in the glorious sunny weather, he quietly wished a wall would rise around his home reaching all the way to the sky, so that he could see nothing and no one from the world beyond its gates.

But he sought in vain to numb himself with his loud, noisy thoughts that things were good like this, that this was real happiness, true family life. In the pit of his heart a hateful feeling pressed down on him that raised malicious objections and spoiled every bite of the noonday meal he shoved cheerfully between his teeth.

During the afternoon, he busied himself lethargically about the stall. Suddenly an irresistible force caused him to stand erect, and he immediately directed his steps toward the house. He must go visit the Countess!

When he reached the door, hesitation had already overcome him. With every word that concerned this plan, he destroyed the blissful little family garden that blossomed here for him in all its splendor ...

His wife stood in her radiant beauty, her face beaming, at the cradle where she tickled the baby awake with her kisses. The child's laughter sounded all the way out into the yard.

"Do you know what this delightfully sweet, this golden little boy of mine has done?" she called out to her husband.

"What?" Dani asked with a quiet smile.

"What? He pooped out such a pure yellow nugget that it was just like gold!" Erzsi's voice rang out in laughter.

Dani smiled warmly and his twinkling eyes reveled with pleasure as they took in the woman's appearance.

"But do you also know what this stinky, tattered, dirty little rascal of yours has done?"

"What?" said Dani, and his teeth shone white.

"He made a mess of his crib, his pillow, his blankets, his clothes, even the tip of his nose. What a pig!"

Dani laughed, and he knew now that he would not visit the Countess.

Not today.

Perhaps never.

It would have been a sin against God to destroy this happy world ...

On the following morning, he was amazed to realize his lack of desire hadn't changed one bit. He was so tired and worn out, as though someone had worked him over good and proper. Once he'd sent the workers out to the field, he returned to the house. His wife watched him warily and uneasily.

"Aren't you going to work, Dani?"

He shrugged his shoulders.

"No matter, sleep!" the woman said.

The man was too lethargic to tell her what he thought about that: the more a man sleeps, the more tired he becomes. He went to lie down and slept until noon.

Erzsi was not as fresh and cheerful as she'd been the day before; her husband's lack of enthusiasm put her in a bad mood, too. She didn't understand what he was after. During the evening, when she saw him tottering about like a man getting over an illness, she asked him: "Are you ill?"

"Me?"

"Are you being stubborn?"

"Hell, no!"

"Why aren't you working?"

"At what? ... For what?"

"Hmph! First you're so busy with work you can hardly see straight, then you loll about doing absolutely nothing."

Dani sat there idly, lost in his thoughts. "Yes, that's how it is, Erzsi. That's how I am. All or nothing."

Erzsi was appalled. "Then it's better you do nothing," she said stubbornly, and threw in for good measure: "milord. ... It's better that way than the other."

Days went by in this sort of listlessness. The woman rallied all her forces in order to cheer him up. But her childlike joy was approaching its limits – it thrived only in happiness, and in this house, joy no longer blossomed. Erzsi struggled, fought, exhausted herself in her efforts, and finally burst into tears.

"It's better if he lives the way he wants to; it's better if he works – at least then he's in a better mood."

Dani was shocked to hear these words, but instead of responding he just gave a dismal wave of his hand. He thought his happiness had run out, forever gone. It only astonished him that he could still live, afflicted as he was by his horribly distracted soul.

But live he did, and during lunch, during dinner he noticed with chagrin how he loaded up his plate. Sometimes he even noticed he was getting fatter. A feeling of chubbiness, of obesity, paralyzed his body, and that made him even more unhappy.

And now difficult days came along, the harvest time. On Thursday, the day of the Feast of Saints Peter and Paul, the wheat cutting was to get underway. But Dani sent the harvest-master off in sleepy impatience. He wanted to be left in peace. The start of the harvest was thus pushed off until Monday.

Erzsi suffered from unbearable restlessness. She had no idea what was happening with her husband. With her feminine instincts she surmised he was in such a state because she hadn't satisfied him. He needed everything ... and amidst all this he also needed her. But she was only a small part of this everything! This embittered her fiercely, and gradually a mood took hold of the little family as though they'd been catapulted into profound grief. Husband and wife only sighed, as neither possessed sufficient willpower to raise their voice in anger.

In this way Saturday arrived, and while on other farms people were laboring like Trojans to get the week's work done, in this house the owners sank into the lethargy and tedium of the aged.

On Saturday afternoon, Erzsi was suddenly shocked to hear her husband singing loudly in the front room:

> Lord, rebuke me not in anger,
> And no longer let thy wrath on me descend.
> Thou hast pierced me with thine arrows,
> Brought me sorrows,
> Bowed me down with thine own hand.

Erzsi crossed herself and sighed deeply. Her husband's strong, somber singing sounded strange to her, but she felt that this song, a Calvinist hymn from his own tradition, signaled an inward change in him. And as she listened, a sense of reverence awakened in her, a prayerful sentiment. A powerful yearning overcame her, just once in her life to kneel in prayer to God together with her husband. In this profoundly personal humility, the two of them stood utterly distant from one another. Each of them went to a different minister, to a different church; each rejected the faith of the other. And for years, to spare each other, they'd brought themselves to avoid speaking of religion at home, to avoid praying when the other was near, in order to avoid angering each other through such acts of piety.

But now the woman was stricken with powerful yearning. She wanted to be one with her husband in that room, now hallowed as a church.

And she went inside.

Her husband was seated at the table, singing as he held his head in his hands. He remained motionless when his wife entered the room; he continued singing, though unable to do it so spontaneously now. He waited in expectation that his wife would leave the room after finding whatever she sought in the dresser behind him.

The woman, however, stood quietly, and the man waited fruitlessly. Then he turned around.

What he saw struck him as incredibly strange. His wife was on her knees, praying with folded hands and tilted head before the little crucifix she'd just retrieved from the drawer and placed on the dresser in front of her.

Dani felt dizzy; his heart quaked and his bile overflowed.

In a sudden fit of rage, he rose, intending to break the painted God into splinters with his fist.

But in the next moment, he choked back his anger. Instead of turning toward his wife, he headed for the door.

He left the room.

He could no longer stand it in the house – he thought it must fall in on top of him.

Outside in the fresh air, he breathed freely. "Oh my God, what a pitiful man I've become!"

From this point on, he was as though unconscious. Everything tormented him like an open wound. He felt like he was in a prison cell from which there was no escape, not even on the gallows, although that would actually have been a relief to him.

He spent twenty-four hours in this state.

The following afternoon, on Sunday, his wife went to church. Now at last Dani felt somewhat relieved. He looked around him like a tormented yard dog when his master goes away. Was there a breach somewhere he could escape through?

Then he saw a peasant girl enter the yard from the village street.

"Uncle Dani! ... The Countess would like for you to come."

"The Countess!?" The peasant was barely able to speak. His tongue was paralyzed. "I'm to come to her!" he stammered, beside himself, his face white with pallor.

"Yes, yes, she's sent for you. Tomorrow afternoon ... When the Count will have gone out riding ... right away."

The girl said nothing more and hurried away.

Dani stood for a time as though rooted to the spot. But in the next moment the hissing, fiery flame of power, of yearning, of life flared up inside him.

A miracle had taken place. The charred trunk sprouted new, green foliage.

XVI.

The young Countess had the feeling in the little village as if she'd been suddenly exiled from the midst of modern, cultivated life into the ancient world. This odd situation was agreeable to her, as it involved no privations. She possessed a lovely little castle, newly wallpapered and furnished, polished to the last shine; an enchanted island in the middle of an ancient forest, equipped with all the necessities of modern life. And the natives were not cannibals, but rather pleasant, handsome, cheerful people whose aboriginal, primitive nature suited them well. And they were well reared, not overly curious, not intrusive. The beautiful Countess, who hid herself from the world here in order to nurture her secret love, had in fact the feeling of being wrapped in a veil of invisibility.

Nor did she permit that the order introduced in the castle during the absence of the master suffer any major changes. The manorial agents had incorporated the little castle into the administrative framework. They'd spared the ornamental garden in front of it, where the branches of some moss-covered pine trees drooped mournfully to the earth. Behind the castle, however, they'd replaced the flower beds with a vegetable garden; they'd claimed the yard, where the stalls and carriage sheds were found, for agricultural purposes. Here the women occupied themselves with breaking hemp, shucking corn, and similar work. Even now a large amount of hemp had been brought into the yard, and in the rush to receive the Countess, the drying mound of hemp had been totally forgotten. The Countess found the hemp's penetrating odor not unpleasant and asked the women to work beneath the north-facing window, as calmly as though she were not there.

She wanted to listen in on them. She was curious as to people's secrets. At the time of her schooling in the convent, she'd felt just as distant from people as later, when in the extraordinary course of social life she threw herself into its feverish, noisy turmoil. And now that she'd come to rob solitude with her lover, her interest in the secrets of the human heart was awakened.

This daring deed of succumbing to her brother-in-law's persuasion and, for the first time in her life, straying from the straight and narrow path, had set her heart on fire and driven her to fits of inward agitation. She was twenty-six years old, and during her six years of marriage she had in fact not spent a single day by herself or with a real man. Her husband, Count Miska, was interested only in horses and ladies of the theater. After a platonic friendship that had lasted for several years, Countess Helene had finally erupted in burning love for her brother-in-law, Count László, who was the only man around her of deeper substance, although his way of thinking was in many ways eccentric.

Her overhearing of the peasant women unexpectedly brought a nascent quality – one that had previously been hidden to her – to full, red-blooded blossoming: her sensuality. When she was alone, she immediately went to the little salon on the north side where one could hear every word spoken in the yard. And the talk of the women and girls as they continually gossiped, laughed, tattled, and subjected each other to insolent teasing so affected her that every single awful word caused a new blood missile to go off insider her. She would have liked to further encourage the women, but was afraid of scaring the gossipers away, who would surely have been ashamed to be caught engaging in such a base pastime.

Among the women working the hemp in the yard was one girl whose loose talk especially piqued the Countess' interest. Countess Helene called the girl into her chambers. She wasn't the least bit fazed – with natural ease she moved among all the grandeur in this foreign, intimidating environment. The Countess took the girl into her service and had her tell all about herself: her life, her village, her world. Until then, the Countess had never recognized that the people working near her were cut of human fabric, but this girl's raw and stunningly beautiful sensuality captivated her.

During the scorching afternoons and evenings when she was left to herself, she called this Bora to her chambers, and the small, nervous, slender peasant girl lay down in her bed and talked until dawn. It was like throwing kindling onto the embers. The girl spoke openly and without fear of shame, and the blazing words poured from her like the sulfuric spray of a geyser. They catapulted her listener into the raunchy world of the little village, surrounding her with the odor of the brutal and unrestrained mating of the animals, the horses, the chickens, the pigeon coops, the unbathed peasant women, and Dani Turi's name and fabled reputation rose before her, and gradually this peasant Don Juan grew to a powerful, incredibly strong Oriental hero, who ruled like a proud cock over the many hens atop the dung heap of life.

For the first time in her life, the Countess felt the wild, sensuous, aimless drive well up within her that takes hold of one's body and jolts it, ripping one's soul from its hinges. And at times she shuddered at the thought of what would happen if she really fell into the hands of this stallion of a peasant, whom these rutting mares surrounded with their neighing and cavorting like a god risen to earth.

Prolonged excitation shot through her, and as she told Bora to invite the peasant hero to a rendezvous, she feared at once that the primitive animal-man could forfeit his halo in her presence. By degrees her ardor toward him cooled, and as the sun bleaches the color from the desirable heroes of our dreams, so did her blood dampen the hot fire of its own accord, allowing the apparition's significance to grow pale. Before long she regarded the peasant woman's passion as a puzzling mania, admired and envied her for her ability to speak of her hero with unchained passion, as though she were sitting just then in his lap, atop the pinnacle of desire.

Every drop of blood boiled within her; if only she could attain this climax in the intensity of sexual love!

XVII

On Monday afternoon, they were in the great salon of the upper floor. The salon windows gave onto the castle façade, and between the trees in the little park was a view of the village tower.

The Countess sat at the piano playing a piece by Chopin. She had a certain aboriginal sense for music and indulged herself with genteel carelessness in variations on the Chopin theme. Her improvisation pleased her more than the composer's work, and after this minimal effort she flattered herself that she'd accomplished something.

Her brother-in-law smiled as he listened to her playing.

"Bravo!" he cried as the lady returned from her capricious excursions to the gently rocking melodies of the piece.

The Countess reciprocated his gaze with a smile. "Come and play."

The Count shook his head. He was seated so comfortably on the chaise longue, smoking his cigar with such enjoyment, that he didn't want to move from his spot. Count Laci was beginning to put on significant weight and his entire figure radiated the sort of fullness that characterizes those privileged enough to enjoy their indolence. His white teeth shimmered; he wore a dense, dark blond moustache; thick, edacious, kiss-hungry lips swelled forth from his chestnut-brown beard.

"A model citizen has been lost in you," spoke the Countess, then glided her fingers across the keys in gentle scales.

The Count stood. Unsettling ideas and thoughts occurred to him, bringing him to his feet. "It's quite strange," he said, articulating his words slowly, leisurely, and yet somewhat nervously, "that a beloved woman to whom we have devoted ourselves so completely that even our innermost feelings are laid bare to her, can ultimately so misunderstand us, as though we'd never spoken to one another."

The lady smiled ironically and stretched herself slightly. She wore her blonde hair in the fashion of bourgeois ladies, in small knots, which lent her head a somewhat strange, bird-like appearance; and her beady eyes sparkled like those of the agile little birds, bright, moist, rash, constantly thirsting after love. Only her large, intelligent mouth bore a human sort of scorn. Her slender, girl-like, barren body was beginning to take on fat in places, getting soft, easing its earlier elasticity. The Count stood before her and saw the entire form of her body as she stretched, her deeply cut dressing gown opening from the back. The soft forms of her shoulders, hips, and backsides played across her nobly-formed bone structure, and he was almost sorry when the lady opened her mouth to speak. "You have a masterful ability to portray your flaws as virtues."

"Flaws ... virtues ... such empty phrases! You are a little bourgeoise, *ma chérie!*"

The Countess gave a slight frown and resumed her playing. Suddenly she stopped again. "How long do you intend to stay here? Forever?" she asked.

"Forever! Where could we stay forever? Isn't it all the same, whether here or elsewhere?"

"One must have something to occupy oneself."

"Must? Why?"

"Because otherwise I'd die of boredom. If I didn't at least think about myself, I would already be dead."

The Count stood there, observing the lady with thoughtful attentiveness. "What does the little peasant girl do here?" he asked.

"What peasant girl?"

"I know you spend entire afternoons with her."

The Countess bent over the keyboard and let her fingers glide across the white keys, as though seeking one of them out. She repeated this a few times, then paused. She suppressed a little smile. "I have her tell me stories. I'm just so terribly bored."

"And does she tell of interesting things?"

"Yes, she does."

The Count began to pace. The Countess smiled secretively and played a few chords, delighting in the sight of her splendid hands. How sad that these, too, were beginning to plumpen, causing the fine blue veins beneath her smooth, soft skin to disappear. The lady lifted her hands and observed them closely. She would undertake a cure. How sad for her beautiful hands.

"Tell me, dear friend," she spoke, startling the Count out of his reverie, "how is it that you don't enter into public service? Wouldn't it be more interesting, as a forty-year-old man, to be a minister, than to be standing here arguing with me?"

"Certainly not ... If I'm going to argue, I'd much rather do it with a beautiful lady than torment myself with politics." He took the Countess' hand and kissed it. Then he looked at it and kissed it again. "And if I'm to fight against intrigue, I'd rather suffer because of the intrigues of my little chickadee than over the pointless games of dumb politicians."

The Countess quickly withdrew her hand and reached with it behind her back for the other, clasping them together nervously. Then with a laugh she looked into the Count's face. Scorn mixed with disdain, annoyance, love, and benevolence marked her features as she spoke: "Aren't you afraid of getting rusty? Does so little work suffice a man to keep his nerves in order?"

The Count smiled. "I'm not a *man*, I'm a *count*, and counts aren't made of iron, they're made of some rare, precious metal. We don't need work in order to shine; we need airtight closure and a worthy frame."

He looked the Countess in the eye and kissed her on the mouth. "I'll turn the little peasant girl out of the castle. It would be an unfortunate lesson for you, if you were to become attached to the idea that we're the same sort of people as the peasants."

"We are gods! We live on Mount Olympus and drink nectar ..."

"Of course."

The Countess drew her mouth into a scornful smile. "But that's so very boring."

"Not to me."

"To me it is."

The Count smiled. "Really?"

"Certainly."

"Why?"

"It's boring ... Living is more interesting than vegetating."

"More interesting?"

"Naturally! ... Don't you think it would be nicer to see a strong, fighting man than a lazy count who doesn't even feel like smiling?"

"You don't know that."

"I certainly do."

The Count furrowed his brow and looked in thought off beyond the Countess. He spoke in a low voice: "A woman is the eternal vibration of light; even in its absolute radiation, light makes 16,000 oscillations in a single moment ... For a man the highest ideal is the life of absolute rest ... Silence is beautiful, the color violet is beautiful, beautiful are the days that leave behind no memory; beautiful is the instrument with a single string, and the wisest music is the single-beat tam-tam of the Papuas. Beautiful are the raindrops when they are all the same, beautiful is the heart when it no longer beats. Beautiful is the philosophical death; for the death of life is but a living-across from one thought into the next, from one form into a new one. Beautiful is a white hand, but only one of marble ..."

The Countess withdrew her hand and stretched out her beautiful, white arms, causing the sleeves of her negligee to fall back from them.

"Have a care, Count," she said coquettishly. "You could learn too late that women prefer the powerful hug of a peasant to the most subtle philosophy of a ruminative aristocrat!"

With a laugh she bent her face toward him for a kiss.

Then she turned and rushed away. From the door she glanced back once more and, her white teeth showing, laughed at the man, who looked after her with a sinking heart. As she disappeared through the door, he stared sullenly out the window at the church tower, whose daring, jaunty, Gallic weather cock seemed to betoken that same truth.

XVIII.

Every afternoon, Count László rode his horse home to his own castle, which stood in the neighboring village of Vezekény. There great economic transformations were underway, and the Count pretended to have taken up residence at his estate because of this work; but in reality he was no more interested in this than he was in anything else in the world.

During his absences, the Countess usually took a bath and then indulged in a nap.

As the Count rode away today, the Countess was already enjoying the cool water. Bora crouched on the floor by the tub. With her strong, small, brown hands she splashed the cool water onto the Countess' snow-white body, observing her lovingly.

The Countess laughed. "Well," she said, "well?"

But Bora just looked at her with her large hazel eyes and forgot to open her burning red lips that threatened to burst in their blood-filled puffiness.

"What is it, Bora?" the Countess asked, unnerved by Bora's strange look and silence.

"How lovely you are, my angel!" Bora said now, and she pinched the pretty lady's chin with her thumb and forefinger in the manner of the peasants.

The Countess was insulted, but simply smiled. "So, what's new?" she pressed.

The girl bent toward the lady's ear and whispered to her: "He's going to come! ..."

The Countess was slightly annoyed. The girl had spoken the words as though they implied a great honor. And Bora looked at her as if hoping to read from her face that she would immediately keel over in a dead faint out of sheer, unbridled joy. She gazed coolly at the girl and asked: "Tell me, Borcsa, hasn't Turi ever hugged you?"

The girl looked at her innocently. "I wouldn't allow it."

"Even so."

"I'm a poor girl."

"And?"

"I can't be had for free ..."

The Countess was astonished; she didn't understand.

"Uncle Dani pays no one. On the contrary, people pay him," she added as though boasting. "The women and girls all go to work on his fields solely in order to get a kiss from him. 'Cause he doesn't give his kisses to just anyone."

"So he hasn't hugged you, because you can't pay him?"

The girl gave a peevish shrug of her shoulders. "I know how to wield a hoe, too! I could pay too ... Him ... But he wouldn't pay me! Obviously you don't know that when a poor girl like me is also beautiful, she can only sleep with a man who pays well. I have to make my fortune. My mother told me when I was a schoolgirl that, if I take care of my good looks, I can make a great fortune."

"What kind of fortune?"

"Either somebody will marry me, or he'll give me so much that I'd no longer have any worries."

"But then no one else would want you for his wife!"

"No! Of course not. When you have a little something, you can get a man. But my father's just a cottager. Only a poor farm servant would marry a cottager's daughter."

The Countess gained the vague impression that an open trade was going on in the world, whereby girls and men freely generated profit from their beauty. "So you wouldn't give yourself to Dani Turi for nothing?"

"I'm a poor girl," Borcsa said simply.

"And he doesn't hug any of them for free? ..." And she looked from the corner of her eye into the clear eyes of the girl.

"Dani Turi is a man! He does what he wants. He doesn't ask. He doesn't give a damn. But the women run after him. They'd give up their life for him just to have him glance once in their direction. There's not a single young lady in the village who wouldn't gladly give up her soul to have uncle Dani hold her by the waist just once!"

The Countess fell silent again and gently sloshed at the water. "But you wouldn't give up yours."

The girl shrugged her shoulders. "I'm a poor girl, I've got to make my fortune," she repeated stubbornly.

"But your Dani Turi is just a man like the others, a peasant."

"There's only one Dani. Only him."

"Doesn't he have any nicknames?"

"Sure he does."

"Really? Which ones?"

The girl frowned and lowered her gaze. "I can't say!"

The Countess looked up in surprise. "What? Is he that nasty?"

"And whoever says it out loud, Dani Turi would kill without a thought."

"Well, he's not here. Tell it to me."

"Come, I'll whisper it in your ear."

The Countess bent her ear toward her, bursting with curiosity.

The girl whispered something to her.

"What does that mean? That's nothing at all! Where is Dani Turi beautiful?"

The girl laughed out loud. "That's it! So, where is he beautiful? Don't you get it? ... Where, then?"

The Countess began to turn red, as though the heat were streaming up to her from the water.

Suddenly the girl wrapped her arms around her neck with a brusque movement and pulled her toward her. She whispered the word into the lady's ear.

"They say," she added, "that the young ladies like him so much 'cause he's very, very beautiful there ..." and she pointed her head down behind the tub.

The Countess closed her eyes and felt a small, voluptuous shiver of disgust run through her. A rush of blood flooded her brain.

Love had become frightfully simple to her since she'd begun taking lessons with Bora.

Sort of like the roosters and the hens going to school together.

XIX.

On this warm summer afternoon, the workers moved lethargically and dirtily along the wall. The hot air was filled with the smells of chalk, mortar, and sweat. Count László looked at the workers, puffed quietly on his cigar, and thought to himself that human life is built into every castle: a piece of the life of many, many people.

"You see," he said to his steward, "they move like sad, sluggish animals, and seen from a distance, the whole thing still looks like feverish activity. Life is the same way. With what agony do we place one brick on top of the others! Nonetheless the strangest rambling, towering, gaudy palace dwelling is growing out of all this. With secret corridors, hidden rooms, spacious parlors ... weighty libraries ... unholy ladies' boudoirs ..."

The manorial administrator was a quick-witted member of the gentry who regarded Vezekény as his own home and not the Count's. He struck the shaft of his boot with an osier tie. "Of course, Your Excellency!"

The Count suddenly furrowed his brow. These castle-building workers were thus those aboriginal creatures who, with their raw, wild strength, could justifiably become the dangerous opponents of the castle-dwelling lords! Reluctantly and yet with objective detachment, he looked individually at all these people. One by one. And he cried out in surprise: "Where is the human being here? These are all degenerate types! Miserable, infirm creatures, with sunken cheeks, alcoholic eyes, formless and dull. They're all penurious, pitiful unfortunates."

The administrator, a handsome, strong young man, now likewise observed the workers and called out in disgust: "These aren't people, Excellency. The village handworkers are the leaven of humanity. They drink endless amounts of brandy, live in an unhealthy manner, eat poorly, and lead an immoral life. You know, Excellency, they belong to the class of intelligent beings. The reason they're so degenerate is that they're resistant to leading a virtuous life. They're nothing but rascals and scoundrels, debauched, dense, unreliable asses. In the entire region there is no handworker to be found who by the grace of God would keep an agreed upon appointment. They're deceitful wretches who've earned their misery. Their kind arrives in the world already intoxicated."

The Count listened in boredom to the words of the administrator, who had distracted him from his thoughts. "And the peasants? The day laborers certainly aren't handworkers, and they're even more miserable, more base and stupid."

"The day laborers!" the administrator responded. "They in fact are lower than the animals themselves. They're not even worth talking about; they live like swine. If Your Excellency were to get to know them like I do!"

"Where then is there a people superior to them?"

"The well-to-do peasants are not like them."

"Who?" the Count asked, wrinkling his brow.

"The more prosperous peasants here in the village. There are so many beautiful young women among them, it's unbelievable. If Your Excellency would like ..."

The Count interrupted him. "And are the men good-looking, too?"

"We have a certain peasant in Kiskara, by the name of Dani Turi. If he had a bit of schooling, he could cut a nice figure in any gentlemen's society. He has more intelligence than the entire village put together. He's just a cottager's son, yet today he's the leading peasant in the village. He's a handsome fellow! The women run after him like fanatics! I could tell stories about him, Excellency ..."

He smiled and again struck his boot with the osier tie he held.

The Count interrupted him with a movement of his hand. "Interesting," he said, then turned and walked on. Disquiet had surged within him. Whenever there was talk of the peasants, Dani Turi inevitably received mention. This name had irritated him repeatedly. He decided to have Turi brought to the castle that very day ... Then his mood darkened and he thought of the Countess. He was nervous ...

The administrator followed him with his eyes and grumbled to himself: "May the devil take you! If I were the

Count instead of you, I'd leave you high and dry without a thought." With this he dismissed the little incident and went happily on his way, while still remaining close by should somebody need him.

The Count began repeating the name to himself: "Dani Turi! Dani Turi! ... So he's the one! Dani Turi!"

Suddenly he made a decision. He turned around, signaled to the administrator and had his horse brought to him. He swung himself onto the saddle and within minutes was on his way back – to his lady love.

To his lady love who, clothed only in a sheer negligée, was awaiting the arrival of the peasant in the corner salon. There she repeated to herself the very same name as the Count: "Dani Turi! Dani Turi!"

Bora stood in the background leaning against a doorjamb and watched the Countess, who stood at the window.

Bright sunlight shone through it, and Countess Helene, standing in the deep niche in her green silk veil, resembled a goddess surrounded by the green mist of the sea. "Bora, a glass of water," she commanded.

The servant hurried away as noiselessly as a cat, and the Countess waited in the light of the window niche. A pleasant feeling excited her, and again she repeated, as though seeking some cabalistic insight from the name: "Dani Turi! Dani Turi!"

Minutes pass. Warm air enters through the window and surrounds the Countess' form with dust, light, the odor of hemp, and the primitive singing of the peasant women.

And it makes her feel good that the setting sun, with its warm red glow, shines on her and seems to produce a radiant haze from her ivory-white body.

A creaking of the parquet floor can be heard behind her. And a gasping, suffocated voice proclaims: "He's here ..."

She turns around.

Bora is standing before her, beside herself, her face aflame, blissful and proud. And she points toward the back of the salon where, in the dim light, before the Countess' dazzled eyes, a manly form stands, a peasant in white trousers and polished boots.

The Countess' first impulse is to step to one side of the window, but she immediately thinks better of this. The effrontery of these meddlesome peasants angers her. Who do they think they are? In a fit of anger and scorn, she wants to turn out the both of them. For several moments, however, she merely stands there.

Then she slowly steps forward. With the pride of a goddess, she steps directly into the bright sunlight. A full step into the radiant flood of light. Then she slips across into shadow, and her sheer dress takes on a massive plasticity.

She fails to find the most fitting word to communicate to them her anger, her disdain and rejection. Something holds her back from pronouncing the one simple, honest remark that forms on her lips: "Get out of here!"

She's a woman. She thrives on guile. She wants to punish and pamper them simultaneously. To humiliate them and hold them fast. Bring them to their knees and raise them up. She wants to be a goddess who keeps her halo, who is as distant from humanity as she is near to it.

At last she summarizes all these feelings in a single regard and looks at the man.

She encounters a gaze from steel-hard eyes, a clear, cold, daring gaze that nothing could perturb, as sure as the blade of a swordsman, a gaze that stuns her with its superiority.

In the next moment, her eyes survey the man's face in timid haste, and she's met with a surprise that robs her of her calm. With astonishment, even terror, she regards this face. Moments pass, and she stands transfixed, lost in thought, completely forgetting that she'd just wanted to turn the peasant out.

The painful silence is suddenly broken by a grotesque noise as the floorboards groan beneath strong manly strides.

Count László enters, his face distorted, his eyes protruding from their sockets, controlling his rage with great effort.

And as the lady sees their two faces next to one another, she realizes exultantly that she was right.

The two men are so similar they could be taken for brothers.

It's just that the Count is taller, plumper, softer. And bearded. And without passion. And helpless ...

For a moment or two, the Count remains indecisively on the threshold. Then he steps into the room and utters hurriedly, more gentle in his tone than his words: "Quelle folle! Sans doute tout cela est délicieux, mais ... Mais ma chérie, tu es une rêveuse, et tu manques de sens social et d'idées générales ..."

"Je ne sais pas," the Countess began with irony, and suddenly she added cheerfully: "Je suis une femme, voilá tout!"

And she laughed out loud, immediately easing the tension in the room.

The Count could relax. The Countess was merely exercising her curiosity. He recognized the peasant girl standing behind the door, the intermediary. He cast a disparaging glance at her, then turned toward the peasant.

He was glad to see he was a few inches taller than his counterpart. "What do you seek, my son?" he asked in the tone of a merciful benefactor.

The Countess sat down in an armchair. The tension in her nerves was tiring her. The Count's demeanor actually pleased her, and she waited expectantly to see what would happen next. She assumed with certainty that the peasant would stammer like an idiot and either give her away, in which case he would deserve no mercy, or keep her secret in an amusing fit of gallantry.

Dani Turi did not look downward, however, but spoke in solemn seriousness: "I come here in the name of our village with a humble request to our gracious Countess."

"Who are you, my son?"

"I'm a poor peasant from the village of Kiskara. My name is Dániel Turi."

The Count's eyes quaked imperceptibly. It struck him that he'd assumed the peasant he saw before him could only be Dani Turi; on the other hand, he was amazed that Dani Turi really was here. "Well, speak then."

"Our humble request of Madame the Countess," the peasant said simply, without excessive subaltern humility, and he looked stiffly at the Count, with the intensity of deeply felt emotion, "our humble request is that we receive a share of the noble domain ... We wish to lease some land!"

For a moment, the Count had acted as though he would listen to him, then he turned his back on him and approached the Countess, without concern for the peasant's words. Dani Turi had spoken his final sentence with unexpected loudness, almost too loudly, crying it out toward the Count whose back was turned to him.

It was as though he'd dropped a bomb. Like a war cry against the landlord.

With a jolt, the Count suddenly turned again toward the peasant and regarded him with flashing eyes.

The hatred of hell burned forth from his eyes at the peasant.

At the moment when the manorial lord had done what all landlords did in the presence of a peasant with a request, and turned his back on him in yawning indifference and boredom, Dani Turi had been assailed by a hatred whose embers had accumulated in the souls of the peasants for the past two centuries.

And the Count too was burning with the pride, the aristocratic hatred, the self-importance of the noble Karays. And although Count László, in conformity with his ideals, always stood on the side of the peasantry in this regard, he was nevertheless overcome by bitter anger.

But he controlled himself.

"Dearest sister-in-law," he said, turning to the Countess, "treat this man to an insult or two, and send him mercifully on his way."

The Countess, for her part, had sensed with her female intuitiveness the full electrical power of the storm behind the two men's silent stand-off.

"Speak!" she said boldly to the peasant. "What complaints have you got against us?"

"I, my dear Countess?" Dani Turi returned with a triumphant smile and flashing eyes – and in this glowing smile his manly visage grew in handsomeness. "We peasants of today have no complaints against our landlords. Our fathers had complaints. Our sole complaint, dear lady, is that our landlords today are still not endeavoring to make up for the injustices committed against our grandparents by the previous landlords."

"What!" the Count cried out. "What does this peasant dare reproach me for!"

"The truth, Lord Count!" said the peasant emphatically. And as this truth shed its warm glow across the peasant's face, anger made the Count's calm, serene, cold-blooded countenance only more ugly.

The Countess remarked in passing that, in this confrontation, it wasn't the peasant who found himself at a disadvantage.

While the Count questioned whether he should risk throwing the peasant out, Dani Turi continued boldly, with the power of truth on his side:

"We know it, we haven't forgotten how our grandparents were driven from our ancestral land, the land of Canaan, to the Hangman's Heath."

"Not another word!"

"You know it as well, Lord Count ... It angers you! Shames you ..."

The Count had in fact reached the point of attacking the other with clenched fists, seeing no other option before him. Yet torpor and numbness overcame him. If he'd been alone with the peasant, he would most likely already have smiled at him, or, had his anger taken over, yelled at him, forced him out with some blows and called for the coachman. But in the presence of the lady he could do none of that. Her proximity tied his hands; faced with this wild, shameless animal of a man, his superior intelligence and refined education were worthless. His very nobility disarmed him. And at the peak of his ire he realized with his subtle and sharp powers of perception that the peasant's cause was just – he was in the right and, from his standpoint, obligated to act as he did.

The Count was bursting with unspent rage. Lacking release, all tension within him turned on himself.

The Countess looked at him with alarm. His face was blue – he seemed on the point of suffering a seizure.

In that moment she rose to his defense. She stood in front of the peasant and bellowed at him: "What do you want?"

The peasant was dumbfounded. For a moment he lost his composure.

Then with tranquil, humble, manly subservience, as though he were sighing, he said: "What I seek, gracious Countess, is that you might from time to time turn your lovely, merciful eyes toward us poor peasants. If these will shed their light on us, then God knows we will no longer have anything to complain about!"

The Countess likewise was flustered. She must sense that she confronted here a creature who was not of a lower stature than she. She must sense that this man facing her was indeed a man. A man who appreciates her strictly as a woman. Who dares to pay her compliments, yet does not consider her worthy of participation in serious discussion with him.

She did not want, did not dare to pursue the matter further. She feared she must somehow humble herself before this peasant. She found that things had already gone too far and her sharp eyes grew dull, as the water's surface in the wind, from the piercing gleam of the man's eyes.

Dani Turi observed the discomfort of these people and his breast swelled fat with pride. The whole idea of the land lease could perish here and now, for all he cared. Even the largest of monetary losses would not have been too great a price for this moment.

This painfully long silence, in which the manorial lord and lady found no words with which to chase out their abuser, was the greatest triumph of his life.

It was he who now spoke the final word. With feigned humility, like the thief who offers the dog a poisoned bone, he said: "Your Grace, we will submit our request in writing. May you decide as your heart instructs you. The Mother of God is the most beautiful of all, and thus also the most kind. But Your Grace is even more beautiful, much more beautiful! ... and therefore also kinder ... We entrust ourselves to your will." With that he replaced his cap on his head, gave a nod, turned on his heels, and left.

With his iron-soled boots slicing into the priceless carpet, he strode across the creaky flooring like a heathen from ancient times, like one of the heroes of Árpád. And not the least of them. A tribal chief who has brought from the East a commandment in his soul: in solemn moments, in church, and when swelling with pride, don your Hungarian cap.

The Count and the Countess followed him with their eyes in amazement. All the blood had gone to the Count's head – his face was beet red. The Countess was deathly pale at first, then blushed, her heart beating wildly. She could have laughed as well as cried. At the bottom of her quaking soul, she felt that this moment that had just passed could easily, in the warm and fertile bed of passionate memory, grow into something larger than life.

Bora stood behind a curtain, half hidden from view.

The Countess gestured toward her as toward a dog. Bora slipped out along the wall, subservient and shy, like a pup who fears its master's whip.

XX.

Dani was filled with unbridled joy when he saw the Countess change color. In his arrogance he would have looked on indifferently had she collapsed in the face of his victory. His chest swelled with pride, his eyes gleamed, his face glowed in wild, animal satisfaction. That's the way it should be, that's what he wanted. To have the woman at his feet. What does a woman matter to him, even if she is a countess? A woman! Nothing! If a real man looks her in the eye, she's bound to wither. And if he touches her ... He pressed his fingers together and felt the power, the desire in them: with a single twitch he could rip her dress from her body ...

As he left the stairway and came outside, someone whispered his name: "Uncle Dani!"

With one eye he looked back. It was Bora. She leaned against the doorjamb, holding it, clinging to it, having followed Dani Turi with her eyes as he'd departed.

A sly smile graced the corner of the handsome peasant's mouth. It flattered his vanity that one of his own people was there, even if it was just a poor girl, to witness his triumph.

Without dignifying her with a second glance, he went on his way.

Bora, for her part, wrapped her arms around the door, as though she must hold herself fast with bodily chains to prevent her soul's passion from launching her after the object of her ardent desires.

As the peasant arrived in the street before the castle gate, he wasn't sure if he should turn right or left, home toward the village or away toward the fields.

After a moment's indecision, he turned boldly and headed for the fields.

With heavy, yet buoyant steps, he strode along the dusty street. He turned down the field path that snaked its way opposite the grass-laden roadside ditch between plantain weed and thistles, then took a narrow path that led among corn plots and wheatfields. He now had the dusty field path behind him. A fresh wind caressed his face, the perfume of thyme and wood sorrel surrounded him, and the young corn plants rushed and rattled in the breeze. He plucked a shimmering yellow flower from a stolid yarrow plant as he passed, then turned left before the sun, which was already hovering low over the crops and stared after him with its gradually reddening countenance.

It did him good to go about at will across God's free earth. Unspent energy poured from within him, like the steam escaping a machine – it all but whistled as it left his body. After a hard half-hour's march, he grew calmer and began to walk at a measured pace. He approached his acreage where today the cutters were tackling the wheat crop.

The workers received him warmly.

He returned their greeting with a smile. He broke off a head of wheat and crushed it between his hands, blew away the chaff and took joy in the beautiful ripe red kernels. Each was fat with floury richness, there wasn't a single shriveled kernel among them. The downpours of the last weeks hadn't caused as much damage as originally feared. The image of St. Mary, Mother of God, was smiling down on them.

"What's next, master?" a cutter called out to him, eyeing his neighbor as he spoke.

Dani understood the question. It was a veiled attempt to get something from him. The poor man always wants to glean from the rich.

"Time for some wine, Péter, some nice wine!" Dani replied.

"That's good then," everyone said with a sigh of relief.

They'd just completed a row and were starting to sharpen their scythes, when Dani called out to them: "Hey, you people, women, boys, girls, which of you is tired?"

But who would be tired on only the first day of the harvest?

"Who wants to work tonight during the moonlight?"

They all wanted to.

"All right, then. Péter, give me your scythe. Ride into the village and have my wife fill a keg with fresh brandy. In the meantime, we'll stay here until we get this little plot cut down."

And he pointed at the mighty wheat plot. Everyone liked his suggestion. It was good to work under the foreman's leadership. Especially when this foreman was Dani Turi.

Dani checked the sharpness of the scythe. "You've got a good scythe, Péter."

"Because a good hand is guiding it! ..."

Dani nodded with understanding.

Péter was already seated atop the horse, the keg safely positioned at his back. Before he rode off, he said: "I wouldn't entrust it to anyone else, by God!"

"Bring back my scythe, too!" Dani called after him. "And tell my wife ..."

"What?"

"Nothing! Not a thing! ... Now, you girls, let's hear a song!"

A sturdy binder laughed to his face. It took very little convincing before she began singing in a loud, shrill tone:

> I wasn't sick a day in my life,
> As long as I hadn't met you.
> Ever since I've been on the edge of death
> For lack of becoming your mate.

"What the deuce?" Dani remarked upon hearing this song. "If you were to die from that, one would have to drown you seven times, like a cat."

"That's easy for you to say," the girl said as she released the binding tie. "You've only ever had to deal with the kind of girls ..."

"What girls?"

"Ones that were crazy for you."

Dani put his arm around her waist. "And aren't you crazy for me?"

"Me? You'd best leave me be."

They wrestled with each other. It was clear the peasant had no special interest in the girl, he was only toying with her. Things ended with her escaping his clutches, even though she didn't necessarily want to. He let her go, as he was already thinking of something else. He passed the whetstone across the blade of the scythe a few more times, then went to the front of the group of cutters. The workers followed in line after him. Behind him was a long-necked, red-faced, taciturn, haggard fellow, followed by another crotchety old peasant, then the small, crooked man that had recently taught him a lesson, and so forth, eight workers altogether.

With a joyous feeling, Dani swung the scythe. It whirred majestically into the crop and, with a single stroke, cut the swaying row of ears to the ground. His strong, manly arms were up to the hard work, and his senses were soon fully occupied by the guiding of the scythe. Carefully selecting the path of each stroke, keen to avoid all clumps of earth, thistles, and weeds, he worked his way forward up the row in mechanical rhythm and with skillful sureness. His tempo was somewhat quicker than the others', so that the long-necked worker behind him could only keep up with effort. The binder followed him with nimble skill and softly hummed the same tunes as she worked that the others crooned out loudly in the warm air. No one gave a thought to the meaning of the words, they just sang as they went, one after the other. And their singing released a sweet aroma, like the sorrel sprouting between the ears of wheat.

Dani strode vigorously forward, his scythe whirred and he harvested the wheat ears as swiftly as his head did thoughts. His fellows remained far behind him in the fast approaching dusk.

"Hey, foreman, God knows," cried one of the men in the rear, "when you gallop like that, we can't keep up with you!"

Dani stopped with a laugh and sharpened his scythe. The others followed his example, and the sharpening of eight scythes could be heard far across the plain. Cutters were walking home down the path at the other end of the wheatfield, and in the dim of evening soon one, then the other called over:

"Tomorrow's another day!"

"For whoever lives that long," came the retort.

"You have a fine foreman, he knows how to make two days out of one."

"Yes, indeed – he's none other than Dani Turi!"

Everyone laughed. It was an honest, hearty, happy-go-lucky sort of laugh.

The cutters continued on their way home; the scythes swaying on their shoulders twinkled in the twilight. The binders' rakes shone against the evening sky, and soon the entire group disappeared behind the neighboring cornfields.

Once again his scythe whirred and Dani soon reached the edge of the wheatfield. He thought for a moment, wondering if he should wait for the others. Then his glance fell on a girl whose face was flushed from work, and who stood before him returning his glance with sparkling eyes, as though she wanted to say: "That was a nice piece of work."

Quickly Dani decided to press on; he took stock of the next row and took a great swing so that the wheat plants could lie easily and the binder would have sufficient room for her work. He moved forward quickly, like the flitting of a shadow. His scythe seemed to float, feather light, as though swinging itself automatically, one need only keep pace with it. The percussive flapping of a quail could now be heard in the dense wheat, the crickets chirped round about, and up above the cries of wild geese shattered the air. The cutters who'd just now reached the end of their row cheered back at the geese. The young men and women engaged in teasing and flirting, there was cheerful laughter and wild shrieking – summer's night. Dani's eager ears picked up their voices, he breathed in the smells around him lustily and guided his wide-open eyes across the purple horizon, the night sky with its myriad twinkling stars and the moon smiling with its fat cheeks. Having grown hot, he shed his vest and rolled up his sleeves. Thick steam emanated from his body. The girl working behind him quietly hummed a tune to herself. She'd exhausted her supply of binding ties and had no time with which to weave more from the wheat straw. She just laid the mowed-down crop in loose sheaves with the intention of binding them the following day. As it was, she barely managed to keep pace with her foreman.

Soon after that, Péter returned on his horse from the village. He brought a generous supply of brandy, also bread, bacon, sausage, and ribs. Mrs. Turi had provided him with enough food and drink for the people who would be working during the night. He was received with a cry of joy, and the cutters immediately sat down to the abundant food. Only the foreman took no part in the meal – he had no desire for food or drink.

"Go join the others and eat, Julcsa," he said.

"Why?"

"In case you're hungry."

"And if I'm not?"

"Why wouldn't you be?"

"With you at my side?"

"I can't fill you up!"

"Oh!" the girl grunted with a soft giggle.

"Hey! Come over here!" those at the table called out playfully. "You'll get sausage!"

"I don't need any," the girl replied, then she added quietly: "even if the foreman were to give it to me! ..."

Dani glanced quickly at her. The girl was standing right beside him, a robust, strong, buxom girl. Her stiff blouse stretched, she let it slip down, extending her strong arms from her; her pinafore dress expanded at her hips, her face glowed – in the moonlight it practically blazed. And beneath the mantle of semi-darkness, she offered herself there among the grain so openly, brutally, and shamelessly, that one would only have had to touch her with one finger ...

For the first time in his life, Dani was overcome at such a sight with anger and disgust. All he really wanted was to give her a good swift kick.

But instead he turned away without saying a word, swung his scythe and began working with great speed, as though wanting to flee from a persecutor. Soon a veritable competition emerged between the two of them. Who could get more work done: the cutter or the binder? In this way they covered two full rows, and Dani observed angrily that the panting girl was always just behind him.

"Be careful," he finally broke off. "Tomorrow I myself will gather the gleanings of your harvest."

"Fine with me!"

Dani trusted in his ire that she was doing her work well, and continued to mow. His anger grew and grew. He resented his own lassitude. Then he began cursing his scythe, recalling that he wasn't working with his own. He yelled out to his group of workers who, having finished their supper, were just now about to resume their work.

"Péter, where's my scythe?"

"Here!"

"Bring it here ..."

Breathlessly he halted his work and waited until the farmhand, who passed through the wheat crop, brought him his scythe, then returned the other back to him.

The worker inspected the implement. "Goodness, sir!" he cried. "What the devil did you do with this scythe?"

"I mowed with it."

"It was as sharp as a razor when I gave it to you, now it's not even fit for the peddler Jew. It's not a scythe anymore, it's a saw ..."

The farmhand looked at the peasant in exasperation, and struggled until morning with the dull-edged scythe. Dani took his own splendid scythe and resumed his work, which now progressed as smoothly as a dream. With inward joy he noticed that the binder wasn't able to keep up with him. With every swing of the scythe he gained ground and increased his distance from the disturbing titillation of the girl's vicinity.

His thoughts turned to the Countess. He reviewed in his mind every moment he'd spent in her presence. His thoughts soared like an eagle from its nest, and his senses grew and swelled along with them.

Now he took on yet another row. No longer did he storm forward as he had; he progressed with light swings, almost absent-mindedly. His heart was in a state of fierce excitement, his senses enthralled by the warm, aromatic summer night, filled with the fertile smells of the wheatfields, the music of the birds and the beetles, the lapping waves sounding from the distant lake. From time to time he stood still and absorbed the rich, tangy air with closed eyes. His knees grew tired and he stretched himself out so that his joints cracked. In the meantime, the girl, who'd rushed after him blindly, wildly, out of breath, caught up with him.

The peasant no longer feared her. He stood, turned around, and let his scythe fall to his side, expecting her.

Once the girl had piled up the last sheaf, she twisted a withe from the broken stalks and used it to bind the grain together. Then she stood up. She looked the man in the eyes as he stood a short distance away from her.

And Dani flung his arms around her, hugged her wildly and brutally, then cast her onto the sheaf of grain. He shattered her with his kisses, with horribly lustful kisses meant for the both of them.

When he came to himself, he raised his head and looked around with teary eyes.

His blood was cooled and his gaze shrank back as before a serpent. The blade of the scythe stood a hair's breadth from his eyes.

He grew sober, meek, then rose to his feet. The girl lay there in the grass. He pulled himself together and tried to return to his work. He heard the chirping of birds, leaned his head to one side, listening, and saw that it came from a quail's nest. One stroke of the scythe would have cut the nest in two. He felt sorry for the pitiful little family. He gathered himself, carefully mowed the grain around the hallowed spot, then took a deep breath. He no longer desired to work.

On a sudden impulse, the peasant placed his scythe over his shoulder and walked out to the road.

He made his way home.

He didn't once turn around, didn't even glance back at the girl, who lay in her disheveled clothes there among the grain like a crushed bit of life.

He proceeded down the road, and soon he had the group of cutters well behind him. Only their ceaseless singing managed to reach his ears from the distance. A cooling dew sank down from above and Dani walked quietly in his boots across the grass. The scythe on his shoulder rocked in an even tempo as he strode leisurely toward the village.

In the still, balmy night, his nerves grew calm, and the image of the Countess floated before him in fairylike magic. He lowered his head like a flower singed by the burning sun and sighed: "Ah, if only I could throw my arms around her just once!"

How softly, how gently, how very differently he would hug her than he was accustomed to hugging other women. So impalpably that he would barely graze her skin; so lightly that he would barely feel her weight. He senses a slight tingling in the skin of his palms and fingertips. He feels the gentle air of the night and the hair on his hands and arms stiffens.

He lets his feet carry him forward at a steady pace, without wanting them to or helping them along. He's turning into a different person from the one he was, he feels new capacities within himself. And every scent is so strong, so penetrating. The alfalfa's pungent, weedy smell and the cornstalk's prickly haze; the dense grasses radiating their sweetness; the artemisia and white wormwood, the sorrel and the pleasant-smelling dog rose all send their souls forth wantonly, penetrating the man's every pore.

Dani is dazed by them, intoxicated. His brain is as though suspended, he feels like he could float in air at any moment.

Finally he reaches the village. He walks along beneath the acacia trees. Here and there a dog or two can be heard barking, but they soon recognize the neighbor man's familiar scent and grow quiet again.

He arrives home. He hangs the scythe in its spot on the porch and approaches the window to look inside. His wife is still up and alert, expecting him. Some sewing work lies before her, but she's not working on it, she just stares into the burning lamplight. Dani finds this all so strange today. He suspects the true nature of his wife. He's seized by weakness in the face of this dark-eyed, delicately built, ivory-necked woman, captured by its call for indulgence. Until now this essence of hers was strange and unpleasant to him; now it captivates his soul and fills his heart with kindness.

He enters the house. From the darkness of the kitchen he steps into the front room. His wife barely moves in her armchair, she only rests her large, dark eyes questioningly on him. Dani greets her with a nod, then approaches, and he walks by her, taking his place in the other armchair. His fingers lightly brush his wife's back as he does so, where it shows bare above her neckline.

A hot shudder courses through Erzsi and she looks at her husband with an uneasy expression.

Dani sits down and looks warmly at his wife, taking her eyes in tenderly, which is quite unlike him.

"Are you hungry?" Erzsi asks softly.

Dani shakes his head.

"Don't you want anything?"

"No."

Erzsi stands up wordlessly, she only sighs and acts as though she might want to undress, but hesitates.

Dani looks at her with keen affection, threatening to tear up.

"What is it?" the woman asks quietly.

"I love you, Erzsi."

A feverish nausea overcomes Erzsi.

Dani gets up, walks toward her, hugs her gently and looks into her eyes.

"Oh, don't insult me."

But the man doesn't let up. He hugs his wife in the same way that he saw the lawyer embracing his in the city; he hugs her as his heart dictates to him.

"What's come over you?" his wife asks, turning her head away.

Dani smiles tenderly.

"You really don't want to eat anything?"

The man shakes his head again.

"Then let's go to bed." She walks over to the table and puts out the lamp.

A minute later and they were already in bed. The man sat beside her, leaned over her and kissed her. He kissed her forehead, her eyes, her eyes again, then her face, her chin.

The many, almost impalpably soft kisses that touched her excited the woman over her entire body. Her head grew dizzy – this was what she'd always yearned for, this, not those wild, rough, vehement embraces. And gradually she submitted herself to being surrounded in her husband's arms.

Suddenly her limbs stiffened. Her body grew as hard and cold as ice. She understood the man.

He's hugging *her*! It's not she that he loves!

It's the Countess!

That's who he was preparing himself for, that's who he was practicing for.

And disgust, anger, a stubbornness and alienation she'd never known before raged within her. She jumped up and tore herself from her husband's arms.

"Get out! Get out!" she screamed at the top of her voice. "Get out, you dog! Go to your Countess, go to your Countess!" Her voice rattled and shook as she screamed. "Go to her! Leave me! Leave me alone and go to your Countess!"

Dani froze. He was stunned.

They stood across from each other for minutes on end in the dark room, sensing their mutual presence as an electrical storm.

With a brusque movement, Dani extended his arms and reached blindly for his wife's neck, dragging her back onto the bed.

"Get out of here!" the woman gasped. "Get out!"

All lust for love had fled from the man and his humiliated manly pride rebelled. "I order you!" he mumbled with clenched teeth.

"Order your dog around, you dog! Never! If I don't want it, never!"

Dani grasped the woman's shoulder with his hand, shook her, shoved her several times against the wall, then threw her from the bed into the middle of the room.

XXI.

Erzsi groaned in pain as she came to. She shuddered and sensed the aching soreness in her body. She pressed her teeth together, her eyes burned, her temples throbbed wildly. Her stomach ached and her collar bone seemed broken. Since having given birth to her second child, she often suffered pains in her lower back, and now she felt like something had burst inside her.

Her eyes seemed to want to come out of their sockets as she tried to stand up. She staggered to the cradle and took her baby into her arms. Then she shook her boy awake. Little Béla groaned miserably as he crouched at the foot of the bed, and at the first nudge of his mother he obediently sat up and slid down onto the floor.

None of them spoke a word. The woman suppressed her very breathing with her strong will. The baby in her arms slept; little Béla walked on tiptoe, as though he saw ghosts.

Away, away from here, the sooner the better.

The creaking of the door as they opened it set their teeth on edge. It seemed to ask them with its frightened, horrified shrieking what they wanted. Erzsi didn't dare close it, she left it open so as not to have to hear the creaking again. Even so it sounded in her ears at length, its sad, eerie rasp traveling up and down her spine. She felt the urge to look back at it in the darkness, but didn't dare to. With trembling hands she felt her way forward and found the handle to the outer door. It wasn't locked and Erzsi was glad she could get outside so easily.

Now to cross the yard! Her bare feet sank in the moist, cool sand. She pressed her baby gently to her breast while the boy ran nimbly behind, holding onto his mother's skirt with his little hand. In this way the poor creatures wandered along in the pleasant, clear, starry summer night.

Erzsi's trembling subsided. One thought ruled her being: run, run toward freedom.

A curse pursues her, blessings await her. Every step tears them away from misery and carries them ever closer toward happiness. It's as though she were fleeing with each step from the agony of the present and toward the joys of the past. This tortured nighttime flight transports her, the suffering wife, back into her happy, carefree childhood. A curse weighs down on the home they're leaving, and blessings rest upon the one toward which their steps lead them. A curse on the harrowing life of the adult, blessings on the years of unknowing childhood. Another step, ten, a hundred more steps, and then she can forget forever all the evil that's befallen her. Nothing will ever happen to her again, she'll simply return to being a child once more. Softly and gently, like the dew of life, she carries the baby in her arms. She'll be a child again, along with her children, she's bringing home three small, tired children. Home to her father and mother.

Full of love she looks on her family home. The feelings are swarming down on her, bombarding her. It's like she's fleeing from a strange land, from frost and ill weather, from abuse, mud, and abjection, to find rescue in her parents' home. She's going to her childhood home to cry herself out. She still doesn't know what will happen – she doesn't think especially of her father, not of her mother, she only thinks how nice it will be at home, how cozy and safe, how in the corner by the door she can cry and sob to her heart's content behind her little child's handkerchief. And she feels like a child with her two children, and she runs home through the dust that clings soft and damp to her bare feet.

She feels a pain in her heart.

Behind the hedge at the schoolmaster's home a man stands and looks after her in wonder. It's Gyuri Takács. He looks at her as though she were a ghost. In his paralyzing fright he stands riveted to the earth, unable to make a sound. He's reassured only once he sees the woman enter a gate, the gate to her father's house. For some time he stands there behind the hedge; at last he sighs in relief, turns and enters the house, where later on people sit around the card table.

A shudder travels down Erzsi's spine as, with stiff fingers, she knocks on her parents' window.

Inside someone immediately moves about. A match flares up, and someone lights the lamp. Then her mother rushes quickly out to the door. Astonished, she sees her daughter standing in the porch, bathed in moonlight.

"I'm here, mother," Erzsi whispers.

"I see that, but why?"

"Let me inside."

Her mother stands there, as though wanting to block her way. But Erzsi slips quickly inside, pulling the boy behind her. The mother shuts the outer door hesitantly, slides the bolt into the lock, and follows her daughter into the front room.

Now the peasant, too, is awake. He sits on the edge of his bed and looks at his daughter with concern.

"What's wrong?" her mother asks her.

"I'm dying, mother!" Erzsi replies, her face distorted with pain. She can't cry, because her sensitive heart discovers in her father's traits the same judgmental bewilderment it finds in her mother's.

Until now she wasn't even thinking of herself, but now, as she puts the baby to bed on the bench by the oven, she feels as though her body is being torn in two. As she straightens, a terrible pain shoots down her back. She runs her hand over her head and discovers two large swellings, one on her forehead, the other where her hair parts. She can't raise her arm, it seems broken. And what the pain in her heart hadn't accomplished, the pain in her body does: she erupts into sobs, crying bitterly, as though the unbearable tension inside her were struggling with all its might to find a route through a plugged-up hole.

Mother and father looked at her for a time in wonder. They said nothing, not even exchanging glances, as loveless spouses are wont to do; they kept their thoughts to themselves.

Once Erzsi had cried herself out and calmed down, her mother asked detachedly: "So what's the matter?"

Erzsi shrugged her shoulders in sullen embarrassment. Her blood had cooled.

"What, then? What?" her mother pressed.

"Nothing," Erzsi responded, and her tear-stained lips trembled with inward pain.

Her father only looked at her, tired, apathetic, sad.

"My, oh my," the mother sighed, stroking and patting her bare, fleshy arms as she crossed them. "You're right, daughter, all men are pigs and dogs. Deceitful and corrupt."

Erzsi furrowed her brow. She began to feel uncomfortable. Here she wasn't at home, but in a strange place, a place worse than among strangers.

"Did you think I don't know what the matter is?" her mother continued, incessantly kneading her fat arms. "You're right, daughter. It's enough that you have two children. The devil take those bovine men!"

Erzsi looked anxiously at her mother, then lowered her eyes. Her blood began to boil, she grew nauseous, weighed down by shame.

"Do you think your father hasn't beaten me as well?" the old woman continued, pursing her lips disparagingly. With this she took both hands and lifted her mighty breasts above her low-cut frock, so that her white skin grew taut with youthful suppleness. Her entire body had maintained its feminine beauty, only her face was old, covered in deep furrows; dark wrinkles even surrounded her eyes, and her brown cheeks were as slack and weathered as the battlefield of love's raging struggles. But her body was hard, one could have crushed a flea on her skin, and one could see from her energetic, temperamental movements, that even today she wouldn't have feared seven men.

"My, how many times he's beaten me," the old woman went on. "But what should I do about it? I always got what I wanted. At first I, too, ran home to my mother, but my mother refused to let me in. 'Go away!', that's what she said. 'You've got a husband, let him rip you to pieces, I don't care.' My mother – now that was a woman! What a woman!"

She stared gleefully before her. She spoke only to herself. Certainly not to her husband – weeks passed without them exchanging so much as a word with each other. Nor was she speaking to her daughter – an entire world separated them from one another. But for all that she was very self-sufficient, and whenever a stranger approached her, she was always so fresh, so hearty and affable, that the whole world called her "golden Mrs. Takács." No one could understand the silly old "Scarecrow" who was unable to live peacefully with his kind, appealing wife.

The haggard peasant sat on the edge of the bed with a somber look. He focused his brown eyes darkly on his daughter and spat. Then he looked over at his wife and saw with disgust how the old woman kneaded and stroked herself, how she stretched and turned her body this way and that, with brazen defiance.

Would that you'd pack yourself off just one more time, he thought to himself, *you wouldn't come back through my door again.*

He sucked on a bad tooth and listened.

All three of them were silent. The miserable little boy squatted beside his mother, staring through his big, sleepy eyes about the room.

The silence was painful.

"So, what do you want?" the mother asked at last.

Erzsi shrugged her shoulders in discomfort. What she wanted? Her? Good God, what could she want? To call death to her side – that's what she wanted. She sensed the baby's presence in her arms, the little boy beside her, his knees weak with fatigue. With her protective hands she pulled them both toward her and stood with them in seeming hostile opposition to the two beings before them. It was clear to her now that she couldn't wait until morning under the same roof with her mother, and that her father was completely useless to her, a powerless man who suffocated his cares in stubborn indifference. She looked with pity and sympathy at the old man, brought low and crushed by life.

She looked around the room. Because the covers had been taken off the beds for the night, everything lay in disorder. She herself was accustomed to putting everything carefully in its place, while her mother tossed things carelessly and sloppily around, a pillow here, a pillow there. Garments and bedclothes lay on every chair, one boot was out in the middle of the room, the other beneath the bed, both dirty and muddy, even though there hadn't been a drop of rain for weeks. On the table stood a plate of unfinished food and soiled utensils from last night's supper, along with an upset salt shaker. The mirror hung askew on the wall, covered in fly dirt, the lamp hanging above the table hadn't been cleaned since spring – the woman had once wiped off the upper and lower ends as far as her finger could reach, but the rest was caked with a thick layer of soot ...

Oh God, to live here? Was it possible? Nothing had changed, everything was as it had been in the past.

"God grants us our trials," the mother said then, "yet because of such trifles you wake us out of the sweetest dreams. Well, is it really such a tragedy? What have you got a brain for if not to figure out how to live with him?" And now she yawned. "Certainly it's possible to work things out with *your* husband! Few women have a husband like him."

Erzsi rose. She was overcome with dizziness. All the emotional slime, all the moral filth that coated her husband and her mother, as though they'd been immersed in the same foul vat, rose as a stench in her nose. She had to witness how precisely this woman came to her husband's defense!

Disgust, deathly disgust overcame her.

She looked around her stunned and confused. Was that living? Life? Dear God in heaven, what was next? From where these many, many blows? What else awaited her? God knows, her needs were so small, she sought neither food, nor drink, nor wealth, nor health. She could live in such a small space, in such poverty, and even in gross illness, if only she could be surrounded by honesty, purity of heart, and healthy morals. How had she earned this sad fate, this worst of all evils, that rained down on her with such violence?

Her mother approached her and whispered in her ear: "Now, now, there's no need to be so alarmed. Why don't you speak? I've aborted eleven children! ..."

Frightful aversion contorted Erzsi's face. "Ooohh!" she roared, crying out in disgust, and as though stricken with insanity she stared with glazed eyes into her mother's face.

Gradually she pulled herself together; with trembling hands she held her infant to her breast, then like a she-wolf she took her poor boy's hand. Away from here, before the house caves in on her! Away, before this pestilent air suffocates her!

Out, out she runs. The mother spreads her arms in dismay, the father stretches his ragged, bony body forth to watch her, but doesn't make it to his feet, saying nothing. Erzsi turns once more at the threshold to witness the hopeless desolation carved in her father's face – it shatters her entire being. She realizes in that moment that she could one day turn into just such a pathetic creature. That's what becomes of those whom life crushes!

Where to go now?

This door, too, the door to her parents' house, is closed to her!

Forever.

Once again she's out on the street. In the emptiness of nothing. In the dreadful void of the universe.

Where can she turn?

Her floundering legs carry her weakly back in the direction from which she'd come. Her emotional excitement abates, like the unwinding of a taut rope. She can hardly take another step, or drag her children along.

"I'll die," she says to herself, "life will bury me alive, like my father. This strong, holy, true man. If he has come so far, then I will come farther, deeper, deeper, down into the earth, beneath the earth. I'll succumb beneath my cross like Jesus. Oh, dear, sweet Jesus. Oh, my redeemer, suffering

Lord Jesus. Give strength to your sinful daughter. Deliver me, my Lord ..."

As she whispered these words of prayer, she grew stronger and calmer. She was like the sacrificial lamb, content with her fate, ready to bear it humbly. A rupture had coursed through her soul. Her lust for life, that's what had ruptured so. Her soul now sought only sadness. She was glad as she felt that her legs could now barely carry her. She rejoiced as she noticed how her physical suffering weighed down the pain in her soul. She feared that, without the pain in her body, she couldn't bear the pain in her heart. If it weren't for the feeling that her arms, her shoulders, her thighs were about to be torn from her frame, she couldn't thirst for spiritual torment, for humiliation, scourging and martyrdom, with such terrible devotion.

Her soul was prepared to die, to fade away.

Suddenly she heard a forceful, yet suppressed and frightened voice call her name, causing her to all but collapse in dismay.

"Erzsus!"

Erzsi halted, pressing her sleeping baby to her breast. A moment later, and Gyuri Takács was standing behind her.

"I saw you when you came by here before. What's wrong? I couldn't rest, I had to go out to the street and wait for you."

Erzsi stared at him silently, her face as pale as death.

"So? What's the matter?"

The woman shook her head and sought to resume her hike.

"Stop ...," he spoke, grasping her arm.

Erzsi wanted to cry out, but no sound came from her throat. Horrible pains shot through her beaten body, and she stood trembling, like doomed prey.

"Say something, for God's sake, don't make me crazy!" Gyuri begged hoarsely. "I can't let you go like this. Speak to me!"

"Leave me," Erzsi said in a rush, her voice fading.

"Not until you tell me what's going on. You're in trouble, aren't you?"

She nodded.

"With your husband ... I knew it! You can't lie to me. Lie to those who don't love you. Lie to your husband, not me."

All his talk was unbearable to her. He himself felt it. "Did he beat you?"

Erzsi stared stiffly at him.

"And you ran home! ... Your mother drove you away with her pestering! Your father ... well, what could he do? Turn his wife out of the house for his daughter's sake?"

Erzsi listened to all this in horror.

"What're you going to do now?"

They stared at each other in silence, each fearing the other might guess at his thoughts.

"Erzsi!"

The woman furrowed her brow in spite at the intimate tone in his voice.

"Do you still love your husband?"

Erzsi turned her face from him with an expression of stubborn scorn.

"Do you love him?"

And when the woman didn't answer, he began again: "He cheated on you – the dog. He beat you – the beast! He let you leave – the sorry piece of trash! ... And you love him?"

Silence.

"Are you going back to him? You can forget what he did? So that he does it all over again tomorrow?"

Erzsi clenched her teeth and narrowed her eyes.

"Do you love him?"

"What is it to you?" the woman hissed.

Having thought himself the victor by now, the man shrank back at these words. "What is it to me? My dear woman! What is it to me? You poor thing! ... I love you. That's what it is to me."

"Then leave me be."

"Are you out of your mind? I should leave you be? Are you a child? Should I be talking to you like a child? It's nighttime! No one sees us! ... Damn it all!" he roared in a sudden fit of anger, so that his voice reverberated through the entire village.

Erzsi's heart stood still. "Quiet!" she commanded him.

"Come here to me. I'll defend you against the whole world."

"Never!"

"Come!"

"Never!" the woman screamed with all her might.

The man stood as though paralyzed by this scream, with its expression of total, final rejection. He let his arms fall and stood passively as the woman went on her way. He watched as she hurried along the dusty road on her wobbly legs, dragging her sleepy toddler behind her. He grated his teeth, then resigned himself, turned the corner and returned to the card game.

And Erzsi walked on, she herself didn't know why or where to. She was walking toward the scaffold, deathward, to the funeral pyre. To suffer with her virtues, to suffer and do penance for her father and mother, for herself, for her children, for the whole sinful world, so full of evil, sin, and damnation. She had a single feeling, that she must make good the sins of others; her sole desire was to remain the lily of purity, and she yearned for a hundred temptations as a means of proving her constancy.

"Oh, Lord Jesus, Saint Mary, Mother of God! What is my suffering compared with yours! Pray for me ..."

She was reviled, cast down to the dust. Her crushed soul will never be revived, never again will she sense herself a woman, a person, a proud creature of God – she is a sacrificial lamb! She is a being slain, the very last of the last creatures.

In this way she arrived at her home, her husband's home. Returned now from her journey to Calvary, she was prepared to see herself nailed to the cross.

She found him just as she'd left him. He lay stretched out on the bed, awake. And he soon guessed at the cause of her return: she'd been subjected to greater humiliation at her parents' house than here ... And he clenched his fist against his chest – he wished he could smash the old people's house and cast them among the ruins for having treated *his wife* so badly! And yet he'd reconciled himself to the thought that his wife would separate from him. It's better that way, he'd told himself. If they didn't belong together, then not even God could keep them together. He detested himself and his life, castigating himself for his inability to serve a woman as her idol.

But what would happen now?

Without saying a word, Erzsi put her exhausted children to bed. How fortunate it was that they were so healthy. She laid the nursling in his cradle and helped the boy into his own bed, laying his head on the large pillow. She herself knelt down by the bed and began to pray.

Dani dozed off fitfully, unable to keep from waking again. Erzsi found no sleep. Nor could she think, she just repeated to herself the litany: "Mother of God, blessed Virgin Mary, intercede for us ..."

As the reddening dawn shone through the window, Dani rose from bed and dressed. He was sad and dispirited.

For a moment he stood still and studied his wife's form. With a soft heart he looked at this woman, some unconscious feeling inside him imbuing her with superhuman power. For hours she'd been kneeling there, as though in a church, in the manner of devout women who rest tirelessly on their knees in the mysterious gloom of dark sanctuaries, fervently raising their praying hands, their heads bent to one side, like the Virgin Mary, and who, with faint movements of their lips, mumble the wondrous monotone words that are ever the same, like the drops of a waterfall, and yet ever quicken the faithful souls with a new, rich feeling, as rushing water does the weary.

Dani's eyes widened as jealousy took hold of his heart. Wild fury began to surge within him. He realized he could not destroy this woman. His own power was nothing compared to that reigning secretly inside her. He saw that, if he were to give in to his sudden attack of loathing and crush the praying woman with his foot, each of her limbs would rise above to heaven and the physical abuse would have no impact on her soul.

Yet still he pitied the poor being. He would harm her no more. He had no right to her! She was nothing to him now. And were they to live a thousand years under the same roof, she would forever remain a stranger to him ...

He stirred, and quietly, heavily, he left the room.

Outside was a beautiful summer's morning, full of promise to lift the spirits from this day to the next.

But his spirit was weighed down by the shadow of misery. With lowered head he looked around him, his eyes dismal and gloomy.

Here and there the cool, blissful morning was interrupted by the lowing of a calf, a rooster's cry, or the curses emanating from a man's mouth.

And Dani sensed dejectedly that here once again work reared its head, toil without purpose, this struggle for things without worth, the blaze that turns everything to ash. The new day had arrived.

He heard the rattling of a carriage.

He looked brusquely out toward the street.

A terrible giddiness seized him as he recognized the Count and the Countess seated in the carriage, the large suitcase revealing that they were headed for the train station.

A vague sense of horror took hold of his head, his heart. He stared at length at the coach as it rolled away. When it disappeared from view, an acrid taste rose to his palate.

What was left for him here?

This miserable village, miserable people, miserable life.

He spat at it all in disgust.

What sort of life was this?

Mud!

And once again he furrowed his brow, balled his hand into a fist, and gasped out loud in a wild rage: "Let it be mud, then! Mud! But at least I'll wallow around in it properly!"

And his desperate gaze fell on the village, his house, and menaced the noble folk as they faded from his sight.

Second Part

I.

Winter arrived early. Already at the start of November, thick snow blanketed the earth. Real winter hadn't even set in yet, and the poor folk, who live as easily as the birds and, because they manage to get by with little, gather nothing at all, nonetheless began stealing the sunflower stalks from the large landowners, in order to have fuel for their fires.

Dani Turi was driving through the village, in the same taciturn and dismal mood he'd betrayed ever since the summer before. He looked neither to the right nor to the left, but straight ahead, at the end of the shaft between the horses. His roughly hewn peasant sleigh with its iron runners jerked heavily across the snowless road, the horses' hooves clopping against the frozen clods.

"What about the bells, Dani?" a peasant girl called to him as she came out from her yard, all bundled against the cold and holding a tub full of wash water to empty. Invigorated by her hard, feverish work, she was in high spirits. "Where are your bells, Dani? Your horses are embarrassed to be without them! ..."

Dani didn't answer. He just wrinkled his gloomy forehead even more; he sat there at the front of his sleigh in his shaggy black *guba* mantle, his sheepskin cap pressed down over his head, as though neither seeing nor hearing a thing. He only gazed in front of him, toward the horses' hooves as they negotiated the filthy, muck-ridden road with its frozen clods, which were ice-hard, just like his soul.

He saw neither the rows of houses to either side, nor the people who stood smoking their pipes and gabbing at their front gates, nor the women who persisted even now in gawking at Dani Turi.

"What in the hell is wrong with that man?" a peasant demanded of his neighbors, who were all taking turns venting about the cold, the winter, the summer, the government, and God himself.

"Why, he's got quite a problem on his hands. He can't swallow the Kiskara church tower in one gulp. That's what's wrong with him."

Dani in fact had become remarkably single-minded in pursuing his acquisitiveness, his work, the growth of his assets. With the same tireless passion with which, as a hungry fire, he engulfed everything he undertook, he accomplished the work of ten men. He paid no attention to his wife, none to his children, none even to his womanizing, he focused solely on obtaining money. During the summer he'd visited the town lawyer day in and day out without succeeding in taking over the dead tenant's land lease. The Count had journeyed to Africa, and the Countess would hear nothing concerning the governance of Kiskara. And Count László, her brother-in-law, had made it clear that he was the peasants' enemy. So nothing at all had happened. For the time being, there was no urgency, a decision would not take place until the new year.

As Dani approached the end of the village where the castle stood, the matter surfaced again in his mind.

Suddenly and without thinking about it, he looked to the right of the street, catching sight of Bora standing before a gate. She was about to go inside, but turned around at the sight of Dani, her hand still on the latch. Dani looked at the girl absently, sensing the lithe, nervous creature beneath the thick gray shawl she wore. Their eyes met. Nothing else happened. Neither spoke a word. They exchanged no greeting, not even with their eyes. All they did was look at each other, Bora with her nervous, sensual, devout expression, Dani with his serious, manly, searching regard. And then the sleigh took Dani away; he didn't even turn to look back at her. He just stared in front of him, toward the ground. Bora opened the little wooden gate and, with crisp, firm steps, crossed the veranda and entered the house.

A sharp wind blew into Dani's eyes; he pushed his cap down over them, lowered his head, and drove harder into the wind. Thick frost coated the tree branches, the entire world was white, and the wind swept snow from the dense white crowns of the acacias down to the road. The horses gave off their vapor, and pearls of ice clung to the ends of their hairs. Here and there great black crows huddled among some refuse, flattering sluggishly as the horses advanced.

Dani looked up toward the end of the allée along which his sleigh was gliding. The thickly frosted street with its endless row of magical sugar trees made for a splendid scene: an ice-locked fairy world that offered ever-new wonders even in its dormant state. Dani blinked his eyes as they rested on this scene, then looked once again at the horses and felt the wind whip his face.

Once arrived at the little bridge that crossed over the ditch, he quickly veered off the main road onto the field, the roadless road, where there was no trace of the cart track beneath the snow. His sleigh flew, swerving across the smooth snow, which was frozen so hard that the horses' swift hooves didn't break through it.

Great loneliness surrounded him on all sides. He heard only the soft rushing of the wind, the crunching of the sleigh's runners, and the rhythmic movements of the horses – across the field's even expanse nothing else stirred. Toward the west the snowfield shimmered with a bluish haze, to the east it glittered a stinging bright yellow. The morning sun broke through the enormous opal arc of the sky, glistening all around just as evenly and languidly as the snow.

Distractedly, Dani observed some rabbit tracks. The rabbit had made its way across here while the snow was still fresh and deep, inscribing it with the form of its belly.

The two horses flew across the field on a wing and a prayer. Here and there a corn stalk poked up through the hard-packed snow, weighed down with ice. From a distant farmstead a dog was heard barking, and it seemed so strange, so alienating as it rang out into the silence.

The sleigh sailed forth for nearly half an hour. The two horses galloped like the wind, as though endeavoring to work out the stall-induced stiffness in their legs with a good hard run. Dani's cheeks reddened and little by little his dismal mood lifted. He sat tall on his seat, stretched his limbs beneath his *guba*, and cracked his joints contentedly. Sensing his power, he knitted his brow like a savage animal. "Giddyup, you horses!"

The snow rises around them like dust. The wind is invigorating. He lifts his cap to allow the air to better reach his face and tugs on the reins to increase his speed. "Giddyup, giddyup, you sorry nags!" Who worries about life? What's so bad about it? Who can hold anything against it? Who even matters anymore? Who the hell cares? The way is smooth, his sleigh is flying, let him who dares get in his way. Sooner or later we accomplish everything as long as we live. And why shouldn't we live as long as life is good, life is beautiful, life is worth living, after all! This is the one joy accorded to man: to live, to act, to fly! "Giddyup, you horses! Or it's the glue factory for you! Giddyup, let's go! Giddyup! Giddyup! Giddyup!"

At last he sees the large pear tree and he recalls where he's headed and what he's after. He looks about him in surprise. The field is bare, his field. Nowhere a sign of the sunflower stalks. He came here to bring them in before they were stolen from him, but oh my God, nothing's left of them but some dirty, trampled remnants, frozen in the snow.

Dani erupts in bitter rage and his invectives against the thief resound in the very sky above. In vain: the plants are gone. It's clear they were made off with quite recently, since after the snow had frozen. Today! Here: fresh boot prints – the snow displaced by the sleigh is so fresh that the thief must have been here only minutes before.

He looks around and sees a dark blot in the distance, a moving rick. That's him. That's the thief.

After him! He grabs his whip and smacks the horses properly. The two fiery beasts take off in anger. Again he lights into them, and yet again. Venting his anger, he lashes their flanks, their bellies, turning them into veritable hellhounds.

Then he slackens the reins and the two animals fly like the rushing wind. Dani replaces his whip and lets the horses run as they will. After the thief. Across clefts and ruts, down into gullies and back up again they fly. Sometimes the sleigh nearly bounces on top of the horses' backs, then leans so far over that the driver all but falls from his seat. But ever onward, straight as a shot, dodging nothing.

It's not long before this struggle, this chase has Dani feeling at the top of his game. He pushes his cap back on his head and searches for the absconded sleigh with flashing eyes. The fugitive doesn't suspect a thing. Calmly, smoothly he ambles along, and the gap between the two sleighs progressively closes. Dani hopes to reach the crook before he can turn onto the road. What a bitter confrontation it will be! Were the bandit to be God himself, Dani would spare him no mercy. He peers behind him and catches a glimpse of the pitchfork. Today it will serve him well. As he approaches the thief, he turns and grasps the pitchfork. The feeling of the implement in his hand causes him to revel in his deepest depths as manly power courses through him. He's a totally different man now from the one who'd left his home earlier on. No longer is he weary and restless, no longer apathetic and anxious. His blood is boiling.

The race runs its course wordlessly. Not a race, a manhunt. The first sleigh with its great burden moves along calmly, its driver oblivious to the fact that the landowner is pursuing him. Carefully, quietly the sleigh jolts along, the rick cautiously tilting this way and that as the driver avoids every obstacle and works to prevent it from sinking into any snowdrifts. His calm drives Dani to distraction, turning his anger to rage. He refrains from calling after the thief, whom he can't yet see, nor does he yell at the man's horses, he maintains control of his anger. When he finally reaches him, he slows his own horses down, pulls up alongside the thief and yells: "Hey! Stop! Whoa there!"

The man takes up his reins and stops his sleigh. Dani climbs down from his seat, the pitchfork in his hands, and closes in on his prey.

A moment later, he draws back in shame.

From the other sleigh, his own father stares down at him.

For a short time they were silent and Dani, dismissing all thought of confrontation, recalled that his father was growing old. His face was as though clouded over, and creased with deep wrinkles. His blue eyes peered shrewdly from beneath his ragged brows, and the poison of bitterness seemed to emanate from his every pore.

As was his wont, Dani was subdued in his father's presence and looked in shame to one side, as though he were guilty. And yet his only fault was that he'd become rich, while his parents continued to languish in the same old poverty. He certainly hadn't done his family any harm, on the contrary, he'd supported them in meaningful ways, earlier on with loans that were never paid back, then later, since becoming wealthier and learning to appreciate the value of money, more with moral support. Nevertheless he felt himself in his parents' debt and, in order to avoid witnessing their misery, steered clear of them. Old Mr. Turi used to say: "I'll slug you in the face, even once you're wearing a gray beard." But that didn't prevent his sons from outgrowing his fatherly power. He alone remained the poor old field worker, even though he'd always strived for bigger and better things. He wasn't a particular friend of work, preferring instead to resort to speculations, to all sorts of little deals in which he invested his meager earnings or perhaps the money he extorted from his sons.

The old man felt that, in that moment, he was superior to his son, and shouted at him, conscious of his bitterness: "You should be ashamed of yourself!"

Dani merely shrugged his shoulders.

"Shame on you! A man raises his sons with pain and misery, and once they've left home they don't so much as darken the door again. For all they care, we could freeze to death. The son doesn't even have the decency to bring his parents a cartload of dried stalks! ... Your mother is ailing, did you know that? Phooey!"

He gave the horses a smack of his whip; they were happy at least for the brief chance to rest, and resumed their drawing of the sleigh, with its load of winter fuel, at a measured pace.

Dani remained behind, releasing a sigh as he watched his father's departure. He mounted his sleigh and, after brief reflection, turned his horses back toward his fields. At least he hadn't completely lost his good mood, and he found himself contemplating a dirty trick that got him genuinely excited.

"I'm not fool enough to return home without any sunflower stalks," he said to himself. "Someone must still have some left in their field."

To his great joy, he soon caught sight of numerous heaps of dry sunflower stalks. His happiness was complete when he decided to steal the stalks of Gyuri Takács. He went merrily to work and tossed a sizeable load of them onto his sleigh, fastened them tight with a rope, and started for home in a pleasant mood.

The good cheer that had found its way into him only continued to make itself felt as the wind's heathen song penetrated his ears. Something within him welled up with such a pleasant feeling, one he hadn't felt in a good long time. He would have loved to stretch himself out properly, and smiled over and over for having stolen from his cousin-in-law, Gyuri. Since the summer, a secret, increasingly tense opposition had existed between them: each took advantage of the smallest opportunity to get the other's goat.

And Dani thought of Bora – he knew that Gyuri Takács was chasing after her. And he smiled, for he, Dani, had only to say the word, to stretch out his finger – a single glance, and the girl would throw herself into his arms ...

He remembered that Gyuri had once courted his wife. And Erzsi had jumped into the well in order to gain him – Dani – for a husband ...

Then his nickname occurred to him, having somehow found its way to his ears. He knew his cousin-in-law had given him the name; in this moment he had the satisfaction of knowing that this word expressed all his successes in love, and all of Gyuri's envy.

Other things occurred to him as well, all of them such thoughts as these, and all in order that he might despise

Gyuri, who in comparison with Dani Turi was a nobody, a louse, nothing but mud!

And yet the string that had been plucked by the appearance of his wife in his memory vibrated on in him, arousing bitter, painful, agonizing feelings.

What use is it that he, Dani Turi, aspires to such great heights, when he has no control over his wife? Erzsi is rapidly withering away, she's fading like the moon, the flesh is melting off her bones, her skin is losing its softness, she looks likes the walking dead ... No path leads back to their former life, their former feelings. If only it were possible to bring life to a quicker end. But living alongside a corpse like this, it's more than a man can bear. A cold shudder courses through Dani whenever he sees or thinks of her ... She's going to die. Let her die, then. If she doesn't want to live, then that's the best. But living like this, where with each passing day something dies inside her ... This way she's only taking her healthy, living husband's strength and lust for life along with her into the grave – a frightful thing! Absolutely horrifying! If in her fit of despair last summer she'd done herself in, everyone would have since mourned for her and forgotten her. Everything would be fine now. He would seek out another mother for his children ... And again he thought of Bora, who stood today as ever before her front door and followed him with her admiring eyes.

He released a heavy sigh.

The horses drew the sleigh along in rhythmic silence. Before long, he reached the row of trees and turned down the main road. The splendid white sleigh once again traveled smoothly along.

Dani sullenly wrinkled his brow. Why not! Today he would put the bells on his horses after all. The sad life wasn't worth living!

With stubborn determination he stared before him and began humming a festive tune. A bent, pathetic-looking figure wandered down the street with quick steps. Having already stepped aside to avoid the sleigh, he tromped through the deeper snow at the road's edge. It was an old peddler Jew.

A sudden thought occurred to Dani. "Halt!" he cried out to the Jew.

The Jew stopped and looked up in frightened wonder at the peasant, who reined in his horses and shot a threatening look at the poor devil from beyond his long, black, fur skin *guba*.

"What have you got in your pack, Mojse?" Dani shouted at him.

"Whatever you wish, master, at your service!"

"So show me, and make it quick!"

"Yes, but ..."

"Make tracks, or you'll get it from my whip!"

The Jew's dirty gray beard trembled, but he didn't speak a word. This area was unfamiliar to him, he didn't know who he was dealing with or what might happen. He was a tiny little man; he peered with his blinking red eyes from beneath his cloth cap, which was perched low on his head and bore earflaps – he looked for all the world like a kestrel trapped in a cage. With his bent, dirty, trembling fingers he fumbled in a frantic, yet vain attempt to unknot his big checkered bundle, slyly eyeing the peasant's face as he did, in hopes of discerning what sort of man he was dealing with. The poor old peddler was as cowardly now as he'd been during his boyhood, when the village dogs had torn off his britches. But that didn't stop him from wandering out into the world with his large bundle, in spite of fearing at the movement of any and every bush that a wolf or a robber was about to attack him. He thanked God each time he managed to return home safely to his family, where he rested for the briefest of times among his sons, who were gentlemen by now, and his daughters-in-law, who were fine ladies; then he set out again on his journey and peddled glass pearls, inexpensive hand mirrors, and silk kerchiefs for the peasant women.

"Hurry up, old man!"

"Aren't I hurrying, then? For you I shouldn't hurry? The next thing you know I'll start dancing, right?"

Dani laughed and, sheltered from the icy wind blowing behind him by the load of sunflower stalks, leaned out from his sleigh and looked with pleasure as the peddler breathed on his frozen fingers that were barely able to undo the knot in his cloth bundle. Apart from this, the old man was actually growing hot; red splotches began to appear on the thin skin of his bony face.

The peasant had him show him his entire stock. A bright yellow scarf attracted his attention.

The old Jew looked up as he waited for the peasant to make a selection. He was moody, uncertain whether the man wasn't just toying with him.

"I need a silk kerchief," Dani said as though each word cost him money, "a large one, a scarf, for a girl ..."

The old man understood what the peasant was after and looked among his wares with eager, trembling fingers. At last he pulled out a scarf.

"This one will be nice!"

"That's not pretty," Dani said tentatively. He'd dealt only rarely with such things in the past.

"If I say it's pretty, then it is."

Dani didn't dare contradict the old man's simple, categorical explanation. He felt the cloth, turned it over in his hands, studying it. "What's it supposed to cost?" he asked.

"Fifteen forints."

"Oh, my! And you have the heart to demand so much?"

The Jew looked him up and down, and waited. Dani tried to bargain with him, but the peddler put him off.

"Just give it back to me, friend. You don't want a pretty kerchief, you want a cheap one."

Dani turned red. "Of course I want a pretty kerchief, but this one is worth ten forints."

"Then be my guest: go into town and look for something like this, then ask for the price. If you can get it for less then twelve forints, come and spit in my face."

In the end he sold it for eleven. Dani always had money on him. He handed him a ten-forint and a five-forint note. The old man returned the difference in small change. Carefully he counted out the small coins, to "avoid a mistake." "Eight plus two makes twenty ..."

"What?!"

"I mean ten ..."

Dani's anger over the apparent attempt to cheat him had caused him to snarl at the man. But when he checked the change he received and saw that not a penny was missing, he tossed the old man a dime. "That's what you wanted to cheat me of, let it be yours then."

The peddler angrily flung the coin into the snow. "I don't need such a gift from you. Give it to your father, to keep him from starving."

Dani was so incensed over these words that he thought of lighting into the old Jew with his pitchfork even as the peddler was calmly packing his bundle. But the peasant suppressed his anger, shoved the kerchief beneath his *guba*, and prodded his horses with his whip. The two beasts had begun to shiver in the cold and lunged forward eagerly – within a few moments the sleigh had left the old Jew far behind, who stood carefully restoring order to the items in his bundle.

Dani stared ahead, whistling happily. He wasn't sure what he would do with the silk kerchief. The first houses of the village appeared before him, the castle's snow-covered tower rose forth above the crowns of the trees.

Aroused from boredom, the village dogs sounded their lazy howls. Dani let the horses slow down and drove at a walk over the ice-hardened surface of the village road.

All of a sudden he saw Bora step out through the same gate he'd seen her enter a few hours before. The girl had clearly been awaiting his return – he'd seen her hurry across the courtyard. Doubtless she'd been looking out for him from the window and gone to the street at the very moment when she saw his sleigh pull up by the entry. She looked at him with the same dreamy eyes she always had whenever she saw Dani. Her entire soul seemed contained within this gaze.

Dani halted the sleigh. "Bora."

"What?"

"Come here."

The girl readily approached the sleigh.

Dani recognized with fright the audacity of his actions. The girl won't accept the kerchief. The entire village would see it. Already a spectator had emerged three houses down. Within an hour the entire village would know. He grew nervous and his eyes clouded over. For a moment he looked into Bora's deep brown eyes, which rested on him with a sparkling glow, then he made up his mind and, without speaking a word, took out the silk kerchief and put it in the girl's hand.

"For you."

Bora took it. Not a word of protest escaped her mouth.

Dani was astonished and stared searchingly into the girl's face. He found nothing special there, neither amazement, nor confusion, nor surprise, nor objection. Bora calmly took the kerchief, as though it were completely natural, and accepted it as a gift. Only her expression revealed a great change. The dreamy romance was gone from her face, the fiendish depths in her eyes seemed to have receded, replaced by a shallow clarity. In place of the agitated, secret devotion, simple, easy understanding appeared. In place of humility and enslavement, superiority and the self-confidence of the woman in charge took over. But all of these were shadows that the man, suddenly overcome by passionate love, neither saw nor felt. Something confused him, something that originated in himself, in the unaccustomed nature of his deed and his position. This moment, in which everyone was staring at him, was perverse, as was his deed, which seemed to rip him brutally from his orderly life.

He had the feeling he was making a horrible mistake. With a certain surprise he gazed into the girl's face, and realized he hadn't yet pinched it, had never kissed it. He hadn't touched this girl with a single finger, hadn't even threatened to. And in the brief moment when his gaze was fixed on hers, a stiff half-smile adorning his mouth, his conscience, his will as though paralyzed, he realized he'd done himself a great disservice by starting things off here with a gift rather than a slap in the girl's face.

He would have loved to scream at her, but hesitated. He had the feeling this girl with her sly, clever eyes – how different they were now from before – saw right through him.

He drew the reins and the horses resumed their pace.

A terrible excitement was ignited within him as he left the girl. He was tempted to look back and see what the slut would do. Show the kerchief around? Most likely she'd already gathered it around her shoulders ... From the other end of the village road Gyuri Takács approached him on foot. Hm. Before a minute has passed, he too will see it ...

Once again he stared grimly at the end of the shaft and at the dirty, snowy chunks the horses' hooves were trampling, and his soul trembled with emotion. A storm of desires and sensations battled within him; he felt ashamed and was overcome with humility; he sensed the unmanliness of his actions and sought to make amends for it. He was angry, angry at Bora, whom he now despised – he wanted to beat her, to spit on her, to kick her down in the mud. And his anger boiled inside him, as within the innards of the earth, and he longed to belch forth fire.

The villagers who saw him huddled in his great *guba*, his cap pulled down over his eyes, sitting grimly in his sleigh, had no idea that this Dani Turi was a completely different man from the one who'd driven out to the fields that morning.

II.

Gyuri Takács followed Dani's sleigh with his eyes.

"What are you looking at, uncle Gyuri?" Bora asked as she ambled past him. She spoke to him out of a sense of propriety, and accompanied the strong man as far as the ditch, so as not to come across oddly to him.

"I was looking to see what sort of stalks cousin-in-law was hauling home."

"Certainly, yours are no different."

"Well, mine grow thicker stalks ... You were there. Remember, how you all were teasing me that every sunflower plant bore seven baby plants?"

"Seeing as how you haven't brought any other babies into the world ... !" The girl stood restlessly, ready to be on her way.

"Say!" Gyuri called to her. "What's that you've got beneath your kerchief?"

"A piglet, don't you hear it squealing?"

"That's not a piglet, it's a lamb, its foot is hanging out."

Bora gave a start, then lifted a corner of the kerchief. She blushed and looked away.

"Be careful, you'll have to give up the pair for that. Someone will catch your little black lamb."

The girl returned his gaze with a suggestive look of maidenly devotion from the corner of her eye. "Let them catch it. It'll cost them!" And she blushed in embarrassment.

"Damned girl ... I myself would give you my *guba* for it. Here!"

The girl's eyes welled up with tears; her inner excitement was choking her voice, and she looked at this haggler as though she'd already sold herself to him. But she kept her wits about her. "You shouldn't start off so high – where would it go from there?"

"For the time being a silk kerchief will do, right?"

"Looks that way."

Once again she looked limpidly into Gyuri's eyes, causing the heat to rise to his face. With that, she walked off, swinging her hips coquettishly and rustling her many provocatively sheer skirt layers.

Gyuri fixed her greedily with his eyes, then likewise went on his way. "Just you wait, Turi with the handsome ...!" he grumbled. "The girl will be mine yet!"

III.

Dani drove through the open gate into his yard. The horses stopped and he looked around for the little stable boy. The broad yard was empty, no one came running toward the master, the father. The bile rose in his throat.

He stood and waited a moment before stepping down from the sleigh. He moved so heavily these days.

Loud shrieking could be heard from beyond the stall; the little stable boy, a mere slip of a lad, was playing in the snow with Irén, the neighbor woman's daughter. Dani watched them in annoyed disinterest. The girl was thin and wiry, but agile, with a hearty laugh, and was squealing at the top of her voice as she roughhoused with the boy. She was barely fourteen – the stable boy wasn't much older. In their boisterous play, they hadn't noticed that "Uncle Dani" was there. The boy stuffed handfuls of snow into the girl's neck, while she delivered punch after girlworthy punch, slapping and hitting him with haphazard clumsiness. The sweet, fresh quality of her voice as she shrieked touched Dani to the quick.

Instead of stepping down from his sleigh, he pulled his big *guba* more snugly around him and moodily watched the children play.

Envy took hold of his heart, his soul.

Not with anger, but with bitterness, with anguish he realized how much he'd aged.

Only recently he himself had thrust a handful of snow in the girl's neck, but how different that had been. He, the uncle, had joked with the child, who'd born it playfully, even coquettishly, but with childish obedience, and fled before him. Now the young hen was playing with the rooster as though they were a couple.

Sixteen or eighteen years ago, the girl's mother had been his playmate. Later, after she'd married, his lover.

And now his playmates were the aged women with their crusty loins, who complained when hugged that everything aches, their sides, their backs, their bones?

An unbearable bitterness, the great bitterness of his life, gathered in Dani's soul.

So life, youth, have already fled from him. Girls were growing up by the dozen in his midst, and the time would come when not one of them would respond upon seeing him with a throbbing heart, burning with desire ... The time would come? ... It's already here! ...

For he's already an old man that no one can love for his own sake anymore. Already he's giving gifts to younger girls to get them to suppress their true feelings.

And he watched the two children, who'd gotten into such a heated tussle that they couldn't be separated.

Now the girl's mother stepped out from the neighboring house and called out loudly to her: "Irén!"

The girl jumped up and ran home, laughing one last time in the boy's direction: "Just you wait, you little stinker!" She pursed her lips and her impish black eyes smiled.

Her mother grabbed her by the arm and shook her as one does a young child. What a detestable old beast she'd come to be in Dani's eyes. He turned away from them.

On the other side his wife now stepped out from the kitchen door of his own house. Her face was pale and drawn. As though she spent her entire time living in a cellar, she blinked her eyes at the brightness of the snow. Her clothes hung limply on her emaciated body, her arms and legs hung slackly, like ill-fitting pieces on her formless torso. Was this the famous village beauty, Erzsi Takács, whom he had wooed and yearned for so? To whom once on a late autumn evening, when she'd told him she was hungry for plums, he'd brought from the Count's own plum orchard an entire branch filled with ripe fruit, as big as a house? ...

He moved, turned, and again his eyes wandered over to the neighbor's yard, where Irén was carrying a pail of water from the well into her house with fresh, agile movements. How lithesome her ankles were, like a deer's; how well-formed, well-developed she was, like a burgeoning rosebud.

Dani heaved a great sigh.

IV.

Once the stalks were unloaded, Dani looked around in search of another chore to do. It was noon. His little son was calling him in to eat. He took the child into his arms. The boy hugged him tightly, nestling up to his father. Touched by this tenderness, Dani pressed his son's small body to his own, but said nothing.

He went with him inside the house.

The front room was excessively warm. Next to the cradle the other little boy played, half naked, his shirt tied so that it covered his buttocks, allowing him to scoot across the stamped earth floor. He was filthy, covered in dirt up to his ears. He stood now, supporting himself on the end of the wobbly cradle, not daring to move for fear that at any moment the unstable object would topple over. He waited there, hoping someone might help him.

With wide, astonished eyes he looked at his father as he entered the room. He reached out to him with his little hand and stammered: "Hey, da! Hey, da!"

Dani's heart was overcome with emotion. He bent down and took the little child onto his other arm.

He stood holding his two sons at the end of the table. When his wife came from the stove with the pot of soup, a sad smile alighted on her care-worn face, as though she sensed a hint of the old, long hoped-for and now forgotten domestic bliss.

The suspicion dawned on Dani too that this was right, this was life as he was meant to live it. He sighed, pressing his two silent children firmly against him, and a kind of worshipful yearning rose up from the depths of his soul. If lightning were now to strike them, killing them all, what a fine thing that would be for them. From how much suffering it would deliver them. But who can see into the future?

One thing is certain. Nothing good can come from anything now.

"Well, take your places, little lambs! Take your places!"

He set the children into their chairs and sat down on the bench behind the table. The woman, who for months now hadn't sat down to eat at the table, likewise brought her plate.

Dani brooded. How was it that happiness had so spectacularly disappeared from their lives? Every time he sensed the warmth of his family circle, he was overcome by a peculiar lethargy. He felt an eternal war, a smoldering, silent battle between himself and his family life. A conflict that was never spoken of, yet never ceased for a single moment. His family seemed to ensnare him with a thousand strands, to draw him down into the mud, into a warm, cozy bog where he must lie, grunting quietly and growing fat like a pig until the day of slaughter arrives. And an incomprehensible drive stirred within him. He didn't yield

– out, out he wanted to run, to free himself from this bewitching coziness with its suffocating odor of fat. If he had wings, he would certainly have flown off long ago into worlds located far from this place. And what most oppressed him was that he couldn't accomplish anything great. He couldn't make a break from life as he knew it. He couldn't leave this irritating woman, his children, his house, his fields, his property, his standing and good reputation among the people, nor all that might develop from today as he lived it. He despised everything, he yearned for another life, greater, busier, bolder, but lacked the courage to pursue the unknown, to start the battle anew in a foreign land, now that his powers were on the wane, so many hopes reduced to nothing. So he subsisted, wasting away, suffering under the sad weight of his cowardice, the palpable shrinking of his strength. *How deplorable are all these wasted days*, he thought to himself over and over, *God, what I could accomplish with them! If I only had the right opportunity!*

He began shelling some corn. He could sit for hours watching the kernels roll through his fingers into the basket beneath the sheller. *This is me*, he thought, *this little stool with the corn sheller that stands here all year long in the corner while the stripper grows dull with rust. And to think how much corn it could shell if it was used day in, day out, throughout the year. Dear God, how much work one could get done with it! ...* But this day too neared its end like all the rest, and sadly, bitterly he reckoned it as just another lost day. If it weren't for the hope that the day must yet come that would lead him to a new burst of activity and make good this endless period of stagnation and uselessness, he would surely perish, consumed from within by maggots, like the old barn whose side fell in as it was being filled with newly harvested corn.

And Erzsi, who likewise had hoped that the good Lord would one day lead her husband back to his family once he'd sown his wild oats, saw sorrowfully that Dani, since having withdrawn himself from the world, was slinking around the house like a soulless being. At times she felt sympathy for the big, strong man who wandered aimlessly about the house for weeks on end. She knew well that she herself was the cause, and often took her conscience to task, asking whether she shouldn't behave differently toward her husband. But my God, how? Surely not by supporting him in his life outside the family! Thus she lived on, convinced in her heart that things could not go on like this forever.

When they'd finished their noonday meal, Dani leaned back in his chair to digest his food.

"Well, my boy," he said to his son, "we'll go this evening."

"Where to, Papa?" the boy asked immediately, with wide-open eyes.

"To the cul-de-sac, to your grandmother's. We're all going. Grandma is sick ... we want to visit her."

This explanation was for his wife to hear. Erzsi hadn't seen her in-laws all year long.

She said nothing. She would have made the visit long ago, but didn't want to do it alone, and she hadn't wanted to suggest it to her husband. She didn't want to come across as submissive.

V.

In the afternoon, as was his wont, Dani looked for some work to do in the yard, in the stable; since the start of summer all he did was go into the house to eat and sleep. Erzsi likewise never set foot away from home. She quickly tidied up the kitchen, replaced the fuel on the fire, and on the hearth, which likewise heated the room, a pot of corn was cooking audibly, its sweet smell spreading throughout house. The children sat on the floor in the front room playing with cornstalks; the little one had his shirt tied across his bottom and was rutching about across the handmade mud floor.

Erzsi and Dani both mulled over the same thing in their minds, the old, sad, tedious, ultimately inescapable question: why their family life didn't make them happy.

Dani had forgotten Bora and all other women; his thoughts turned now only toward his wife. "It's not my fault!" he said in a low voice. "It's God's fault!"

Once again he sought to gather up all the feelings that could lead him back to his wife. Maybe things would look up again.

It's true, he thought, *it doesn't please any wife for her husband to be involved with other women.*

He laughed faintly – his male sensibility didn't allow him to see such things with a woman's heart. From somewhere the notion had taken root in him that everything was allowed a man. Everything! And if his wife were as he wished her to be, she would accept matters with a demure, wry laugh and, at best, punish him with a few smacks, for that in turn would be allowed her. But to take things with such deathly seriousness! To turn away from him so! That is not allowed! The wife's thoughts should always favor her husband. She should do in love as her master commands. The wife should be like a living hotbed for all her husband's capacities, where he can rest and gather new strength. What he wouldn't do for her if she were like that!

But does he really know what he wants? He only senses that his wife *isn't the way he'd like her to be.*

He would have liked to picture a woman's nature as being as uncomplaining, tender, and peaceable as her master would ever have her be. When for the first time he heard the words from his wife's mouth: "I'm certainly not going to rip myself apart for you," he couldn't believe his ears. When for the first time he noticed that his wife wanted to force her will on him, it struck him as unbelievable, like something that lay utterly beyond his calculations. When it became clear to him that he and his wife were two independent beings, each with a will of their own, who could only live together when they came to a mutual agreement about something, he found the entire world so disgusting, so unbearable, that he would have preferred to burst apart, to flee from the face of the earth.

That was not the fate he was destined for, having decided himself man enough to look after a wife and children – even if he had a dozen of them.

At first he was beside himself with rage and went about like a madman, and each day he faced fresh disappointment as he saw that his wife stuck by her will just as stubbornly as he attempted to force his will on her.

There was one especially touchy point between them, a matter that ruined every minute for them: the arrangement of their lives. Dani had grown up amidst the poverty of a day laborer family, becoming a landed peasant on his own. Erzsi had brought into the marriage the thriftiness of a home of modest wealth. Dani's parents didn't save – where could they have scraped the funds together from? The meager savings of a poor household didn't amount to anything. The penny-pinching of Erzsi's parents had rescued for their descendants a small inheritance which, in the limited circumstances of village life, could not be enlarged. When Dani turned out to be such an incredibly talented money-maker, into whose lap forints dropped by the thousands, the two of them gradually shed their true nature. Dani demanded more and more impatiently the "good life," a home, a wife, a way of life fit for a lord, and the mere thought of saving angered him, although he never gave or left anything of his to others ... without a tenfold profit. Erzsi, for her part, felt that her old, miserly lifestyle was no longer appropriate, and if her husband had acted toward her as he should, she would have completed the transition to a new way of living. But as things stood, instead of adapting to a new approach to life, she had no idea what would come next. She was losing the ground beneath her feet. It was a constant source of aggravation to her that she hated her husband's money as much as she hated life itself, and she waited and waited to see when the misgotten wealth would meet its deserved end. And Dani gradually realized that the daughter of the landed peasant to whom he had once been attracted, because she stood a level higher than him in the social order and was accustomed to a particular lifestyle, now sought to thrust onto him, through her obdurate, single-minded effort, a lifestyle suited only to her father, the *Scarecrow*.

No, that wasn't a life fit for a human. Both of them knew that. And both of them spent the entire afternoon waiting for evening to come; and both Dani and Erzsi sought to consult with each other in old Turi's house, the place of this proverbial good family life, concerning how the happy family should be constructed that could bind a man like him to his home.

And Dani, involuntarily recoiling before the foolhardy step he'd taken today, before Bora and the great dangers that swirled around in his brain, was determined to make one more attempt at bringing order into his life.

But if that isn't possible! If things go on this way into all eternity! Then everything should cave in on itself this very day.

Bloody and hideous urges seethed inside him, his hand balled itself into a fist and prepared to strike, his secret quivering there menacingly. If this secret breaks out, everything will scatter mercilessly in all directions, all of life together with all its creatures will be trampled without pity like an anthill.

VI.

The children were dressed. The older boy took the basket, wrapped in a snow-white cloth, into which Erzsi had put a large sausage and other food items. She wrapped the younger boy in her big blanket, and he immediately began to kick and yammer. She was forced to unwrap the little bugger and change him.

Dani waited patiently. His *guba* was already about his shoulders, his cap atop his head, and he watched his family absent-mindedly. He had no precise thoughts, a vague mood eddied within him. He was sad and uneasy; he feared his parents' house, feared the misery he would find there, the reproaches; he was afraid of himself, of life as a whole. He stood there and waited until his wife got the little one wrapped back up, scolding him as she did because "such a big boy couldn't manage to speak up when he needed to." At last she took the child in her left arm and, with her right, grabbed a container full of milk. Now they could go.

Dani pulled the door shut behind them. He called out to the stable boy and told him to look after everything, then followed his wife and children with brooding steps as they walked before him onto the village street. He lowered his head and strode forth with effort, as though he must thrust himself forward with every step.

This and that went through his head, but he was already tired of his financial plans and tossed them aside. What else was there to think about? The work of earning money had grown odious to him, his family life only made him tired and depressed. Since the summer he'd barely come into contact with other people. He didn't drink, didn't gamble, didn't smoke, had no affairs. Such a deep weariness had taken hold of Dani that he would gladly have hanged himself.

Erzsi's mood was similar, but the children kept her alert. She kept one eye continuously on little Béla, talked to him from time to time, told him to watch out so he wouldn't fall, asked him if the basket wasn't too heavy, he shouldn't strain his little arms. The boy looked up at his mother with laughing brown eyes and she forgot all her troubles over him. Suddenly she laid eyes on Gyuri Takács who stood conversing with someone in the middle of the street. She recalled now that she hadn't walked along this street since the summer, and suddenly all the awful bitterness welled up inside her that had oppressed her back then.

She tossed a glance at her husband as though to ask him, would he ever be different? And her tired gaze tightened with distress. In her husband's face she saw the easily inflamed anger, in his eyes a burning hatred, in his cheeks a suddenly flaring redness. As though unconsciously, the man had rushed ahead several steps, leaving his wife to trail behind. Erzsi looked more closely now and saw that Gyuri Takács was talking to a girl, Pál Güzü Kis's daughter, Bora.

Immediately something fluttered through her heart of the surging anger she sensed rising within her husband. And she too erupted in an abrupt fit of rage. Since the summer she'd ignored the crazed lusting after women that had aroused such disgust in her. And in spite of all the bitterness, in spite of the growing alienation, it comforted her to know that her husband, regardless of how he was, belonged to her alone. If she felt bad, ailed or suffered, then he did too for her sake. At times it filled her with joy and satisfaction to realize she meant something to her husband. She well knew Dani's changing, easily inflamed, easily forgetting nature, and it had a profound effect on her when she could say that this man, who could push his lover aside so quickly, was bound to her by such a long-lasting, deep and powerful attraction. Months passed without her husband's heart wavering, and Erzsi quietly thanked her creator for that.

Now a painful sense of jealousy awakened in her again. She trembled, dreading the thought that her husband could have changed, could have left behind the old, accustomed, almost beloved quiet fool at her side ... that he could again have stepped as though outside a magic circle and become the fool of alien gods.

No, she wasn't wrong. She'd clearly perceived the groan of passion in her husband's face, clearly too the resolute hatred, the wild, unbridled wrath toward the other man. And she was certain that Dani Turi wasn't stalking Gyuri Takács because of her, rather it was because of another woman. Because of the girl who'd come to spell doom between them.

Gyuri Takács saw them, he saw Erzsi and blushed. He parted abruptly from the girl, who likewise had caught sight of them, then taken off girlishly, with easy, racing steps. From a distance she looked back toward Gyuri, and Erzsi saw that her husband caught her eye, and then grew as hard and grim as a stone idol. And Erzsi sensed these things alongside her husband and was surprised to recognize that she was indignant because the snotty girl hadn't fallen for him, but for Gyuri Takács instead.

Gyuri greeted them, though neither returned the greeting. Dani gazed before him, as though his rival were just so much air for him. Erzsi managed things such that in that moment she bent down to her little boy, then continued walking without even looking at Gyuri.

Gyuri Takács understood them both. He assumed that Dani didn't return his greeting because of Bora, and Erzsi didn't do so for her own reasons; what they saw disturbed them, and he just smiled. But he was off base. Erzsi was angry because of Bora, she wasn't even thinking of herself, for it was only natural that he owed her nothing, and that was as it should be. Dani, for his part, was angry with him on behalf of his wife. He wasn't blind to Gyuri Takács's feelings for her, and he expected Gyuri to be true to those feelings, to guard them with the same discretion, the same steadfast devotion he'd admired and esteemed in him over so many years. For some time now he'd been bothered to the depths of his soul by a certain unaccustomed strangeness in Gyuri's behavior, but only now did he see clearly what was behind it. The beast had broken the loyalty he owed to his wife. And Dani did not accept that Gyuri Takács should be unfaithful to his wife in the same way that he himself was.

VII.

Not until they'd walked on a good piece did this superficial feeling abate; it was at this point that the true cause of it all emerged, the jealousy over Bora. Gyuri Takács was no longer the object of their objection; rather Dani perceived an unusual and incomprehensible change in Bora's behavior. Where had the ardent, dreamy admiration gone to that had shone forth so fully from the girl the day before, during the past week, during the summer when they'd been in the Countess' company together, when she'd looked over at him from the Count's gate, and when yet this morning she'd eyed his sleigh? What has happened to this girl? Does she despise him, now that he's given her a gift? Dislike him because of the gift? How shamelessly she returned Gyuri's gaze, while she looked at him, Dani, only with indifference, or even scorn! If he ever got his hands on her, he would break her in two!

He bit down on his lips.

Now they turned into the cul-de-sac; his parents lived at the end of the alley, directly across from the village street. Their gate marked the dead end.

When Dani opened the little gate to the house, which was woven from reeds and only rotated on its axis when it was lifted just so, and they stepped inside, his mother, who was busying herself in the yard, called out:

"Oh, my God! My God!" She clapped her hands together, dropping the sunflower stalk she was breaking up for fuel, and walked up to them.

By now darkness had fallen. Dani looked searchingly into his mother's face and found with displeasure that she was even older, poorer, and uglier than last year. The old woman's mouth had fallen inward, her toothlessness had rendered her older than the years had. When she pressed her withered mouth against the plump, firm, hard lips of her son, a shiver of desperation ran through Dani at the touch of her brown, greasy skin with its odor of smoke.

The old woman, as though suspecting her son's aversion, timidly stroked the fur of his *guba* where it lay across his shoulder. "Oh, my son, my son!" And she heaved a sigh.

Mother-in-law and daughter-in-law looked at one another silently, then Erzsi leaned over toward her and they kissed each other warmly on the mouth.

The boy kissed his grandmother's hand, and she bent down to return his kiss. He then turned away to wipe the spot where her mouth had touched him with his coat sleeve.

"Oh, my dears!" grandmother cried, and she took the smaller child into her arms, all but crushing him in her happiness. The fearful child tolerated her hug in brief, anxious silence, only to start wailing at the top of his lungs. His mother had to take him back to calm him down again.

"Oh, you, are you that afraid of your grandmother? It's true, you seldom see me ... the dear child has only seen me once before."

They all sensed the painful reality of these words, and fell silent. Erzsi handed the container of milk to her mother-in-law, thus freeing her hands to take care of her children. "I've brought you a little milk!" she said. The old woman pursed her lips in unabashed disdain. Erzsi was ashamed of the paltry gift and her discomfort only grew.

"Well, let's go in then, come on in," the old woman spoke. "How happy father will be, yes he will!"

They entered the dark porch, and the old woman squeezed past them, hastily opening the door by means of a pull made from rope. The strong odor of sauerkraut came at them from within the low room; old Turi sat by the table reading some book or other that he held away from himself. He looked up at the guests and lowered the book. He didn't exclaim to them, making a great fuss as he had in the past; he stood up soberly and shook his son's hand, then his daughter-in-law's.

"You see, they came!" the old woman said appeasingly to her husband.

"They could've stayed at home as far as I'm concerned," the old peasant responded. "They haven't come in three years, and there was no need for them to come today. What do they need to see my misery for?"

"I've got enough of my own misery to deal with," Dani said dismally.

His wife eyed him and thought to herself: *Right, right, go ahead and complain about how your wife doesn't make you happy! That's just what we need! They'd love hearing that!*

Everyone felt terribly, terribly uncomfortable. They took off their coats and sat down around the table.

The old man pursed his lips.

"What are you reading?" Erzsi asked.

"Hell knows. People think up all kinds of crazy things. I only read because I've nothing better to do ... If the winter lasts must longer, I'll lose my mind."

"You could build me a sleigh," his son suggested.

"Maybe so!" the old man responded, and immediately his face lit up somewhat.

"What are the boys up to?" Erzsi asked.

"Well, the one is doing the same as the other," old Turi replied. "They're both obsessed with chasing the skirts." He laughed at this and ran his hand over his face. "And the cripple is off somewhere too, you know, Béni," the old man added.

"I was afraid something could happen to him," the mother piped up.

"Let him break his neck, that'd be for the best," the old man retorted.

"How can you say such a thing?" the old woman whined. "Don't be such a heathen."

"Am I not right, then? Is that a life? Not even for a healthy person ..."

"And what about Miska and his family?" Dani asked in reference to his brother who'd married young and lived in the neighborhood.

"Fools remain fools," the old man answered. "They fight like polecats, practically scratching each other's eyes out. The wife lights into her husband, the husband into his wife. Someone should nab them and hold their heads under the Tisza River, right there beneath the ice, so they won't be so damned hot-headed."

Everyone laughed at this, but it was a stifled, embarrassed laugh. They didn't know what else to say. If no one has any accomplishment worth bragging about, they might as well not visit each other.

Dani ventured to return to the subject of the sleigh. "I could haul that tree trunk for you, it's good for four runners."

"The one in front of the gate?"

"Right!"

"Good."

"But where will you sit during the summer?" the mother asked jokingly.

"She's always got sitting on her mind. Spit a little and sit on that!" old Turi responded with his boorish sense of humor, arousing everyone's laughter again.

"Come here, little one," the grandmother called to the tyke who sat wide-eyed in his mother's lap. But he only thrashed with his hands and feet and nestled anxiously against his mother's breast.

"He won't go to you because you haven't any teeth," old Turi said, his accustomed good humor now restored. "He'll only come to me – come here, you! Come here, you little rascal, you!"

He took the child from his daughter-in-law, which the boy willingly allowed; he felt entirely at home in his grandfather's lap and reached out for the book that was lying on the table.

"You'll become a college student one day!" the old man cried. "You'll be a lawyer, you little stinker, and you'll skin the entire world alive!"

They all rang out in laughter at this, forgetting for a moment how uncomfortable they felt.

So that's what a family needs to be happy, Erzsi thought to herself, *not to take anything seriously. How many hundreds of times have the old couple gone murderously at each other's throats, and yet they hold nothing against each other and live on. The husband lets off some steam, the wife cries herself out, and done.*

She looked at her mother-in-law, who during her youth had been quite the beauty. But she'd been a very poor girl; the little chest there behind the oven, decorated with tulips, had held her entire dowry, and been only half full at that. Now she bore the marks of utter neglect, the entire village knew her only as Auntie Borcsa; she knew a spell for curing snakebites and had sage advice for all kinds of troubles. She got on well with all the world, just not with her daughter-in-law. She'd raised half a dozen children and worked herself to death for them. Erzsi had once seen how her grown daughter had sat comfortably at the table while the mother was sweeping the floor clean. She'd washed for them, gladly run all around, gone hungry, gotten sick, and suffered for them. Her children were her entire world, and she wasn't afraid of digging up from the earth or procuring from the church offertory box whatever they had to have to meet their needs. Both the old people were endowed with a healthy dose of carelessness, especially in financial matters. Erzsi found her husband's characteristics reflected in mixed form in both his parents.

Dani glanced at his wife and saw with what thoughtful, piercing eyes she studied his parents. He too grew sober, recalling his thoughts from earlier in the day, and while grandpa and grandma were busy playing with the children, he wondered what it would be like if he were once again a child in his parents' home.

Suddenly he was seized by nervous excitement. He wanted to jump up and run from the world. Impatience took hold of him. He grew angry with his parents, who were largely at fault for his reaching such a point with his wife, as they'd thrust so many wedges between them. As conciliatory as they were toward each other in their family life, they were equally demanding and impatient toward their children once they'd outgrown their sphere of influence. Receiving all and giving nothing, this was the attitude with which they drove their daughters- and sons-in-law to distraction. Endless battles. Money worries. The old moochers, trying to feast off their children as though they were bees, scraping their honeycombs the minute some golden liquid accumulated there. And then there was his moody wife, who watched over what was hers, over her chicks, like a brood hen.

I haven't a clever father, or a clever mother, Dani thought to himself, *who would ever be smart enough to compensate their son for something that isn't working out – how often they could have helped me with some small kindness here or there ...*

And toward his wife he now felt as he had back then, when his love for her had been uncompromised. He forgave her everything and had an explanation for all that she did. For her sake he was strict with his mother, and he passed judgment on the entire world with her in mind. The husband's heart surged within him, the marital heart that doubles its individuality, making the wife a crucial part of himself, placing her in the foreground, upon an altar before which his own soul, like a priest, holds worship, and where idolatrous reverence is demanded of the entire world for this wife. He sensed all this with renewed clarity. In spite of his parents, in spite of his old family. For he'd toppled the old idol inside him and demanded from it the same level of devotion to the new idol which he himself dedicated to her, even more, much more. And Dani had a heightened sense of the feeling that had come over him earlier in the face of Gyuri Takács. He himself can behave toward his wife however he wants, but he expects others to honor her as he demands. Especially his parents!

He looked about him with a resolute gaze, his head held high. No one paid any attention to him, they were all busy with the children.

He imagined then that everything depended on one's will, his will, his wife's will, the will of his parents and of the world. Because of this, everything would once again be as it was, or even better! As things *must* be.

And he believed he had only to state these things in order for them to become reality!

This belief suddenly filled him with blissful peace. It had been a very long time since he'd felt as calm or as hopeful as he did this evening.

Here, in front of so many people, he can't talk. But on the way home he'll talk. He'll speak his piece, he'll empty his heart. And he saw in his mind's eye how his wife would hug him; with warm glances he caressed her as she glowed red in the overly warm room and, cheered by the joy of her children, recovered some of her gentle charm.

VIII.

Later, the "Baron" came visiting, a neighbor peasant who'd come to share the name he'd given his dog. Old Turi had taken over a reed cutting operation with him, and the two peasants consulted with each other concerning how much reed the brook was likely to contain and where they should next start their work.

The "Baron" was a taciturn, black peasant. He lived by himself, as he'd turned his wife and children out of the house some twenty years before. Old Turi was always teasing and ribbing him, but only mildly, because the "Baron" was a hard peasant who could be quite tough on anyone who stepped on his toes. He couldn't take a joke. He'd gotten used to his nickname, but didn't let just anyone call him by it.

"So, Baron, where's your grandson?" old Turi asked him as he played with his own grandson.

The old peasant said something incomprehensible, shrugging his shoulders.

"Look! This little tyke here, I wouldn't give him up for life itself. If you can call that life, living this way, like a dog."

"Go poke your snout into your own shit," the wild peasant grumbled, being anything but selective with his words.

Old Turi laughed out loud. "Hey, Baron, you're just jealous."

"Not a chance. After all, how many more times will he sit in his lousy grandfather's lap while he lives?"

The crude remark, which reopened everyone's old wounds, was followed by painful silence.

"The wet stalks are smoking so," old Mrs. Turi remarked.

"Let them smoke. Better here than elsewhere," her husband replied by way of camouflaging his ill humor. But only two people in the room understood the allusion, he himself and his son.

"Aren't you tired?" Erzsi asked her little boy, bending down to him.

Dani rose to his feet. "We should go home now."

"If you're in a hurry, then it's time," his father said.

The old woman, who crouched on the bench before the stove, added placatingly: "Stay and play a card game. Where are you rushing off to? The food is warm, too ..."

But Erzsi found the air in the room unbearable, and was determined to leave. She got the children dressed to go.

Dani, too, felt ill. He longed to get out of there ...

They left in a bitter mood. Dani's mother repeatedly assured them that the young folk would soon be returning from the spinning bee, but they just left.

When they reached the street, Dani strode sternly ahead. He thought to himself, now they would go home and to bed. They would sleep through the long night. In the morning his head would ache from so much sleep, and a new day would come with new inactivity. He began to think where he could refresh himself a bit. He wanted to enjoy others' company. He yawned and recalled how, an hour ago, he'd intended to patch things up with his wife. Now he'd lost interest in that. That's not how things worked ...

"I'm going to stop by the schoolmaster's place for a bit," he said, yawning again.

Erzsi said nothing, even though she was hurt by these words. She, too, was waiting for something to happen, anything. A miracle, dropped into their midst by God himself. Something would happen between them, and today yet everything would be as it was before. She'd had the feeling her husband had left his parents' house for her sake, and she'd expected him to continue this considerate behavior ... Thus did his words affect her like a cold shower. But what could she do? She said nothing. If only there were a word that could avert doom.

But when her husband really did leave them and cross to the other side of the road, in the direction of the schoolmaster's house, she all but burst into tears, stricken with the same grief as during that summer's night, when she'd fled half-naked with her two little ones to her parents' house.

IX.

"Bora!"

The girl stood still.

Dani Turi felt the heat suddenly rise to his face. His tongue was barely capable of speech. "You're still wandering around in the street?"

"Me? Why would I be doing that?"

"I meet up with you at every turn."

"I'm just coming back from the neighbor's. We were spinning at the Paps' place." With that she wanted to go.

"Wait!"

The girl shifted her weight to one leg and waited.

"What's wrong?" Dani asked.

"With me?"

"Yeah."

"Nothing's wrong with me." And she giggled. "Why?"

Dani had never felt such suffocating heat. He wanted to grab hold of the girl – his hand trembled and shook. She only looked at him with cool disinterest. He didn't know what to say to her. It shamed him to recognize his feelings, his childish nervousness. He saw that a single word could for ever compromise his reputation in the girl's eyes. "You're so strange today," he mumbled.

"Me?"

Dani took a deep breath.

For minutes they stood there in silence. Dani felt the redness in his face. He was behaving toward this young girl as though he, too, were a youth. It embarrassed him. "You."

"If you please."

Dani gulped, and he just managed to choke forth the words: "Tell your father to come by and see me tomorrow. I want to let him have the cabbage field in the Tisza bend."

The girl leaned her face toward his and looked into his eyes, as though wanting to kiss him in thanks for the monumental gift: leasing a field, to them! "Thank you, dear uncle Dani!"

Before Dani's head had cleared sufficiently to allow him to surround the girl with a hug, she'd already taken off. She ran blissfully, flying like a bird. She could never have believed she would make such a *fortune*! Never something like that! That uncle Dani would pay her! Dear God, now it was time to be smart!

Dani Turi just stood there, and as he stood his blood pulsed, it churned and boiled. He thought he must keel over with dizziness. But he just stood there, following the girl with his eyes as she ran along the street, her shoes crunching in the snow, and soon disappeared in the darkness.

His heart sank, and he was filled with shame.

X.

He was still trembling when he entered the schoolmaster's house; his heart felt like a lead weight, the dizziness lingered, and his secret longing for the girl tore at him.

The schoolmaster was surrounded by his rambunctious children in the front room. One could hear from the darkness of the kitchen how the father playfully scolded the rowdy little brats. He was keenly fond of engaging them in constant competition with one another.

When Dani entered the room, the tall, gaunt man, clad in a filthy old coat, jumped up from his chair with astounding liveliness and rushed noisily up to his guest.

"Welcome! Welcome, dear brother!" he cried. His beard, or rather his stubble-covered chin, was full of tobacco dust from the cigarette he'd just rolled. He used familiar address with the more well-to-do peasants of the village, as a way of showing mutual respect. "So, haven't you started to rust yet? I thought surely you'd been named deputy county chief by now, or at least county hussar, since you work so hard to stay out of the poor folk's way. – Get out of here!" he yelled at his young daughters, who crowded around the two men and gaped at Dani. They didn't budge an inch, they just let their father shout:

"Where's my pipe? My cherrywood pipe?"

He paid no further attention to them, as though they weren't there, and stepped over them with his long legs when they got in his way.

Whenever Dani met him, he always looked at the schoolteacher as if wanting to ask: "Aren't you insane?"

No, the schoolmaster wasn't insane, and his great roars of laughter, his scatter-brained, slap-dash manner, his affected openness, were all calculated to conceal the misery of his life.

The schoolmaster's wife entered then from the adjoining room.

"My, but you're all done in, dear friend!" Dani said to her.

The thin, listless woman staggered about as though she'd just stepped out from the grave. Her voice sounded so hollow – it seemed to emanate from a perpetually hungry stomach. Her large, dark eyes strayed uncertainly. Dani's words elicited a faint smile from her, then she scolded the children for bothering the guest, but they no more listened to her than to their father.

Dani's heart went out to them. He looked at the troop of girls, of which there were five, wide-eyed, pale and shameless little creatures, strikingly similar to their father in appearance. One of them, a five-year-old, was extraordinarily beautiful. She was Dani's goddaughter, and he sat down and took her onto his lap, hugging her warmly. The girl's hair fell around her shoulders and smelled of some sort of perfumed oil, and Dani felt she was already a young woman: with her slender body, pale face, and burning eyes, she already bore within her the secret that would one day bring danger to the male sex. He was overcome with dizziness; he gave her another hug, then held her with his two hands and lifted her down from his lap.

Now the biggest girl, fully fifteen years old, entered the room, and the moment she appeared, it was clear she was the one who held the household reins in her parents' stead.

"March! Out with you!" she yelled to her younger sisters. They all stuck their tongues out at her, upon which she grabbed the one by the hair and slapped another on the back, quickly ushering them all out with a punch here, a slap there, into the adjoining room.

"Hahaha!" the schoolmaster roared with laughter. "Oh yes, Mariska will make a great wife, just you wait, she'll have her husband dancing like a dervish."

He lit his skinny cigarette and finished smoking it with but a few deep drafts, not speaking a word, and forgot his children once again. His wife sat on the bench before the oven, staring at the two men in sickly desperation, overcome with sadness.

Dani, who already felt like a stranger here, couldn't imagine how this sad, profoundly abject house could serve as a bastion of drunken cheer! ... For here card games and alcohol-induced revelry were a nightly affair.

The schoolmaster didn't speak as long as he smoked, blowing the fumes out through his nostrils. Dani broke the silence:

"How are you getting along, ma'am?"

"Surviving."

Dani nodded absent-mindedly, as though agreeing with her a dozen times over.

"Maybe things will be better in the new house, no? The construction on the new school building is moving right along!"

The woman gestured dismally with her hand.

"The new house!" the schoolmaster laughed out loud. "That's all off now. Already the first confessional complaint has rolled in. Did you know, my friend, that they've now named the headmaster? Did you?"

"No, I didn't."

"No?" the schoolmaster laughed with a twinkle in his eye, as though he were about to tell a good joke. "He's a papist!"

Dani furrowed his brow and grew red with rage. The school system had in fact been nationalized. Until then, the Calvinist church had supplied them with a teacher who was to instruct a hundred and twenty pupils. Now the state had taken over the school, promising to hire a Calvinist as one of the two teachers, who must simultaneously fulfill the duties of choirmaster. Everyone assumed the government would retain the currently employed teacher, which was completely natural, and the entire village was glad the unfortunate family, so bruised and battered by fate, would finally enter the haven of a secure existence. But sadly the government with its ancient politics, controlled by one national state after another, and feeding richly off the bitter legal pretensions attendant to centuries of religious aggression and blundering, had once again abused its power.

Dani listened to him angrily, then proceeded to bluster and curse, but the schoolmaster only laughed out loud, as though the whole affair meant nothing to him, although his sad eyes, crisscrossed with tiny red blood vessels, were filled with tears.

"We're moving," he said, "to the other side of the Danube. I've already submitted my application."

"You're moving my foot," Dani said.

"What? Me? Who's managed the whole affair for you? Who for six years has been preaching so you wouldn't have to agonize about turning the school over to the state, and I'd have a decent place to live and some level of job security, and now I'm to be the *headmaster's* worn-out shoe? The devil take the peasants – there isn't a one of them who'd lift a finger for my sake. We're leaving for the other side of the Danube, and you'll have two papists for teachers! That's it!"

He began to whistle, lit another cigarette, and refrained from speaking for as long as it took him to smoke it.

An oppressive mood reigned in the room where the adults sat in silence, while from the next room the children's pandemonium could be heard, drowned out from time to time by Mariska's screeching as she attempted to restore quiet.

Suddenly the door opened as the noise was going full force, and in the doorway appeared a diminutive two-and-a-half year-old.

When he spotted the child, the schoolmaster burst again into uproarious laughter. "Hey there, little tyke! Come here, cutie-pie! Come here, my son, I'm gonna eat you up!"

He rose, bent down to the child and held him up toward the ceiling. The grease-stained sleeves of his jacket gleamed in the light of the smoky lamp.

"How many sons are you?"

"Six!" cried the tot from up near the beam across the ceiling. He, in fact, was the *sixth* child.

"And how many more will there be?"

"Six!" the boy cried again.

"That's right!" the schoolmaster brayed with his hoarse, wine-tainted voice, and he stood his son in the middle of the table, then laughed at him. "Six? May each of them resemble his father! They should all leave theology school before their last exam, take a wife, wander from village to village, have six children, then croak in the roadside ditch!"

Dani looked at the schoolmaster, who guffawed to keep himself from sobbing.

XI.

"Well, no use crying about it," the schoolmaster said later. "What does a man live for? Is his lousy life worth all the work it takes to keep it going? What am I? A caterpillar who works solely to fill his own belly? Didn't God give me two legs, a straight back, an erect head with eyes facing upward, so that I should dedicate my genius not just to myself, but to others? Well then, I've been devoting myself to others, I've looked after hundreds, a nice place is assured me up there, there I'll be the headmaster! I'll treat priests, peasants, and ministers to a few slaps! I can hardly wait!"

For a moment it seemed as if he were tired, then he stroked back his disheveled blond hair, rubbed his jagged moustache with his fist and looked at Dani, leaning his rough, wasted face on his hands.

"Your affairs likewise, brother, I've managed so well that you wouldn't believe it, yes sir! I've worded your petition to the Countess such that, if she has no more heart than a hen – and such perverse countesses do indeed have a heart, not like the robust, naïve, villageois ladies at court – the Karai property will certainly not be left to the Jew, but to all of you. Admittedly the petition must also come into her hands. Whether that will happen, I can't say!"

Dani had come to see the schoolmaster for precisely this reason. It had been so long since the petition had gone off

... He'd long since given up hope of success. He wasn't in the mood to respond to the teacher's report, nonetheless it had gotten him excited and aroused new hope in him.

The loud patter of horses' hooves became audible below the schoolmaster's window; heavy boots crunched across the snow. Guests were arriving. The door soon opened and Gyuri Takács, along with Vincellér, another landed peasant, appeared, both wrapped in their traditional fur coats.

There was vigorous handshaking, noisy greeting and talking.

Gyuri Takács, accustomed to chastising the others with his taunts, said to the schoolmaster: "It's not Candlemas yet! Why are you coaxing the bear out now?"

"He came out by himself," Vincellér remarked in wonder, his voice hoarse and gruff. He stroked his short-cropped, brown moustache with his thick black fingers, which obviously had not been washed in some time. "Isn't that right, Turi?"

Dani was in no mood for jokes. He stood erect and acted as though their words didn't concern him.

In the small room, a child began to cry miserably, as though he were roasting on a spit. The schoolmaster's wife, who'd extended her hand from a sitting position to greet her guests, now rose and went inside, but her appearance failed to silence the children's noise.

"Sit down and don't gab so much, brothers," the schoolmaster said.

The men threw off their *guba* coats and sat down. Soon they were joined by two more peasants, a young landowner named Kása who spoke little but laughed a lot, and an old one named Kis, who could have sold his skin for a gulp of wine.

They conversed about this and that; the schoolmaster, whom the peasants bored to no end, finally laughed out loud in his own uncouth manner: "So? What's happening? Where's the schnapps bottle?" He got up, went to the wobbly cabinet that only stood because of the brick that supported it, and withdrew a green bottle. "It's empty!" he said, tapping on the bottle with his finger.

For certainty's sake, he took the stopper, made from twisted paper, out of the bottle, sniffed at it, and slurped the last few drops left inside. "I'm telling you, it's empty."

"The hell with you," Gyuri Takács piped up, "how could it not be empty when you drink it all?"

"To hell with you – why don't do the Jew in, if he won't loan the headmaster any more money. What a lousy village, where the headmaster no longer has any credit."

"Headmaster!" Vincellér whinnied with his cracked voice.

"The minister's certainly fired that man up!" said Gyuri Takács. "It'd be better for you as well, schoolmaster, if you scraped something from out of the fire for yourself."

"Oh, shut up, the hell with you, you cussed, stinking peasants," the schoolmaster whined with groggy, watery eyes. "So what's gonna happen? Who's gonna pull a forint out from his behind for a drink of wine?"

"Wine?" Gyuri Takács said. "Some leftover pomace brandy isn't good enough for your sorry belly?"

Dani Turi felt very uncomfortable here today. He took his old soldier's billfold from his inside coat pocket and removed a five-forint note which he handed to the teacher.

As the teacher took it, Dani noticed that his hand trembled continually, as though he were shaking with fever.

"Mariska! Mariska! Come here. Go over to the Jew's place and have the bottle filled with wine. And bring some bread and a pound of bacon too."

"Look at the greedy vulture!" Vincellér snickered.

"Not a pound," Gyuri Takács kidded, "bring at least a side of bacon!"

The girl laughed. She too had been coarsened by this life of misery.

"Bring as much bacon and bread as the money will get you, girl," Dani said. "Here's another forint for the wine."

"Yeah, tricky old Dani Turi," Gyuri Takács cried, "he can even afford to buy little girls!"

The blood rose to Dani's face. He knew his cousin-in-law was alluding to Bora, but he said nothing. Today he was so tired and depressed he barely spoke a word, even though normally he was quick with words, and also with his fists. The misery of life that stormed at him in this house unnerved him with all its filth, noise, squalor, and stench.

His six-forint contribution made for quite an uproar among the other peasants, and even the taciturn Kása couldn't keep from adding a word of affirmation to their remarks.

"Well, cousin, if you've got that much money," said Gyuri Takács, whose mood grew increasingly wild and jocular in the face of Dani's calm composure, "if you've got that much money, then let's get down to business. Schoolmaster, where's the Bible?"

The schoolmaster gave a stifled, grunt-like laugh and brought out the dirty, worn-out cards from the drawer where they lay scattered among bread crumbs and cutlery. "21 or 31?" he asked.

"21!" Gyuri cried and leaned with his elbows on the table. "That's the game for us. There's no need for a fuss. One, two, I've won!"

They laughed frigidly.

The low-ceilinged, spacious, poorly furnished and badly whitewashed room became a den of iniquity in one fell swoop. At the head of the table sat Gyuri Takács with a feverish expression, full of greedy excitement, his eyes flashing; the others threw themselves with wild abandon into the abyss of the card game. They could hardly wait for it to get underway. They sat together this way evening after evening until midnight and often later, waiting in ambush for the dumb vicissitudes of this most primitive of games. Normally they played for small amounts, only the schoolmaster was a reckless player. He could afford to be, because whenever he lost, he didn't pay. He repaid his debt by drinking up the peasants' wine and then allowing them to subject him to all sorts of abuse.

Dani watched the others crossly. He would have preferred to leave; he was captivated by the others' mood, but didn't want to touch the cards. "I don't understand the game," he said.

"There's not much to understand!" Gyuri replied. "Whoever plays might as well marinate his brain ... What do you want to put on this card, cousin?"

Dani reached apathetically for the card. It was the ace of diamonds.

"A crown!" he said.

"Oh-ho!" the others cried in alarm, having sat there for hours playing for pennies. "You can't start off with a crown! We haven't had a bet like that yet! That's too much even for the end of the game!"

"It's all right, I'm holding the bank," Gyuri Takács said. "It's not often that a man is confronted with so much fat. Time to drain some away." He handed Dani another card. This, too, was an ace.

Now Gyuri dealt his own cards: one card, two, three. He hesitated for a bit, finally taking a fourth. His eyes twinkled and he cried out triumphantly: "Twenty-one, cousin!"

"This is more," Dani said calmly and uncovered his second ace.

The company reacted in shock. They all sensed that heavy storm clouds were moving in above them.

Gyuri Takács, bored by his lonely, austere life with its lack of any goal or foundation, had become as passionately devoted to card playing as the schoolmaster, who was pursued by singularly bad luck in this as in everything else.

Mariska came with the wine. They filled their glasses, clinked them, only to empty them in one gulp.

Then they threw themselves into the game. After the first lucky hands, Dani began playing more carefully, and they spent the first hour more or less exercising their nerves and testing their luck. In the second hour, near midnight, Dani grew suddenly bolder, and when he saw that fortune was staying on his side, he looked the increasingly tipsy Gyuri Takács more and more defiantly in the eye. With the greasy, sticky cards in hand, the two entered into a duel while the others, who had no reason to lose their heads, were gradually eliminated.

Their breathing grew heavy. Naked greed shone on their faces. The bets got higher, like an avalanche. These peasants, who earned their pennies through hard work and drudgery, slammed their daringly high bets angrily and noisily down on the table.

When Gyuri ran out of money, he yelled at the schoolmaster: "Write what I tell you! I'm holding the bank!"

All the money was in the bank that the peasants had brought collectively: seventy-four forints.

Gyuri Takács lost.

"I'm holding it again."

He lost once more.

"Once again, the whole thing."

This time he won.

Dani grew pale, his hands trembled. The unaccustomed excitement gave him an unbearable headache. He shoved the money over to Gyuri Takács and began to shuffle the cards.

Dani again looked haughtily into his cousin-in-law's face. They were both on edge; sweat ran in large drops down their foreheads. Dani panted as he did during haymaking, but his red face was aglow and a sort of heroism shone there. Gyuri was wild and coarse, he slung obscenities indiscriminately and talked smut left and right. Luckily the girls in the next room were already asleep. The lamp had burned down quite far and shed only dim light on the table. All speaking ceased, and the wine that sat untouched in their glasses grew warm, spreading an unpleasant odor throughout the room. No one drank except to relieve the dryness in his throat.

Dani felt waves of heat running down his back; he sensed a lustful, tortured excitement akin to that he'd felt the evening before when talking to Bora. "How much is the bank?" he asked, taking the first card. He noticed how his voice faltered.

"A thousand forints," Gyuri Takács answered.

"I'll hold it."

In harrowing anxiety, his teeth clenched tightly together, Gyuri Takács picked up the cards. Dani remained the naïve player who simply uncovers the cards without raising the tension by slowing sliding one card off the other, something the peasant card player who seeks to make the game more titillating never fails to do.

Gyuri once again let his arrogance get the better of him and laid down his twenty-one, even though nothing compelled him to do so in advance.

Dani then showed his cards: again he had two aces!

He'd won. He was absolutely raking in the money. The eyes all but sprang from the onlookers' sockets.

Dani wanted to take the bank again.

"I'm not giving it up!" Gyuri cried. "You pig, you dog!" he cursed. "I'm holding it now!" And again he shuffled the cards.

"How much is the bank?"

"A thousand forints!"

"I'll hold it."

Dani stopped with the third card, even though they only added up to seventeen points.

Gyuri looked him in the eye, but in his breathless excitement he could read nothing there. Hastily he picked up his own cards, and when he had eighteen points, he took one more card.

"Over!" he uttered flatly, hoarsely, and when he saw that Dani had only seventeen, he nearly had a fit.

"One more bank!" he bellowed, startling one of the children next door from his sleep.

"How much is the bank?"

"My paternal inheritance!"

Dani flinched in shock, staring at him. "No nonsense, Gyuri!" he said.

"I spit on you, phooey, you miserable peasant! You're withdrawing, you filthy piece of shit!"

Dani said nothing.

"My paternal inheritance, all the fields my father has left me. Those along the Mill Creek, the ones along the pasture hedge, the reed acreage, the cabbage fields along the Tisza, and the Six-Cord field."

"I'll draw." When Dani took the card and looked at it, a strange premonition came over him. It was an ace! That was his lucky card today. "Gyuri Takács," he said, and his lips trembled, as did his hand, and in his hand the card. But he finished what he was going to say: "Don't tell anyone I'm a nobody. Against your paternal inheritance I'll wager everything I own, my God-given naked body excepted."

The sweat ran in great drops from Gyuri Takács's forehead, his chest rose and fell like a blacksmith's bellows. He was terrible and monstrous to see.

Dani took the second card.

He looked at it, sighed, and glanced up toward heaven.

Then his heart was again filled with goodness, peace, and profound calm.

He'd once again drawn an ace. The two aces in his hand could not be beaten, unless the other man likewise held two aces.

But he did not, for he took a second card, and then a third one, then a fourth, a fifth, and a sixth, and still they totaled only eighteen points.

Gyuri Takács suffered horribly. He saw the calm in Dani's face and thought he would lose his mind. Now he took the seventh card: it was a nine.

"Over," he groaned.

The cards fell from his hand.

And then, as he saw Dani's miracle, the two aces, he thought he would go mad. Drool flowed from his half-open mouth as from a dead man.

For a time silence reigned.

Dani rose now to go.

"Wait a minute, stop!" Gyuri Takács cried after him, and fending off drunkenness as he rose to his feet, he cast about with his hands for something to hit him with. "Are you fleeing, thief? Shoving off, you outlaw? Robber, highwayman, henchman! Running away? Hey!"

Dani stood and looked at him.

Calmly and quietly he asked: "What should the bank be?"

He took the deck of cards and started shuffling.

"What it should be? Let me tell you! I'll tell you, you dog! The most dishonored thing in your house, the thing that is the least worthy in your eyes ..."

"What's that?" Dani asked intently.

"Your wife!"

Dani grew dizzy, as though stunned by the blow of an axe. "And what will you match that with, Gyuri Takács?" he asked, his voice rattling hollowly.

"The one thing you desire most on the earth."

"What would that be?"

"Bora."

Dani stood as though rooted to the ground. Then he let the cards slip numbly from his hand, and they fell across the floor. "There's no bank," he said. He didn't know when he'd returned to his senses, he heard his voice as though in his sleep, and he could feel his lips moving: "Schoolmaster, take two sheets of paper and write."

His teeth chattered like two parts of a machine. And when he saw through his glazed eyes that the schoolmaster was prepared to write, he dictated:

"I, the undersigned, Dániel Turi, have won, in the presence of the below-signed witnesses, two thousand forints from my cousin-in-law, György Takács, which I hereby give to the children of the schoolmaster Pál Vásárhelyi, with the condition that this sum be administered by the guardianship authority."

Dani signed the document and saw that his hand, this alien instrument, was not shaking, rather it executed cleanly the "T" with its accustomed flourish.

Once the two witnesses had signed the document, Dani began to dictate a second one. He still hadn't awakened from his feverish delirium. "I, the undersigned, Dániel Turi, have won from my cousin-in-law, György Takács, in the presence of the below-signed witnesses, his paternal inheritance, to wit: sixteen acres along the Mill Creek, thirty acres along the pasture hedge, four acres of reeds, six acres of cabbage fields in the Tisza bend, finally the Six-Cord field with seventeen acres. I freely give this entire property in perpetuity, in gratitude for the favors she has shown me ..."

He stopped and waited until the schoolmaster had written all of this down. Then he closed with the crushing words: "I give it to Bora Kis, Pál Kis's unmarried daughter."

All those present felt like they were bearing witness to a kind of doom, the destruction of the world.

Gyuri Takács sat there, devastated, speechless. And Dani watched once again as his murderous hand wrote the honorable name: *Dániel Turi.*

Once the witnesses had signed it, he took the document and kept it on his person, giving the other to the schoolmaster; then he bundled himself in his *guba* and left.

Nobody said a word to him, they just watched him leave, and when he was gone, they stared at each other and trembled, as though they'd witnessed the starkest horrors of an earthquake.

Dani observed himself as he left the house, closing the gate with a calm hand. Once he was outside, he didn't turn left onto the street as he would if he were going home, he turned to the right. And suddenly he was standing in Pál Güzü Kis's yard. He saw himself knock on the window with a firm hand. Then he saw the girl come out in her bare feet to open the door, and saw her shiver in the cold. He handed her the document and told her in clear terms she could readily understand just what it contained.

The girl threw her arms around his neck, slipped beneath his shaggy fur coat, and stood there barefoot, shivering with cold, hugging and kissing the big, strong man.

Then she pulled him inside the warm, dark room, walked back and forth, whispered something to someone, upon which two people rose in the darkness and went out. Pál Güzü Kis and his wife went to sleep in the barn, as they had no other room for a guest.

And someone took his *guba* from his shoulder, then took his boots from his feet. Yes, he knew who was doing that.

And as he lay in the warm bed and pressed her maidenly body to his own, he knew he was not hugging his wife.

His heart hurt so badly, so very badly, he thought it must burst right then and there inside his chest.

XII.

Dani had barely passed through the schoolmaster's gate when Gyuri Takács jumped up from his chair, took his coat, and hurried after him. The other two peasants (the third, old Kis, had already left the moment the two landowners had risen from the table) had sat awkwardly on their chairs as this scene unfolded. "We'd better go now, too," they said to one another.

"Well, go then," the schoolmaster said. "Don't you realize he wants to knife him?"

"That's quite possible!" Vincellér laughed coarsely. "I'd like to see that!"

"It'll be good!" said the other, and they left.

"You should all drop dead," the schoolmaster grumbled to himself – he'd had all he could take of the peasants and their affairs; he was thoroughly disgusted with disgust, and felt a kind of elevated mood rise within him. He wanted to do something noteworthy, something beautiful and great. He looked around with his dull eyes, scratched his beard with his dirty fingernails, and sensed keenly the absurd hollowness of his situation, the impossibility of experiencing here a single stimulus, a solitary gesture that would be commensurate with his human dignity. The room was full of smoke, the odor of wine, spit, and the blight of the smutty jokes just told, which had practically eaten their way into the rotting furniture as they'd thickened the air. The glass of the wobbly table lamp sweated out this same filth, adding to its ash and eating into its flame. And then there was man, this being created in God's image, his life, his society, corrupted by congenital, acquired, and imposed weaknesses, this humanity whom alcohol led on detours, promising false hope of liberation – how could this fragile mankind keep from staggering and quaking with failing limbs, in the tortured sweat of irretrievably helpless weakness?

And suddenly the divine spark lit up within him: reason and human glory. He almost fell over as the inspiration to accomplish a beautiful feat of greatness motivated him to take quick action.

He opened the window.

As the clean, sharp, free air poured in and the icy gust of wind swept through the room, the startled lamp flared up and was blown out, and the man shuddered and trembled in his thin clothes. But he resisted, and rather than close the window, he reveled in the divine spark that lived on in his mind, and as he stood there in the cold, freezing, clear night, the stars began to quiver and shine in the reflection of his moist eyes, and suddenly this new, great, beautiful deed broke forth from the depths of his being:

He began to sob.

XIII.

Gyuri Takács stood before the gate and looked down the village street. As the other two peasants caught up with him, he turned around and said: "Do you see the wretch? He's going to see the girl." And after a bit he added: "To the girl's, that's where he's going!"

"And you're going to the wife's!" Vincellér said to him with a raucous laugh.

It disturbed Gyuri to hear the thought that was silently churning within him thrown so openly into his face. "That's just what I'm going to do," he grunted.

"Yes, you should. He goes to the girl, and you go to the wife."

"That's it!" said the other. "Just as it should be."

Gyuri Takács turned grimly and looked off in the direction of Dani's house. The others' shameless suggestions had totally ruined his mood, effectively cooling his impulse to act. Had the thought occurred to him independently, the decision would have burst forth from him, like an act of heroism to be carried out with immediate resolve. As it was, he stood there indecisively, sulking.

Vincellér, the peasant with the hollow voice, thought he must spur him on, and said over and over again: "Go to the wife. If he dares go to the girl, then you've got to go to the wife."

The other peasant thought he'd figured out why Gyuri hesitated. "But maybe Dani will come back," he said. "Maybe he just wants to hand the document over to her and then come back."

"If only he'd come back!" Gyuri cried. And they could clearly hear in this outcry that that was just what he wanted; it would give him a chance to confront his rival.

"Like hell he'll come," Vincellér growled. "He won't come back. He's no fool. Dani Turi isn't fool enough to leave a girl untouched."

"Could be," the smaller peasant said.

Their words, spoken with stifled voices, sounded thinly in the cold, frozen winter night with its secretive, frigid, ghostly atmosphere.

Gyuri started off slowly, without saying a word.

The other two followed him.

The snow crunched beneath their feet as they moved along with heavy steps, their caps pulled down over their eyes. They could only guess what would happen yet this day.

"Right is right," Vincellér said. "If he's going to the girl, then you go to the wife."

"May the sky fall down on him ..." Gyuri remarked darkly, "alongside a piece of the Lord!"

They continued on their way, and as quietly as they snuck along, they soon reached Dani's gate. They stood there in the middle of the street, Gyuri in front, the other two men directly behind him.

"Just go boldly inside," Vincellér said in his usual way, "go right inside. If he's gone to the girl's, then your place is here."

"But what will the wife say?" The other peasant asked, thereby giving voice to the thought that weighed on all their minds.

"What'll she say?" Vincellér grunted. "Women aren't upset when a man visits while the husband's away ... And if she were to say something, then you've got to answer. What has a man got a tongue for if not to respond to a woman. And when talking does no good, then you just make short work of things ..."

Gyuri took a hesitant step: should he go in or not? He looked back at the road as though wanting to know whether Dani was coming.

"He won't come back before morning," the smaller peasant said, "don't worry about him coming back."

These words cut Gyuri to the quick. He didn't fear danger, he craved it, yearned for it viscerally, his muscles swelled with the urge to tempt his fate.

He suddenly moved forward, leaving his companions behind without a word, and stepped through the little gate. The other two stayed outside and watched him.

"He's going inside!" the smaller peasant said.

The other only nodded.

"Think how he's gonna fly right back out ...," the little man giggled.

They waited, but didn't hear a sound. The tense wait turned each minute into an hour.

"Nothing's happening!"

"What should happen, anyway?" said the other, shrugging his shoulders. "There's no need to worry, they know each other well. Gyuri was making eyes at the girl already during his days as a young man. Who can know what embers are still burning among the ashes ..."

They waited a few more minutes as it grew stupefyingly cold; then quietly they left for home.

XIV.

Erzsi hadn't gone to bed when she'd gotten home, but took up some sewing instead, while the little one went to sleep. When hours had passed and Dani still hadn't returned home, she began to sob. She recited all her woes and cried herself out good and proper. She felt relieved then and recalled her pledge to endure everything fate had in store for her without grumbling. In her suffering she even found comfort. Dear God – for some time now she hadn't suffered any real sorrow, she couldn't remain unpunished for having allowed these peaceful days to pass with such sinful heedlessness. Not until now did she see how foolishly and uselessly she'd allowed those minutes to pass in which she could have grown more intimate with her husband. She had him close by her side, he was in a tender, kind mood, and indicated at every turn his honest love for his wife. For the past six months he hadn't gone anywhere and had done nothing to cause her to complain. But she'd grown stubborn and refused to yield. And yet of the two it was the wife who must be more tender, more conciliatory ...

Now with her husband out of sight, Erzsi found as many excuses in his defense as she had complaints against him when he was right there in front of her.

Once she'd dried her freely flowing tears a bit, she set her sewing aside, which had lain untouched in her lap in any case, and looked for some other, more strenuous work. Impulsively she set about preparing sourdough to make bread with in the morning ...

Until midnight she passed the time away, growing frightened in due time. Where was her husband gone to for so long?

Again she tried to console herself. The man hadn't left the house for so long that now he was detained everywhere he went, whether while spending time with relatives, or visiting the schoolmaster.

Surely by morning he'd return home! And she began mixing the batter for a cake to give to the children. The large wooden bowl soon filled with watery batter. Erzsi sprinkled it with flour, made the sign of the cross over it, and washed her hands. Then she put away her apron, straightened herself up, and lit a small fire on the hearth, as it had begun to grow cold and both the children and the dough needed warmth.

When she was finished with this, she burst into tears again and allowed the bitterness to well up inside her.

She didn't know how long her quiet crying had lasted, when suddenly the little gate outside was opened, the door shortly after that, and then strange footsteps sounded in the hallway.

She rose from her chair. At first a vague fear took hold of her, but in the next moment it was clear to her that something must have happened to her husband.

All the blood flowed to her heart.

The one matter she hadn't thought about all evening long now reared up in her gut as an absolute certainty.

Her husband had gotten into a fight with Gyuri Takács and things had taken a bad turn, *because of that girl*.

Before so much as a single curse could cross her lips, the door opened and Gyuri stood before her.

They regarded each other at length. Neither found a word to say. They gazed at one another with a numb, spectral stare.

At last Gyuri gathered his courage and stepped toward her. This movement in turn brought Erzsi back to her senses.

"What do you want here?" she yelled at the man.

"What I want? I want to sleep with you!"

Erzsi was so shocked she nearly fell to the floor.

Gyuri took another step toward her, then stood and stared at the woman with bulging eyes. "That's what I want!" he cried again. "I want to find out for myself how your husband's business operates! ... Is Dani Turi the only one who's allowed everything? Is he the only one who can have his way with all the women? Let him be the one for once who learns what that means!"

"Are you insane?"

"Insane? Not in the least! For a change I'm actually quite sane! ... I won you from your husband in the card game, and now you're mine."

"You're lying!" Erzsi yelled.

"Me?"

"Yes, you! Otherwise you wouldn't be coming here to me like a thief in the night! It's not true, my husband didn't gamble me off in a card game."

"How she knows him!" Gyuri said. "All right, so he didn't gamble you away. But when he'd won everything from me, my paternal inheritance, all my money, once he'd reduced me to a beggar, he took off."

"That's not true either!"

"I asked him: what of the chance to get even? But he just left."

"You're lying!"

"I told him he should place as his bet the most negligible, worthless thing he has in his house! ... You! ... And I bet against that the one thing his soul most keenly desires: that girl!"

Erzsi grew pale. "And then? What then!"

"The bastard ran off. He said: 'There's no bank! No bank!'"

Erzsi sat down and crossed herself. "St. Mary, Mother of God! ..."

"Go ahead and pray, pray well! Where's your husband? If he loved you, his place would be here! Where's your husband? He must really appreciate you ... Well? Why am I here? How did I get here? Am I your husband?"

Erzsi said nothing, but her heart was calm and resolute; this man could say nothing bad about her husband to her. She was filled with an uplifting feeling that made her forget all her life's suffering, because of those few words: *There's no bank.*

"But today you'll be mine," Gyuri continued, gasping. He looked at her keenly, while she spared him only a few scornful glances.

Neither spoke a word. A painful silence ensued.

"Where's your husband, good lady?" Gyuri Takács started up again. And he behaved rudely, as though wanting to take revenge on her because of her husband, for the unshakeable trust she wasted on him, for the rejection with which she greeted his persistent overtures toward her. "Tell me where this hero of yours is! Do you even know? If you knew, you'd tell me." And he stared the poor woman shamelessly up and down.

Erzsi stared stubbornly in front of her.

"It would be good for a woman, a faithful woman, to know where her husband is hanging about at two o'clock in the morning. You don't know it, do you?"

"Yes, I do!" Erzsi shot back.

"Out with it, then, if you know it! Let's hear it, if you know it! Just tell me, don't be afraid – I'll let you know if you get it right!"

"He's where you wish you were, you miserable coward! You come here to gossip because your jealousy is eating you alive. What a shame that Gyuri Takács can't succeed with a girl like her. Phooey – you come whining and crying to me, because my husband, who's married and has a family, is more appealing to the girls than an old bachelor. Well, I'll give my husband a good scolding, so that he won't take the bread from my little cousin's mouth a second time. Shame on you, you numbskull, it'd be better for you to have a suck at your mother than to chase after the girls! Is there a girl anywhere who would so much as listen to you?"

Gyuri narrowed his eyes as he listened to his cousin's words. He was getting a taste of the sharp tongue of the Takács race, and he actually liked it. Rather than grow angry, he responded in a pleasant tone: "I can go after my mother, you're right. The world has nothing else to offer me. Dani Turi picked my flower in front of my nose – don't worry, he bought her with my money! He paid for the kisses he's now lapping up with the Takács inheritance ... Did you know, all this inheritance from my father that he won from me he's now given to Bora Kis, Pál Kis's daughter, as a gift, just to spite me?"

"What are you saying? Are you insane?" Erzsi shrieked. "You dared to gamble the Takács fields away?"

"You realize that just now, when you hear that you're not getting them, that they belong instead to someone else?"

"Of course, now! I have a claim on those fields."

Gyuri smiled and put her off with a wave of his hand.

But the woman argued, sobbing tearfully: "You're a wretch, a dog, and you dared to lay eyes on me, you nobody, you nothing! You sorry, wretched man, you misbegotten creature! You've ruined my life, because if it weren't for you, it would never have occurred to my husband to do what he did today. You miserable cripple, you world-class rogue! ..."

Gyuri grew more serious and cast stern, dark glances at her. "Listen here, you unfortunate woman. Instead of thinking of your own problems, you talk a lot of nonsense. You're sore with me? ... And not with your husband, who climbs into another girl's bed?"

"That's none of your affair! Look after your own business. I can take care of mine."

"And I of mine!" Gyuri yelled, suddenly moving toward her, removing his *guba*, and wrapping his arms around the woman.

"Get out!" Erzsi cried with a stifled voice, and she struggled with all her might to free herself from her attacker.

"This is what I came for," the man groaned, and he hugged the woman and kissed her on the face, the shoulder, her dress, wherever he could.

This assault was so sudden, so unexpected, that Erzsi was overcome with shock. She was powerless in the man's strong arms, and as she fought, all the blood rushed to her head.

"I'll show you," Gyuri grunted, "I'll help you if you're such an ass that you won't even allow yourself to be happy for once in your life. You lunatic, you stupid cow, your husband cheats on you day after day, and you don't cheat on him even once! All you do is eat yourself alive with suffering? I mean, the flesh is melting away from your bones, you're wasting away in worry and bitterness! You think I don't know how much you suffer? How much you cry, you unhappy wretch? What's become of you? What has that scoundrel done to you? But he's gonna pay for it, he won't die a pretty death, that I know for sure – his dog's life won't come to just any old end. I'll rip the insides from his body, I will. But only because of you! I shouldn't have waited until today to start things with you, I should have done it three years ago ... Why has God granted that I should love you, if not to see me have you, make love to you? The world has nothing more to offer me, all that's left is for me to make love to you today and kill your husband tomorrow. God has granted both to me, but only one at a time. You'll be mine, Erzsi, just once in my life. Go ahead and struggle, flail all you like! You know how I am, the more a woman resists, the hotter the fire burns inside me. If I weren't this way, how would I have it in me to pursue you for so long? Huh?"

Erzsi listened to his words in horror, and a cold shudder passed over her body. She asked herself how she could get her hands on something to kill him with, but then she remembered she'd put all the knives in the drawer beneath the table. If she could just get hold of a knife, then she would do it.

"Ah!" Gyuri hissed in her ear. "I should have done it earlier, when you were prettier ..."

"Ssss!" the woman uttered, then she bit into the man's face anywhere she could, and as his lips pressed themselves onto hers, she bit off half his lower lip.

Gyuri roared in pain as blood ran from his mouth, and with all his strength he pushed the woman away from him so that she fell across a chair, landing on her back.

In this moment they heard a child's blood-curdling scream.

Erzsi jumped up like a mother tiger. Her son stood on the bed and, shaking with the dread of the insane, his entire body jolting uncontrollably, watched his own mother's slaughter.

Gyuri made a movement as if he intended to carry out his plan no matter what, even if the world were to crash down on his head, but Erzsi managed to grab the wooden bowl standing on the table and flung its contents into his face.

The batter stuck to the man like a mask, impeding his breathing until he was able to scrape it off. The bowl fell to the ground, and prompted by some vague, deathly exasperation and murderous yearning, he groped, searched for the door and, finding it, staggered out.

Erzsi ran to her child, who was beside himself with terror. He'd fallen onto his back on the bed and his body twitched and jerked like mad; his eyes turned upward and soon froth was bubbling from the edge of the poor child's twisted mouth.

"Great God above!" the woman's voice rose as a shriek toward heaven. "My son! My son! My son!"

XV.

Bora went out into the stable as dawn broke, handed the paper documenting the gift to her father, and advised him to go immediately into town and present it to his lawyer. Freckle-faced Güzü understood his daughter and ran off with the paper in hand like a dog with a stolen bone.

Then the girl went inside. In the room it was completely dark, and as Bora stepped inside, she sensed the man's presence. His smell was here, his warmth, his memory. And once Bora had finished the task at hand, she felt in her conscience as calm, as pure, and as warm as the young women on the very first morning.

She sat on the edge of the bed where Dani lay and listened for a while to his breathing. Her traits softened, her eyes moistened, and it did her good to know that this great, famous man whom she'd admired so much as a young girl, and who was indeed an idol, was now at her side. She smiled quietly as she considered with what hopes, with what yearning she'd desired him and offered herself to him in the countless nights of the past summer. She smoothed the man's hair gently, so that he couldn't feel it, wouldn't be awakened by her touch.

Then she took off her shoes and sat beside him in the middle of the bed. The man stirred in his sleep, making room for her as though for his wife. The girl's heart filled with great happiness, and she sat there musing as she held the man's head in her arm.

She sat like that for some time and thought of nothing, sensing only the pounding of her heart.

She felt herself so very womanly! The mother beside her child's cradle ... Yet she was a dishonorable person ... selling herself ... She smiled: but she loves him! ... So she wouldn't be selling herself to him if she'd gotten married to him? Would she love him more then? Or if she gave herself to him like a fool for free, in a moment of waggish passion, would it be different? Wasn't it better for them both this way? She would demand nothing more of him ... And if the man were to leave her, she would wait for him, with patient understanding, pray for him, and raise his child ... If she's free from all worries, she'll stay faithful to him, honoring her purity and his good name ...

She crouched beside him, her joy complete. She cuddled against him, purring like a cat.

She wouldn't have become any other man's woman like this, since she loved no other man in the world like this one ... Because if she hadn't received this property from Dani, but from another man, such as Gyuri, then by God, how lousy life would be for her, what torture it would be to live as a couple with someone she didn't love ... How good was God that he'd heard a poor girl's prayers and refrained from destroying her life.

"You prayed well!" the girl tells herself quietly.

Then she thinks of the momentous thing this man, her Dani, has done for her. What he's given her for the bit of nothing that she was in a position to give him. The kind of thing that, no matter in what house, no matter from what woman Dani Turi might get it, if he thirsted for it, he need only hint and his thirst would be slaked ... How had she earned the chance to be the chosen one whom he thanked with so great a gift?

And she feels like the best girl who's ever lived. Suddenly she's overcome with passion and she throws herself on him, covering his face, his mouth, and kissing him greedily, eagerly, all but inhaling him with feverish wifely devotion.

Dani starts, then patiently endures her overtures. He senses in the girl's kisses something strange, something soft and clinging, as though his wife lay next to him, the old wife of their first years together, who for such a long time now has meant nothing to him, and his starving man's heart is aroused and takes, accepts, plucks the pleasure overtaking him ...

And then, then even greater fatigue and languor seize hold of him.

He pushes the girl's body off himself and turns his back toward the cold wall. The mud walls of the poorly heated room are as cold as ice. The cold feels good to him. It penetrates his entire body.

His wife ... She hasn't slept all night long ... He knows she closed the curtains over the windows so that no one would see her keeping vigil. For his wife was the best woman of all, none was better than she ... that was why he did so many horrible things to her, and would continue to do them.

Suddenly he felt in the strange bed as though he were lying in the warm liquid manure behind the stable. He thought he would vomit, and he belched; his head swam, as the bad wine of the previous evening got to him. Misery afflicted his body as well as his soul.

He moved a little and reached out with a clammy hand. As though he'd touched some creepy reptile or other, he drew back in horror, sat up, and suddenly realized he'd overslept. Where should he go? To clean himself up. Before he faces his wife.

"Sickening," he gagged, "phooey, what's become of me?!"

She would wake up any minute.

How much better his wife was than he ... Was it possible to imagine her in such a spot? Or any other woman? How much she had to put up with ... dear God ... how rotten their life had grown during the years they'd spent together.

As though he were appearing before the judgment seat of God ... How naïvely a man enjoys the bounty of his life, how little he dwells on the unhappy days when he will reap the fruits he's sown ... "Am I a sinner? ... Or just unlucky?"

he asked himself. "Should a man just let the good that presents itself to him in life go by?"

He recalled his wedding, the huge breakfast, and that first night ... How had a mother like that managed to raise such an unspoiled girl? ... What deathly horror had overcome the poor girl when she recognized what lay in store for her ... how she'd fought, like a wildcat ... and the battle on that night, when divorce had reared its threatening head ... and yet, it wasn't with blood that he'd cemented his hold on her, but via the heart: his charitable heart chanced upon her agonized suffering and took charge of it ... whoever "suffered as much for him as could be born should be his delight ..." There wasn't a saint in heaven who could meet her standard. His wife.

But what of it! He was no saint and had no desire to be one. Who could alter the fact that the woman took so little joy in love and couldn't bear her husband's kisses! How well he remembered his first infidelity, that too was just as shameful as the one today. They'd been married all of three days ... and his wife had caught him right away.

She shouldn't have forgiven him! She should have taught him a lesson, made him obey her ... But how? Was he the type of man who could be taught a lesson? What would have come of it? Murder! And nothing else.

The bones in his head were fairly bursting.

His heart was suffocating, as though a boulder weighed down on him.

He wanted to jump up and run out, but couldn't bring himself to; instead he thought how terribly great the distance was between thought and action.

He remained there as he was, once again incapable of thought; instead a senseless desperation took hold of him, and the blood vessels in his neck throbbed as they would if he were being transported to the scaffold ...

She'd conspired in every way possible to prevent him from finding happiness in life. What sort of happiness was it that came from his many short-lived escapades in women's laps or the mere earning of money, when he had to forgo the quiet happiness that brought true fulfillment? What did he gain from his home life and what did he accomplish for his wife? ... Was there anyone besides the two children she could exchange even two words with? And who was at fault? Erzsi? Couldn't he also have lived such that everyone would respect and envy him? Precisely what he loved in his wife was that, even in the circumstances in which she lived at his side, she was not an object of public scorn, as any other woman in her position would certainly have been – no one felt sorry for her, no one derided her, rather they respected her and said, as his own ears could attest, what a fine woman she was! That beastly Dani Turi, that dog of a man, doesn't deserve her!

And that reminded him of his parents, and hers as well, the entire boggy morass whose lives stretched themselves out behind her.

"She's right, the poor thing, she's right," he concluded, thus deciding the quarrel that had been underway between his wife and his mother since the very beginning, "she couldn't have acted any differently." He recalled what a warm-hearted, loving relationship his wife had had with his mother in the early days of their marriage, as though she'd been her very own daughter; how horrified she'd been upon learning for the first time that her parents-in-law had nothing to eat in the house, how she'd brought them flour, and lard, and given them money, even clothes for the children, and paid what they'd owed to the Jew ... And she'd loaned them money that she never got back ... Dani had merely laughed about the loan. Such a large loan it had been – ten forints! And they would pay it back! At such and such a time! They would pay the ten forints all back at once. The average day laborer would not be doing that! Only a wealthy peasant would do that, for whom honor means something and who can be held to his commitments. But a poor man? "Well, he'd pay if he had it, but if he has nothing!" And he never has anything. Not even when he does. Because there's nothing in his soul that's there. Because he has no security for the future, he has no idea what tomorrow will bring. And because from childhood on he grows up knowing he's a poor man who can use whatever he can get and who gets it however he can. He called to mind his wife's gentle indignation, which only aroused his laughter, and then her fits of anger that drove him to distraction. And the small insults that followed one after the other. The debtor always gets angry at the person who's extended the loan to him. Even when the lender doesn't ask to be repaid, the debtor has a hard time forgetting what he owes, but how much harder do things become when the lender abstains from such lenience! Then the debtor grows impatient and subjects the lender to abuse. Especially when the situation involves having one's own daughter-in-law as the lender. Here, too, the good relationship came to an end, and Dani repeated what he'd said already a thousand times: "They're not smart, my father and mother! Instead of supporting me in the difficult task of keeping my marriage going, they've made things worse, much, much worse!"

Cold sweat beaded on his forehead.

He stretched and waited, as though expecting the world to end. It wasn't good to think about such things!

And he fell asleep.

When he awoke, it was already light. Bora was puttering about in the room and greeted him tenderly, pleasantly, like a mother greeting her waking child. She spoke sweet, mothering words to him, but Dani was cross and turned his eyes away.

He practically had a stroke when he saw that the day had begun and he must get up, get dressed, leave the room, go out onto the street among the people, before the eyes of all the world, and take responsibility for his actions.

It was truly a sin that he hadn't gotten up when he should have, in the dark, that he hadn't slipped away like a thief while everyone else still slept. Now he had to flee accompanied by his shame, which would cry far and wide, preceding him wherever he went, so that even the children would take the news from the streets into the schoolroom.

For the time being he worried only about that, and he sat up in a horrible temper, moving his legs off the side of the bed, and with sleepy eyes he looked around stiffly for his boots, then hesitated for a moment.

And in this moment, Bora prostrated herself before him, transported by love, and bent over his feet, his snow-white, perfectly formed feet that never went about unshod, unlike those of other peasants, and she caressed them, embraced them, covering them with countless kisses.

"Leave me be," Dani said, shoving the girl angrily to the side, so that she fell against the oven and her skirts flew shamelessly open. Dani, who'd followed her with his eyes like a rabid bear, noticed this before the girl could cover herself, and spit at her. He spit onto her, into her.

Bora crouched in deathly fear in a corner on the floor, trembling over her entire body. She looked up at her master, her face aflame, like a beaten dog who has absolutely no thought of disloyalty or vengeance against his owner – he can do whatever he likes.

Dani turned his gaze away, ignoring her as if she were no longer there. He sucked on his teeth and could have knocked himself senseless for having stupidly fallen back to sleep this morning.

He dressed, and when he was ready to wash, Bora stood up, took the nicest basin she had from the wall rack, poured water into it from the jug resting beneath the table, and set it on a chair. The poor creature feared the man wouldn't accept her services. She was happy when Dani, without saying a word, proceeded to wash himself vigorously. She waited, with clean towel at the ready, until he was finished. Dani took the towel from her as coolly as though he were taking it from a clothes hook.

The cold water freshened him up a bit.

Bora fetched a comb and wiped it off while Dani dried himself. Then she offered it to him in fearful abjection, adding timidly: "My comb ..."

Dani took it. The girl was so touched upon seeing that she didn't disgust him that tears welled up in her eyes.

He was ready now and wanted to leave. And yet he stood, took out his pipe, cleaned it, filled it, passing the time until he figured out what it was he should do.

Bora watched him with a heavy heart. She dared not approach him. She feared him and feared for him. She knew what was going on in his mind, knew that he despised her, that they could never meet again. And this thought was unbearable to her – she had no idea what she could do to keep him there but a minute longer, to exchange just one more word with him during her lifetime.

Suddenly she was filled with happiness. An idea occurred to her. How could she have forgotten it!

"Dani," she spoke, and she herself was struck by the familiar tone she used. The man likewise gave a start.

Silence followed. The man packed his pipe, displaying not the least interest in what she had to say.

"Do you remember," she asked in a somewhat more formal manner, "how I made a promise to you last night?" She spoke softly, nervously, not knowing what she should say to him or how.

The man was as silent as stone.

"Something I promised ... you ..." She stumbled over her words, using instead of the formal form of "you" the familiar form customary between spouses; the urge to use the most familiar form, *"te,"* like she had in the night, was nearly impossible to resist ... "What I'd like to say ...," she continued in painful embarrassment as the man stood, like a totem pole. Then she fell silent.

A cry sounded from outside. Then an ox was heard bellowing, a well-sweep creaked in the neighbor's yard, and a wayward wind rattled the window. And the two of them stood there for minutes on end, neither speaking a word.

Stillness reigned; even the man's restless fingers were still.

Finally Bora broke the silence. "The Countess is here!"

As though a bolt of lightning had landed beside him, Dani suddenly turned toward her. His expression was distraught, horror-struck, mad with shock.

"How do you know?" he asked hoarsely, on the point of exploding.

Bora knew she might as well be dead in his eyes, but she accepted that. She was glad to be the one to pass this news along to him. She would have committed theft for him, would have murdered, sat in prison for him, as long as it meant that he needed her.

"No one else knows," she whispered, "only me. She let me know yesterday, the steward brought me a letter, everything's in there."

"Where's the letter?" the man gasped.

But the girl wanted to tell him everything and rushed on with her story, refusing to be interrupted. "The letter said that the Countess would be here today and that I should tell you to appear in the castle without fail because of the fields, because the Countess is going to give you the fields, that's why …"

"Where's the letter?"

"But that's not why you should go to the castle, not because of that," the girl's words bubbled forth, "but because of the Countess, of how sick she is with longing for you …"

"Where's the letter?" the man cried, shaking the girl. "Where's the letter, you slut, you harlot, you!"

"It's here, it's here," the girl groaned as cold sweat beaded on her face and forehead. "It's here, *my sweet, sweet man.*"

She slipped it out from the corner of the bed where they'd slept.

Dani tore the letter from her hand and read it and read it again, and as he did so his face grew calmer and firmer.

Then he folded the letter and put it in his pocket, took a match from his vest, lit it, and as the sulfur slowly caused a flame to crackle on the end of the match, he stuck the pipe in his mouth and lit it in perfect calm.

But his eyes narrowed slightly, and as he left, calmly, with resolute steps, heading directly for the street in full view of the passersby, in the midst of the women's stares which he did not return, he didn't squander a single thought on her, nor would he ever again; the girl didn't dare speak a word to him as he ventured onto the street ...

Just let him go – if he ruins her own life, Bora thought, then he might just as well ruin some other woman's life as well, even the Countess's ... Let him live, let him enjoy life, let the man wade up to his knees in the flowers.

She followed him with tear-filled eyes, her heart a ball of confusion, sadness, rejoicing, desolation, hope, sickness, and healthy excitement.

XVI.

Dani cut his way through the Sunday quiet of the village as though he were cutting his way across the Tisza River on horseback. He could hear how the waves of curiosity lashed this way and that, while the sharp rays of spying eyes pierced his face.

But he walked along firmly and proudly, not meeting anyone's eyes, not observing a thing, as though wading through a muddy bog. His face was cold, resolute, and inspired; bold decisions led him onward. He was fully prepared to row with all his might, and also to go with the flow.

Men, women, and children stood about everywhere, in the yards and before their gates; everyone knew where he was coming from and what had happened, and it didn't occur to Dani that they knew even more than he, that their gossip didn't just concern him, but was directed against him.

No one dared to address him, no one dared get in his way.

He walked fearlessly and resolutely through the gate. Up to the yard. In through the door, and then into the *tiszta szoba* or fancy room.

Although it was cold there, he didn't feel it. He got out his shaving gear, stropped the razor on the leather hanging by the window, poured water from the jug into a bowl, undressed, worked the shave cream into a lather, and shaved himself carefully.

As he drew the blade back and forth across his neck, he thought to himself that it would be better to cut his neck in two than to make himself handsome.

He smiled complacently, and while stropping the razor once again to sharpen it further, he leaned his head back and closed his eyes partway, and the image of the Countess appeared before him as in a kind of mist, the way he'd seen her last summer. The way she'd stood in front of the window with the sunlight shining through her.

His eyes flashed, the image disappeared, and he calmly continued to shave the other half of his face.

"Well," he told himself, "if you were ever somebody, or even if you weren't, today you'll prove yourself a genuine dandy."

His clothes, his undergarments, everything was there in the room; and while he looked through the two wardrobes to gather what he needed, he didn't think once of his wife, either with hostile or tender feelings. As though she were the most foreign of women, a servant in the other room, with whom he had nothing in common, to whom nothing bound his heart.

He's filled with thoughts of the Countess. For him there is neither life nor death, no village home, no friends, no wife, no parents, no past life, no future happiness, no other purpose in the world apart from this: to go to her, run after her, seize her, take her into his arms! ...

He doesn't hurry, doesn't rush, he completes his work precisely, thoroughly. He won't arrive late, nor will he arrive earlier than necessary. He polishes his tall, weathered boots to a brilliant shine, as he learned to do it during his military service. And once he has on his snow-white undergarments, he thinks to himself: *No other woman in the village knows how to wash clothes like my own, sickly wife.*

He's ready. He takes his expensive *guba*, the one he bought for a hundred and fifty forints, down from the nail and wraps it around his shoulders, straightens himself and knows that there isn't another man like him in any county near or far.

He presses his traditional lambskin peasant's cap down over his forehead. Truly his place is among the ancient heroes of Árpád's reign!

He leaves, keen that nothing and nobody should get in his way.

The minute he steps outside the room, the door to the next room opens. His wife emerges.

Dani glances at her in a calm, cool, unaffected manner, and when he sees his wife's deathly pale face, no guilty conscience awakens in him, nor does he get angry at her. In this moment she is as foreign to him as though a thousand miles lay between them.

Erzsi stands on the threshold. She wants to say something, but when she sees her husband like this, her words stick in her throat from the painful, bitter feelings welling inside her, and she simply gapes at him in shock and wonderment.

One moment later and it was too late, as Dani left, like a brilliant, cold, disaster-bearing comet one sees only once in one's life.

XVII.

The Countess was sitting in the window in her overheated room. She was no longer as pretty as she'd been during the summer. Her face had lost its tender softness, its roral fullness, due to certain emotional and physical ailments she'd suffered since then. Her crown of golden hair adorned a face that was inordinately white, even anemic. One could see the traces of premature aging characteristic of blondes. Her blue eyes had sunk in their sockets and the skin beneath them had grown limp, revealing those fine wrinkles that were a greater source of desperation to women like her than death itself.

She stared out the window, lost both in and to her thoughts.

Outside, tall trees stood beneath the window, their branches coated by thick layers of snow and frost. The sun shone down on her room from an opal-colored sky, and snow crystals shivered in the faint breeze, casting rainbow light on her eyes.

Inside it was unusually warm, as the Countess was wearing the same green moiré dressing gown she'd worn during the summer ...

She huddled there as though she'd lost her very will. Her half-opened eyes blinked from time to time; she herself couldn't explain how she'd come to this place. Something beyond human comprehension resided in the entire affair. And as she drew her diminutive, emaciated white hand across her forehead, fever and bitterness overcame her. For a moment she acquiesced and shook in a cold fever; it occurred to her that she must come down from the clouds! She held onto herself and felt ill. She would have liked to lie down in bed, to hide beneath a down comforter, and take some bitter, nausea-inducing drug, like during her childhood. How it would have pleased her to have someone sit down on her bed and give it to her, someone she loved, whom she enjoyed seeing and hearing ... She now feared everything both foreign and familiar.

Throwing herself into the soft chair and shivering in the cold that crept in through the window, she closed her eyes and thought of Dani.

How very much she'd thought of him since their last meeting.

She didn't remember him clearly, after all she'd only seen him a few short minutes, and even then the man had dissolved before her into a colorful, awe-inspiring phantom. How often her soul had nourished itself since then from those few pregnant minutes. The nausea induced by society, by people, by the world, by life had driven her to this point. How nice it would be to have some brutish man come to her, someone suited to crudeness, who was free to indulge in it, characterized by it. And at the same time that she yearned for this, she also felt many times over the smallest lack of tenderness, and life's minutest crudity pained her, but none more than Count László's considerate tenderness, which tried her patience in much the same way as the noxious air bearing down on a bedridden victim of illness.

A sudden decision had brought her down this foolhardy path, one that had nonetheless ripened slowly. Since the summer she hadn't lived the life of a normal human. She'd passed from one excess to the next, until her sanity was stretched to the breaking point by her empty, senseless and aimless life. At that time, Dani Turi's petition had fallen into her hands, the one written by the schoolmaster. The unusual document both alarmed and thrilled her; she secured the services of a young intellectual with whose help she investigated the past history of the Karay family, and she found with pleasure that she could arouse the young student, who handled the entire Karay history with patriotic hatred, to an even greater, more visceral level of hatred. Filled with youthful passion, the student saw in her a saint, and spurred her on to patriotic action; she should convince the Count to give the fields back to the peasants in exchange for money, parcel by parcel. The Countess discussed the matter with her lawyer, who explained that the noble estate could not be touched, as it was entailed and thus could not be dispersed. It gradually became evident, however, that in the case of Dani Turi an exception could be made, since these fields were exempted from the estate property as a whole. So the Countess had a contract drawn up whereby the one parcel, the "Pallag," would be granted to Dani Turi in exchange for cash, while the other would go to the village community conjointly; this contract was drawn up such that Dani Turi alone could sign it in the name of the entire village.

The documents lay finished on the table, and the Countess, who sat wearily in her chair, cast a glance at them.

She smiled.

It would never have occurred to her that she, too, would be paying this peasant Don Juan, who was accustomed to being paid by the women.

For a long time now, she'd felt herself in the power of the enigmatic peasant, who perhaps had totally forgotten about her, pursuing life in his own little world as calmly as he had before their meeting.

The Countess looked out on this world, which spread itself before her beyond the magnificent trees, into the tiny little peasant cottages.

The conviction dawned in her that this peasant – this man – could not be totally indifferent to her, and feverish passion welled within her.

She crouched tightly in her chair, and secretively, resolutely, cynically, smiled into her hand mirror.

In that moment she uttered a short sentence. She wasn't hallucinating, wasn't fantasizing, she simply and unexpectedly uttered as her thoughts unfolded a brief, short sentence, clearly, audibly, emphatically, with a strange voice and strange intonation: those of Bora Kis.

She uttered the same naughty little sentence that Bora had whispered into her ear during the summer. And she smiled, and wondered, and a tingle passed down her spine, moral disquiet filled her soul, and a torrid kindling crept over her body.

Slowly, with sharply burning sensations, the room where she sat awakened all the shameful, sweet, awkward, blush-inducing surging of her blood she'd endured last summer.

And laughing, her teeth pressed together, lustfully, disdainfully, she uttered the peasant Don Juan's insulting nickname, and saw in her mind the queer, shameless girl who'd likewise uttered the word, with an unmistakable snicker and boorish charm.

For several moments she held her small teeth and lips this way, seized by a fit of lust ...

And once again she uttered the word.

When she looked up, Dani Turi, who'd just entered the room, stood before her.

XVIII.

The sight of the peasant cooled the Countess' flaming heat considerably.

Within a moment she grew sober.

With restored calm she remained seated, her bearing casual and aloof. She looked at the man with cold disdain as he stood before her like some sort of bizarre, tamed bear in his great furry *guba*.

His ill breeding irritated her, and his failure to remove his peasant cap stirred up old, bad feelings.

She didn't speak, she merely waited; waited for the peasant to speak, and for his bearish speech to wipe away completely the last remnants of her earlier acute discomposure.

She wanted to see the peasant in his vulgar lack of refinement, as a means of punishing herself. She wanted to see him as an ungainly half-animal who is nothing, nothing, and unworthy of a single glance.

She looked at his lambskin cap, his shaggy *guba*, his peasant's boots disparagingly, without hatred, without disgust, with complete detachment. As she looked at him, her eyes rested on his boots. They were beautifully formed, slender, pointed, gleaming.

She smiled and glanced up at his face. It was anything but homely. Again she realized how much he resembled Count László.

"So that's it," she said to herself and turned up her mouth derisively.

The peasant stood there with relaxed self-assurance. He didn't speak.

The silence that followed was long and painful.

In the end, the Countess realized she no longer despised the peasant, she was neither indifferent nor favorably disposed toward him. It seemed to her that what was at stake here was a joke, one she was playing on herself.

She felt so calm, was so utterly the master of her own self, so superior, as though she were seeing a peasant who was there to collect alms for the burned-down village church.

Her voice returned, and she spoke in an easy tone, as naturally as the wind blowing through weeds. "I received your petition ..."

But the peasant said nothing. He stood like a statue. Even his face was motionless. Nor did he blink. He just stood calmly, his peasant's cap atop his head.

The peasant's very peasantness angered the Countess.

Her voice grew harsher. "I've taken care of your request. There on the table are the two agreements. The Count has signed them both ..."

The peasant neither spoke nor moved. He simply stood.

This idiocy revolted the Countess. "There is the ink, the pen is on the table. Just sign them."

She waited to see what would come next.

The peasant tossed his head back. The Countess brightened at the prospect that a noble impulse would move him to reject the offer.

But no. He shifted his *guba* onto his left shoulder and stepped up to the table.

He took the first document and calmly read the typed script from beginning to end.

This was the agreement regarding the entire village community, with all the conditions included in the offer.

He grasped the pen, and holding it against the paper, he signed.

He picked up the second document.

As he read it, something caused him to take offense. It was the agreement concerning the Pallag, the property to be sold to him. He was astonished to see that the selling price had been reduced to half his original offer, and instead of payment by installments, immediate cash payment was expected.

He hesitated for a good half minute, then his eyes lit up, and with a quick movement of his hand he pushed his cap back to reveal a lock of hair, which fell across his forehead; then he bent down and signed the agreement. He would get the money to complete the purchase this very day!

The Countess was able to read his face as clearly as a book, only his last thought eluded her powers of prediction.

She observed the peasant briefly, who stood before her in a handsome pose, fit for painting. She liked him this way. Like a picture.

The peasant laid the document down, and turning his head to the side, looked silently at the Countess.

She in turn stood up, and made overtures to do the thing she so desired to do.

She took the pen, dipped it in the ink, and hurriedly wrote at the bottom of the document, beneath Dániel Turi's miserable, laughable chicken scratches: "Entire sum received in full," followed by her name.

Dani Turi didn't see what the Countess wrote, he saw something else.

As she bent down, the woman stood there before him in complete self-forgetfulness, and he saw her entire body.

All the blood went to his head, which was practically black, it was so red.

He sensed the lady's secret desire. Regardless of her tone of voice, he suspected what the woman had in mind for him, what she expected of him.

As for the Countess, she spoke in scornful disdain: "Well, Dániel Turi! ... The people of Kiskara no longer have any reason to complain about the traitor! ..." She sighed – how differently she'd pictured this scene!

She laid the paper on the table and looked at the peasant's face.

And she grew alarmed.

The peasant was looking at her with eyes that rivaled those of a bloodhound or a starving wolf in their fear-inducing horror ...

The woman stood there frozen. She wanted to reach for her gown and gather it together; she sensed throughout her body the threatening gaze of the beast in rut.

She was unable to lift her hand, she just stood there helplessly, at the complete mercy of the salivating boar.

He, however, stretched out his arm, reached for her throat, her gown, and with a single motion he tore the green silk veil in two, from her neck all the way down to the tips of her feet.

XIX.

Her eyes opened in response to a bang, two bangs from far off. Her intelligent blue eyes looked out from beneath the long lids, wearily, with broken sheen. They remained open like this – for some time the supple shimmer of life could not penetrate the tired corneas.

At last her consciousness awakened inside her brain.

And the Countess noticed she was unbelievably weak ...

She feels no pain, but is unable to lift her hand ... Her legs hang off the sofa ... her right leg dangles somewhere off in the emptiness, and she's powerless to draw it toward her. How nice it is that her arm hasn't fallen, how lovely that at least this limb lies next to her on the soft velvet of the sofa.

Her consciousness again recedes.

Then she hears a small noise, a steady, monotone sound ...

Drip, drip, drip.

It's wonderful to lie there, so leisurely, so completely.

It's just that something is weighing down her right leg ... She'd like to free it, to move it at the knee, let it fall where it may ...

A person isn't even in control of her own body. Why can't she move her leg? Why has it grown attached at the knee? How lucky the person is who has a wooden leg. He can simply unstrap it when it's just dangling there in the emptiness ...

She smiles ... She thinks she smiled at this naïve little thought. She's toying ... she thinks she's toying with herself ... How nice, how terribly nice it would be if her limbs didn't hang together so. If they just lay there one beside the other.

That would be perfect happiness ...

Then she rests there silently for a long time, a millennium, two millennia, knowing nothing of herself.

Soon a light goes on within her, and she realizes she's lying naked on the sofa.

And then she knows everything.

Her face grows rigid, and she smiles. She thinks she's smiling, although her face is rigid ...

And again millennia come and go ... What a long life man leads.

Another sound.

Drip, drip, drip ...

How happy she was today ... Now. How very, very happy.

That was good. That was worth death itself. It was so good.

Something breaks within her, and now her blood flows. It's not bad ... it's good ...

How does she know it's her blood that's dripping?

That was worth dying for. That was good. That was good.

Who said that her blood was dripping?

She feels no pain. She's so pleasantly weak; it's nice to feel so weak, how nice it is to be so very weak.

It's really good to lie there so softly. To lie in warm liquid; it's very, very nice to lie in one's own blood.

Who said that her own blood was dripping?

The chambermaid isn't allowed to come in unless she rings. How nice it is that the maid can't enter as long as she isn't dead. That's very good, very proper.

Poor peasant ... Poor dear ...

A terribly heavy weight lies on a person's body.

Why does a person's blood drip?

Poor peasant. Handsome ... Strong! ... Love! Love! ... That's love ...

My God, my Lord ... hallowed be thy name ... it's really nice to lie like this ... My God, but it's nice ...

Drip, drip, drip ...

XX.

His hat had shifted a bit to the side, his *guba* hung loosely from his shoulder, and his face glowed with the feeling of utter satisfaction. He was filled to the brim with satiation and his stomach, mouth, and heart felt so full that he desired absolutely nothing more! What were food, drink, and women to him now? What could come now after everything that had happened?

He stood on the top step and looked around at the dazzling white world. He didn't blink, on the contrary, his eyes opened wide to the white whiteness of the midday sun. Let the person go blind who no longer wants to see.

He shook his head and, clenching his fist, slashed his arm through the air.

Like a god, to bring the world to its knees.

Then he started off, headed down the stairs.

He went, without stopping. He had to go. But where to? Why? Why?

Life appeared so worthless to him, so empty. What should he do after this? All at once the village grew small for him, a snow-covered trash heap. And he himself grew so large, powerful, strong, fortunate, proud.

He proceeded across the crunching snow as though he were rushing headlong into blind fate.

And indeed, he walked right into his Doom.

As he approached the great wrought iron gate, the smaller gate embedded in it opened, and he stood face to face with Count László.

They were both struck with mortal dread.

The Count reached for his rifle and cocked it immediately. Everything that he feared and suspected glared at him from the peasant's face.

But the civilized man did not give in to this animal instinct, and his finger rested idly on the trigger.

They stood eye to eye from each other and the Count failed to notice, failed to discern the dishonorable transformation the other man's face underwent in that moment. In the mere twinkling of an eye, an entirely new man was standing before him. A fork-tongued face presented itself to him that belied every psychological truth.

Heroism, or knavery, or the splendor of fortune had first shone forth from the peasant's countenance.

But then a common, cunning, small-minded peasant's mug emerged from it that gazed wide-eyed at the cocked gun, not knowing what the nobleman intended with it, and wondering with simpleminded curiosity whether the other is insane and what his beef is.

The Count didn't know if his eyes might be fooling him. The gun quivered in his hand, and shame began to gnaw at him.

This peasant! This brute!

And he blushed in the Countess' stead and for her sake.

If the two of them truly met, then good God, what a disillusionment it must have been for the poor lady. In his eyes, too, this peasant had, from a distance and through the suggestion inspired by her, taken on enormous stature. He'd grown larger than just any peasant, larger than just any man, greater even than all mankind, he'd risen up to the very mists in the sky.

And yet here before him stands a small-minded, scheming, nasty dog.

Should he raise his gun to him?

A whip is better suited to the task! A few slashes across the muzzle! Two lashes in the face, then send him away with the hussar.

He lowered his gun. "What are you doing here?"

And the peasant submitted to the disparaging question of this aristocrat as his grandfather had to the twenty-five lashes across his back.

The Count took a deep breath and his facial expression softened. For several moments he stood silently, luxuriating in his relief.

Then he called out sternly to the peasant: "March!"

His rifle was still lowered, but he held on to it menacingly; he no longer thought he would use it, but signaled that he was prepared to if necessary. He was only outwardly angry – while his features appeared to threaten, his soul was amused, and he would have preferred to rush to the lady – he anxiously pictured himself at her side.

In the very moment when he was at his most amused, something flashed at him, as though lightning had shot a monster his way. The peasant's eyes flashed dark and green, and thunder struck as well.

Dani Turi blazed with rage, lunged at the Count's face, at his eyes, wildly, with bared teeth, and like a hungry wolf he grabbed him by the throat, flinging him down in the snow.

He cast him face down and shoved his head into the snow, wringing his neck with his vice-like grip, and held the unfortunate man like this until he twitched miserably, kicking his feet, floundering, and finally growing limp. His struggle was dreadfully brief. The proud man fought in his clutches no longer than a hen in the Countess' hands. And the peasant, who clearly observed the writhings of the large body even in the mercilessness of his bloodthirsty rage, impatiently loosened his grip. As the body moved once again and renewed its thrashing about, he let his right hand fly as he grabbed the neck with his left, precisely where he could grip the man's Adam's apple, and punched him left and right, left and right, over and over again with his fist.

As though his muscles had taken on a life of their own, he began to thrust this bony weapon with rhythmic strokes into the soft, bearded, bloody and flattened head, striking and hitting, shredding the flesh from the face, and macerating the dangling pieces of cartilage. And he struck him and hit him, and when that wasn't enough, he jumped to his feet, grasped the body by the heels with his arms, swung it, slamming the head with such force into the gate post that the skull split in two, and again he swung the damned body, smashing it against the stone wall, as though the latter were the ancient adversary he had to destroy with this despicable object of carnage, this execrable, disintegrating pillar of flesh.

And when he held little more than a rag, a useless, formless heap in his hands, and threw it down into the snow, he sensed his work was still not complete; he balled his fists and snorted and stomped about, and still couldn't extinguish the wild fire raging inside him.

He grabbed the rifle, clutched the barrel in his hand, and stood at attention like a soldier; he stood there rigidly, like a bloody gallows.

His arm was stiff like a steel rod, and his face was stony, and burned with the fire of divine wrath.

In this moment he felt the most sublime bliss a man can feel. Suddenly he felt the fire-breathing power of his might.

Regret, empathy, the trappings of human morality all fizzled into the air.

He burned, he seemed to melt the snow-frozen world as rays of heat spouted forth from him.

He'd passed through the highest of all human passions.

He had murdered.

And he sensed now a hundred times over the superhuman condition of the soul that had seized him before, as he'd stood at the top of the steps.

What more could he seek down here on earth? And in his brain a thought crystallized, much like the divine revelation on Mount Sinai:

"I've eaten, I've loved, I've murdered."

And he smiled with that arrogance with which he alone on earth had the right to look out above and beyond life, mankind, and his own self. He alone, who has robbed from life more than thousands of people could even dream of.

And as he stood there in the open gate, like an unquenched, bloodthirsty archangel of the Last Judgment lusting after new hells, a poor, breathlessly running man sprang out before him. It was his cousin-in-law, Gyuri Takács, who'd traced his steps all day long and knew he was with the Countess, the lonely Countess, and who'd heard of the Count's arrival and rushed to be there, to counter Dani Turi and assist the Count, as well as to satisfy his curiosity, his desire for vengeance, and to protect his own interests.

And as he witnessed the shredded human remains and the bloody man grimly standing guard there, the carnivorous monster lusting after violence, he stopped short, staggered backward, deathly pallor and cold sweat covering his entire body.

Dani Turi looked at him calmly.

He looked at him, and he didn't move. He was still, but like a maritime tempest, blood and rage and the splendor of titanic beastliness rose up within the dispassionate sheath, in the very depths of his soul.

The other man was rigid with shock at this sight, like a bird standing eye to eye with a snake.

And Dani Turi lifted the gun. Properly, soldierly, as he'd learned to handle his soldier's gun.

He fired.

And the unfortunate man bent in two, his spine broken – his body hadn't presented the slightest barrier to the whistling bullet.

And Dani Turi took aim once again.

And again he fired. Blindly, hurriedly, thus shooting one more being, decimating yet another life. A happy life, a peaceful existence that had nothing to do with him, that had gotten in the way of his vast and swollen ego, his god-assaulting power.

And a black raven, drawing slow circles in the sky, was shattered in the air.

Its feathers scattered, fluttering in downward spirals to the ground.

XXI.

Moments passed that seemed like eternities. From somewhere in the depths he sensed the profound nature of his position like a tempest rising up from hell. His self-awareness phased out for minutes at a time, he just stood there in one spot, like an empty statue of his true self.

Suddenly, fleetingly, like the momentary whirlwind that precedes a violent storm, the dread seized him that some cruel danger loomed nearby.

He didn't know whether he stood within or beyond some ill-defined something, and his eyes glassed over and erred uncertainly in the air.

Then his consciousness returned. He knew he'd murdered the Count, and he knew he'd shot his cousin-in-law to death. He even knew of the shattered bird. He knew all of it, and regretted nothing; one cause lay behind it all, and he stated the cause: *My rage!* ...

In that moment he raised his hand; he sensed something strange about it and looked at it.

He grew pale, his eyes narrowed, and he looked at his hand with revulsion and terror; the urge to vomit assailed him, desperation and horror seized him and he thought he must fall down.

Blood covered his hand.

Fresh blood. Human blood.

He shuddered with mortal dread.

And yet he knew perfectly well that he didn't regret doing what he'd done, he wasn't sorry for it, he was glad precisely because he would have regretted *not* doing it – but this glad feeling caused him to tremble, every cell in his body shuddered, and he lacked sufficient control of himself even to move his bloodied hand this way or that. He held it there in front of his eyes and saw that it was shaking as though electricity had jolted him in the barrack-room bath. Fear, horror, and disgust overcame him. He sought to flee. What if somebody saw him? What if someone came upon him here? If a child saw him and snitched on him?

The earth began to spin, he felt like he would keel over, and as though his feet were frozen to the ground, he couldn't shift his rigid legs.

He closed his eyes, lurched forward in the resulting darkness, toppled over, landing on his knees, and crouched there, shivering, teetering on his two bent legs. In his fear-induced daze, his head and body were engulfed in a nervous, suffocating intoxication, as though he were being breathed in by the very air itself.

He attempted to stammer some curses, swore at God, but barely managed to close his clattering teeth together.

Two or three times this senseless, uncontrolled trembling came over him. He was as pale as wax and his heart felt so cramped that several times he had to open his mouth to gulp some air, as though he were drowning.

It took some time for his body to pass through the first feverish wave of dread. Cold sweat covered his forehead, his torso, and he was powerless to move.

When he finally recovered to the point that thoughts could form in his brain, increasingly awful notions beset him with each passing minute. What if someone had heard the shots? What if someone were following Gyuri? He'd come, after all, others might too! What if someone came across the street and looked behind the gate? If only the gate were at least locked! He had to remove the corpses! ... He had to run, to flee from here! To race out to the fields, bareheaded through the snow, across the ice, across the world! To start a new life somewhere else. But here every minute meant death! He must run to America!

Some strange, unfamiliar, craven specter crept over him, it spoke from the inside outward, yet his decent, intelligent, strong, self-confident spirit cowered above in fetters, observing ironically all that occurred around it there inside the cage of his human husk.

Again he felt this double soul that lay harbored inside him, but now its alien nature took him by even greater surprise than the night before. Again it was new and powerful, but it only seemed that way, for it was destroying him, stripping him of all his powers in the eyes of others. It made him more cowardly than a child, more humble than a worm that crawls on the ground.

And suddenly anger flared up inside him. Why did this stupid cowardliness not come sooner? From where in hell did it come, to destroy one that shares nothing with it, that has never known it his entire life? He made a fist with his hand and wavered back and forth, not knowing where to hit himself in order to strike this wretched alien within him! But then he only stretched his limbs with all his might and shook over his entire body.

He breathed deeply after that, filling his lungs two, three times. This seemed to make him feel more human. Now at least there was defiance in him and he could stand up to the destiny staring him in the face.

He took advantage of this momentary strength, lifted his *guba* from the snow and put it across his shoulders, donned his cap, pushing it low above his brow, and with murderous thoughts flickering inside him, he left the courtyard, not once looking back.

He was grim and resolved, choking with pride in his ability to overcome his own self. And yet he felt that if he stopped he must sink to the ground, if he remained where he was, he must become as nothing, if he didn't pursue this bitter struggle to its end, wading through blood all along the open street, writhing across the earth, he would lack the strength even to cry.

He simply walked along and swallowed every pang of conscience, trying to look like a normal human, to conduct himself in human manner. A child stood in the first gate he passed, stared at him in silence, and turned to follow him with his gaze. Dani looked at him and nearly collapsed with dread. In the child's regard he noticed the great bewilderment caused by his *bloodied boot*. And from that point he began to feel as though his foot were surrounded by warm, thick, searing liquid. He reached down as though trying to free it, but it was impossible; the sock on his foot only grew warmer, it was as if his boot were burning it from the outside inward. And the child's gaze likewise singed his soul. He acknowledged the boy as his terrifying judge, who has the right to stare at him, to marvel at him, and to condemn him, and before whom he must sink to the ground in dread.

He looked around, trembling like cornered prey. His eyes sought a breach through which he could escape from the world, and he suffered like the dog who is threatened by his master's club.

Thus only his wild animal horror revealed the man whose powers of reason survived and still worked within him: "Where to, then? If I'm so cowardly, so wretched? What's going to happen? What am I after? Where am I going?"

And he went and went. The child's bewildered gaze flashed before him, traveling through his entire body.

Will his own son stare at him like that?

A terrible yearning, an irresistible drive urged him on: homeward! At home nothing is amiss! And he quickened his steps, stricken with horror, cowering with dread, terrified that someone would pursue him, and he bent his back and tucked in his tailbone and sensed a painful tingling hounding him, chasing him down, as though he were being whipped. He was fast becoming an animal; in his brain, reason began to shut down; he stared in front of him, looking neither to the right nor the left, as though he wore blinders like a horse, racing forward with machine-like steps, like an animal who, startled at the one end of the road, rushes headlong toward the other.

There, there he must run, to his house. Home! He slips into the lair of which he knows only that *that's the place*. That's where he must flee to. That's his home. There he can take stock of things and from there he can bravely fend off his pursuers.

For but a brief time, his brain generates a few clear thoughts. The village's narrow street is so long, so unbelievably, devilishly long ... It occurs to him how hard he's running. This could raise suspicion, so he slows his steps. Later he's terrified that his face might reveal his desperation, making anyone who sees it immediately aware of his deed! And he forces a more cheerful expression onto his face, draws it up in a smile, but a rigid, vulpine grin contorts his features. Soon he realizes that, were anyone to see him grinning that way, later they would recall how he cackled upon returning from committing murder. This causes terror and mortal desperation to draw their lines on his face, and once again his sole desire is to flee, just go, go, get home and hide! Flee to his hiding place and tremble as he had just now, back there ... And already he feels the trembling in his limbs and suffers excruciating anguish.

All kinds of people are standing about before their houses, men, women, at their gates, in the street, and every eye is turned toward him, and he's deathly afraid they might try to speak to him. He knows that a single utterance from them would suffice to cause him to dissolve into dust, like the fairytale corpse raised to life by mere magic.

His jaw grows rigid and numb, his eyes glaze over, and his heart beats chaotically; gruesome pangs torment him, and cold sweat issues from all the pores in his body.

He atones for every sin he's committed as he passes down the narrow street, and endures more terrifying pains than all the sinners of Dante's hell; while their souls burned as their bodies went up in flames, he feels his body dissolving in the flames of his soul.

Now he sees his gate, a hundred steps more, now only twenty, and the closer he gets to it, the further away in the distance it seems.

Half dead, he enters the gate at last. He can't even raise his feet, he just drags them across the threshold. He barely manages to avoid falling over himself. Were he to fall, he wouldn't be able to get up again! From behind him he senses powerful fists reaching for him, clutching at him.

As he crosses the threshold into the porch, he finally comes to a stop and pushes the door closed behind him, and as he lets down his guard, he breaks into an uncontrollable bout of feverish trembling. He can't control a single sinew in his body, and he starts shaking, his blood vessels bulging, his eyes all but popping out of his head, making the door behind him rattle on its bolt as well as its hinges.

And he hears this rattling, like the clattering of a wagon as it approaches, sometimes fading out, then returning, more loudly ... like the jangling of fetters ...

He feels weak and exhausted, as though he were deathly ill. His innards are writhing and squirming, wriggling their way up into his mouth. His head is reeling and heavy as a vat; he can't even hold it atop his neck – it sinks, like the gourd on a withered stalk.

He hears his wife get up inside. Her chair creaks. His hearing is terrifyingly sharp, he even hears *screaming* somewhere in the distance. He listens simultaneously to the outside, where there is nothing, and beyond in the room, to the harmless commotion of daily life. Both horrify him equally.

The door opens and his wife steps out into the porch. She appears in the light emanating from the kitchen window. When he sees her, Dani senses her presence as a fresh breath of wind driving back the fog – his fever, trembling, and angst ebb away. Never before had he seen his wife in this way. No hatred smolders in her large black eyes, instead they are grief-stricken, broken. She looks at him sadly, as sadly as someone resigned to the wrath of fate, whose loved one lies buried and who is reduced to despondent mourning. Her husband looks at her with wide eyes and soaks in her sadness like the field soaks up silent rainfall, and his breathing eases as the sweltering fever leaves him.

For some time, they look into each other's eyes.

Erzsi sees that her husband is a broken man, she senses that his eyes are imploring her. She doesn't know why, but she suspects that great, profound regret has come over him. And she's already cried herself out, in the tears she shed at her sick child's bedside her rancor, too, was spent, leaving only her pain. She's filled to the brim with heartache, and in her husband's eyes she reads sympathy for her distress. She quietly accepts him into the stronghold of her grief – in this their feelings are rightly shared in common.

There is a long silence that nonetheless seems full of life, of meaning. The wife's angelic suffering does the husband good, as the husband's brokenness likewise does her good.

And the relationship between them reaches a new threshold; the beauty of sadness covers and fills them.

The woman signals to her husband, wearily but not without affection, with a certain misgiving devotion. She signals with her eyes, but accompanies this movement with her whole body, calling on him to follow her, which he does; with calm, tired – but not painful – steps.

He follows her into their room.

The woman stands in front of the bed, which is stripped of its covers, and there lies a small body. Their son.

In the first minute he thinks the boy is dead. He shrinks back in fear, but it's not the unbridled terror from before; within this fright is a measure of joy; death is good! It's the only thing that's good!

The child is white with pallor, but he's breathing. His small body is moving. Only his legs are covered with a blanket. How strange and sad this little person is, with his big person's undershirt and drawers. As his father looks at him, he frightens his own self with his thoughts. If only he were lying there dead on the bed! As a child, *guiltless*, sick! A blessed state, forever unattainable!

He looks questioningly at his wife.

Erzsi has already accepted the thought that her husband knows everything. His questioning look startles her. She sees that the man has heard nothing. And that doesn't pain her; in her relieved woman's heart a new fear surfaces: what's wrong with him, then? Immediately she banishes this thought – never mind! It's his problem!

Silently he sits on the edge of the bed. His head droops wearily to one side as he gazes at his son breathing heavily in sleep. He hears the regular breathing of the younger boy in his cradle. He, too, is asleep.

"You weren't at home last night," the woman begins, and her voice is so sad, so resigned, soft, and reproachful without being angry. "A robber broke in on me. The child was terrified. He's still in shock. He's had the spasms a good ten times. Now he's sleeping."

A thought flashes through Dani's mind – he knows who came. Who must have come.

He lowers himself onto a chair and begins to talk. Quietly, calmly, soberly. "I killed Gyuri Takács."

A lump forms in the woman's throat, she becomes even paler, she grows faint and starts to tremble.

The man speaks again. "I killed the Count too. Count Karay."

There is no barbarity in his words, and yet a certain apathy is there, a cold heartlessness. He knows that his words are killing her, but it's also what he wants. As though this would relieve him. For he's in pain, never in his life had his heart hurt like this in upsetting her so.

The thought flickered in his head that he should reproach his wife, because in point of fact it was her fault, everything was her fault, his whole ruined life was her fault. An exasperated cruelty distorted his mouth, prompting him to say something powerful, bitter, heartbreaking. But he refrained, he merely opened his *guba* and showed her his bloody clothes.

Then he was glad, bitterly, gravely happy to see that he'd thus transferred his own trembling to his wife.

For a long time, they sat there in silence.

The woman gradually began to cry. Tears started falling from her eyes. It must have been momentous pain that could still press tears from her dry, exhausted eyes.

The man grew serious, more and more serious, as he sat there. Suddenly he cried out hollowly: "They'll hang me!"

His voice was ghastly. He was numb with unspeakable fear. In this moment his fate in all its terror became crystal clear to him. All the horrors of death were fossilized in his face. His lower lip hung limply after he'd spoken, his tongue stuck between his teeth, his eyes protruded from their sockets, his breath stopped, and a gray film seemed to glaze over his eyeballs.

Erzsi looked with dismay at this face, as though she were already seeing him dangling from the gallows.

And in this moment she forgot everything he'd done. The suffering she'd endured all her life, the many injuries inflicted on her, the insults, the brutality, cruelty, the all too human sins, everything, everything. What was all her suffering in comparison to this? What her atonement compared to this! And were her suffering yet a hundred times greater, she's enduring it because of her love! Undeservedly! And this knowledge carries within her the seeds of inner absolution and comfort. But this man is atoning for his sins! And the soul is his strictest judge! He won't be able to stand up to himself as judge!

She was seized by such profound mercy that she knelt down before him, folded her hands, not even shrinking from his bloodied clothes, and with her woman's heart she summoned comfort and prayed forth words of courage!

"Dear husband, don't despair! Don't despair!" And she bent over his bloody hand. "Your actions were justified!" she cried, and her voice was drowned in tears. "They will condemn you! But you'll go free! You'll come home to me! And then we'll retreat into some peaceful corner! And you'll make peace with God. We'll live happily ..."

A sort of Christian faith and love sounded in her words, causing the man to find his way back to himself. The hand of hope restored his self-control. The truth appeared to him as a flash of lightning. The truth contained in his wife's thoughts.

He won't be condemned to death: *his actions were justified!* And he'll be freed from prison! And by then his hot blood will have cooled. And his wife will have redeemed him from his sins.

This woman now appeared to him as a Savior.

And an overwhelming feeling of submission caused him to collapse, he fell at his wife's feet and kissed the earth before her. In the next moment he saw that it felt good to lay his tired, exhausted head upon the cold earth. The dry earth turned with him and in a moment he could have gone to sleep: in gentle, eternal rest.

Erzsi placed her hand on her husband's head and tears fell from her face. Her faith in the future was as steadfast as her faith in her salvation after death.

Suddenly Dani lifted his head in fear. He cocked his ears like a hound in a pointing stance.

Indeed, steps can be heard outside. The door opens, and before the man can jump to his feet, men armed with pitchforks enter the room.

"Don't be afraid!" Erzsi cries.

She wraps her arms around her trembling husband's head and kisses him firmly.

"Don't be afraid!" she whispers into his ear. "With enough courage, you can get away. You'll come home. We'll be happy!"

And Dani isn't afraid.

He's so calm, so sovereign that it's wonderful to see. And it's wonderful for a woman to know that she gives strength to her strong husband. This strengthens her as well.

Dani Turi stood calmly among the pitchfork bearers, with dignity, trusting in the future.

And as he looked back once more from the door, as though expecting the woman to run after him, he saw the sick child convulsing on the bed. And Erzsi hesitated for a moment, wondering whether she should rush after her husband or run over to her son. She did the latter. She knelt down before the bed, and as she caressed the suffering child with her quavering hand, she turned her tear-streaked face toward her husband: bidding him painful farewell; calling him hopefully back.

And the man understood.

He knew, he sensed it was God's will to give the woman the sick child to tend to: it lent strength to her hope!

His mind was clear, but his heart was oppressed.

Yet what was this meaningless distress compared with the bliss that he knew – today for the first time – awaited him in the future.

He'd sinned many times over. He must and will atone for his misdeeds.

Pay his debts.

Then he'll start a new life. His blood now cooled, he'll avoid new transgressions ... And he'll be happy alongside his wife. His sweet, sainted, delicate, pious wife!

And he walks so blissfully among the people with their gaping mouths, as though he were being exalted rather than led to his death sentence.

Something unexpected happens.

With a blood-curdling scream, Bora runs out and throws herself at Dani.

The girl had heard nothing as yet of the news coursing through the village. She saw only that Dani was being led along like a prisoner.

She screeched like a madwoman.

For a moment she looked at Dani's bloody hands, his bloodied clothes.

"I did it! I did it!" she screamed, and with her arms spread wide she blocked the men's way.

"You did what?" one of the men snapped at her. "Get out of here!"

"I sent him there! I put him up to it!"

"Grab her!"

Dani gazed tenderly at the girl. "Foolish girl!" he said gently.

Somebody grabbed the girl by the arm.

"Let her be!" Dani signaled to them. "What does she know? Go ahead, ask her what happened! Who did I kill?"

"I know it, I know it!" the girl screamed senselessly, and she struggled, stomping with her feet and shaking her fists. "It's all because of me. I'm the harlot. Take me. I'm the slut. Hang me. I put him up to it. He spent the night at my place, with me he spent the night. So we made an agreement. I hired him. I'm the whore!"

"Beat it!" said one of the men with a pitchfork, and he struck her across the neck.

In that moment, Dani jumped on him like a raging wolf. He struck him in the face, knocking him down: he threw himself on him and dislocated his jaw with a single blow. He seized him by the neck.

But then a forceful blow struck him in the back of the head. The men with their pitchforks attacked him, striking him left and right, wherever they could.

The girl screamed and flung herself on the ground, then ran at the men, until they'd subdued her as well with their pitchforks.

Her mother now ran out to help her, wailing in dismay, cursing at the murderers and Dani Turi.

They brought Dani to the town hall in a handcart. They put him in the woodshed, locked the door, and posted two guards there. Then they sent for the gendarmes.

It was dark before Dani awoke.

Slowly he came to his senses and realized where he was and what had happened.

*

The surging rage in his soul had ceased. Left behind were pain, sadness, disgust for life.

He thought of the two women. Of that dear saint who deserved to be worshiped and who would have assured his salvation, and then of the poor unfortunate sinner who would gladly have sacrificed herself for him.

And he knew that both of them had squandered their souls for him in vain. No more would the heart of a woman come to his aid. In his mind's eye he glimpsed a wondrous, dreadful truth.

One wife! If only one single, true woman had entered his life: he would have made her happy! But two, three, ten, a hundred ... they brought him to his ruin a hundred times over.

He saw his destiny fulfilled.

Previously he'd had confidence in the future, a beautiful, quiet, happy future with one woman. Now this confidence was gone.

"Were I to be resurrected a thousand times over, the women would devour me ten thousand times over!"

He lay there limply a long, long time.

A single thought calmed his dazed head.

He'd done his part, for everyone.

The rest was none of his affair.

His fate now lies in the hands of a higher power. That of the human administration of justice.

And it calmed him completely to know that the torch that was destined to blaze and set the world on fire at last rested in the hands of eternal judgment ...

"What have I lived for?" he said. "Why in the hell was I brought into this world?"

What is life?

Mud.

And man within it?

Gold in the mud.

So who is at fault if nothing has become of this gold? "Who?"

God, who has made nothing of it.

ABOUT THE TRANSLATOR

Virginia L. Lewis earned her doctorate in Modern German Literature in 1989 from the University of Pennsylvania and has studied numerous languages including French, Bulgarian, and of course Hungarian. She attended the Debreceni Nyári Egyetem on two separate occasions and has written numerous articles on German and Hungarian literature as well as literature from across the globe. Her book *Globalizing the Peasant: Access to Land and the Possibility of Self-Realization* was published in 2007 by Lexington Books. Dr. Lewis currently serves as Professor of German and Chair of the Department of Languages, Literature, and Communication Studies at Northern State University.

Made in the USA
Lexington, KY
10 September 2014